The SECRETS of the ETERNAL ROSE

Belladonna

FOR MOM.

Thanks for supporting me in all of my crazy endeavors.

Philomel Books · An imprint of Penguin Young Readers Group.
Published by The Penguin Group. Penguin Group (USA) Inc., 375 Hudson Street, New York,
NY 10014, USA. Penguin Group (Canada), 90 Eglinton Avenue East, Suite 700, Toronto, Ontario
M4P 2Y3, Canada (a division of Pearson Penguin Canada Inc.). Penguin Books Ltd, 80 Strand, London
WC2R 0RL, England. Penguin Ireland, 25 St. Stephen's Green, Dublin 2, Ireland (a division of
Penguin Books Ltd). Penguin Group (Australia), 707 Collins Street, Melbourne, Victoria 3008,
Australia (a division of Pearson Australia Group Pty Ltd). Penguin Books India Pvt Ltd,
11 Community Centre, Panchsheel Park, New Delhi–110 017, India. Penguin Group (NZ), 67 Apollo
Drive, Rosedale, Auckland 0632, New Zealand (a division of Pearson New Zealand Ltd). Penguin
Books South Africa, Rosebank Office Park, 181 Jan Smuts Avenue, Parktown North 2193, South
Africa. Penguin China, B7 Jiaming Center, 27 East Third Ring Road North, Chaoyang District, Beijing
100020, China. Penguin Books Ltd, Registered Offices: 80 Strand, London WC2R 0RL, England.

Edited by Jill Santopolo. Design by Amy Wu. Text set in 12.5-point Winchester New ITC Std.

Library of Congress Cataloging-in-Publication Data   Paul, Fiona.   Belladonna : a Secrets of the
Eternal Rose novel / Fiona Paul.   p. cm.   Sequel to: Venom.   Summary: "Cass's fiancé Luca is
arrested for heresy and Cass must travel to Florence to uncover the mystery of the Order of the Eternal
Rose and save Luca's life."—Provided by publisher.   [1. Mystery and detective stories. 2. Adventure
and adventurers—Fiction. 3. Secret societies—Fiction. 4. Social classes—Fiction. 5. Artists—Fiction.
6. Orphans—Fiction. 7. Love—Fiction. 8. Venice (Italy)—History—1508–1797—Fiction. 9. Florence
(Italy)—History—1421–1737—Fiction. 10. Italy—History—1559–1789—Fiction.] I. Title.
PZ7.P278345Bel 2013   [Fic]—dc23   2012029564
ISBN 978-0-399-25726-1
10   9   8   7   6   5   4   3   2   1

The SECRETS of the ETERNAL ROSE

Belladonna

FIONA PAUL

Philomel Books · AN IMPRINT OF PENGUIN GROUP (USA) INC.

"Fire is power. Blood is life."

—THE BOOK OF THE ETERNAL ROSE

Cass leaned over the side of the Rialto Bridge, the wind lifting her auburn hair away from her face. Wispy clouds swirled low in the sky.

"Cass." The word fluttered on the breeze.

She turned. Falco stood at her side, his square jaw backlit by the sun, his mouth curving into the lopsided smile she loved. "I thought you . . . ?" Cass couldn't finish. *Left*. He had left her, weeks ago.

"I came back for you," he said.

He stroked her face with his hands, one fingertip tracing the smattering of freckles across the bridge of her nose. She wobbled in her chopines and he reached out to steady her, his hand lingering on her arm. The platform overshoes made her taller than Falco, but he didn't seem to notice. Tilting his head toward her, he pulled her body in close to his.

Cass trembled as he closed the gap between them. Their lips met. Hungry. Wanting. Falco's hands wrapped around her waist, caressing her through the layered fabric of her dress. Her body went weak, and she gripped the stone railing of the bridge to keep from pitching over into the water. Her other hand found his hair. She twisted it around her fingers.

"Come with me," he whispered.

Cass didn't even ask where they were going. Falco took her hand and pulled her across the bridge, through the streets. Light became gray. Day became night. His grip tightened around her fingers. Too tight. Cass looked up at him. She gasped. He was falling away in pieces. His hair. His smile. His skin peeling back to reveal teeth and bone.

The street dissolved, and Cass wasn't outside anymore. Dark hallways threaded out in all directions, weblike and impossibly long. She clawed at the damp walls, and the stone chipped away beneath her fingernails, leaving long gouges in the rock. She was being dragged forward, through an arched door. A lantern flickered to life. They were in the wine room. Cass and the man of bone.

Only now he wore a new face: Cristian, her fiancé Luca's half brother. Cristian, the murderer. He started shouting at her, horrible black things about the women he had killed.

A droplet of water fell from above. Cass lay pinned to a low stone table. And Cristian was on top of her, his weight crushing her chest, an icy blade pressed against her throat. She felt death in that pinch of steel, but she was more afraid of the hand that wasn't holding the dagger. The hand that was busy tearing away the fabric of her dress . . .

Cass sat up in bed, her heart banging in her chest, her eyes still shut against the monster from her nightmare. Her nightgown clung to her moist skin.

"Not real," she murmured. She had the dream every couple of

nights. Each time it was a little different, but it always ended the same way.

She opened her eyes. The candle on her washing table had burned down to its nub. Burning tallow all night was expensive, and dangerous, but Cass couldn't bear the dark. Not since Cristian had attacked her. A thin shaft of silvery dawn sliced its way through a crack in her shutters. It was morning, and she was all right. Another night survived.

She tried to put the nightmare out of her mind. She hadn't told anyone exactly what had happened to her the day of Madalena's wedding. Even Luca didn't know that his half brother had more than murder on his mind when he lured Cass down into the wine room.

Her insides twisted like she was a sheet being wrung out to dry. Bile rose in her throat. Resting her head back on her pillow, Cass willed herself to be calm. *Inhale. Exhale. Just breathe.*

Something rough scratched against her cheek. A rolled parchment lay in her tangled bedsheets. The edges were crumbling and the ink was fading in places. It was Falco's letter, the only one she had received since he left Venice. Cass had been reading it last night before she fell asleep. She'd read it a hundred times, knew each word by heart, but she unrolled it again anyway. The words were sweet and soothing. Even in his absence, Falco could make the nightmare fade.

Starling,

> *I haven't stopped thinking of you—I can't. I know that you are engaged and want to do right by your family, but you and I belong together. Call it fate if you like. I prefer to think of it as the natural order of things. Just as mixing ochre and*

sapphire produces the most vibrant green, you and I, when
combined, become more alive.

 I've stopped doing business with Angelo de Gradi. I've
left that life behind. I'm working as an artist in residence
for a wealthy patron now. The work she has me do is a bit
pedestrian, but perhaps it will lead to bigger projects.
I meant what I said. One day I will paint whole chapels
for you. I spend every waking minute becoming a better
artist, a better man. One day I will offer you the life you
deserve, the life we both desire.

 One day I'll be good enough, or I'll die trying . . .

Cass glanced at the portrait of the Virgin Mary above her dressing table. She should have lowered the black veil attached to the frame before reviewing her love letter. It wasn't proper to let the Virgin see her swooning over a man who was not her fiancé.

But she could ask for forgiveness later. Cradling the parchment against her chest, she thought about the last time she'd seen Falco. She had been strolling the streets of San Domenico with Luca when she saw Falco flagging down a fisherman for passage. Cass knew he was going away, but she didn't know where. Part of her had wanted to drop her fiancé's hand and run to Falco's side, to escape the tiny island with him.

But she had stayed put, her arm entwined with Luca's, watching Falco's back fade into the setting sun. Following him would have meant abandoning her aunt Agnese and dishonoring the memory of her parents, and Cass just couldn't do it. Besides, she wasn't completely convinced she could trust Falco. Their whole relationship was based on secrets and lies. Even if Falco had stopped stealing dead bodies and selling them to Angelo de Gradi, did that mean he wouldn't turn to crime again the next time he needed more than his art could provide? She didn't know.

But she *did* know Luca might never be enough for her. Cass's heart fluttered in her chest. She felt Falco's lips on hers as if he were there in the room. She remembered their first kiss, in the studio where he apprenticed, the way she felt as if she had lived her whole life inside a frozen shell, melting for the first time at his touch.

She sighed. Luca had been so patient with her the past few weeks, content to enjoy her company at mealtimes and during an occasional stroll along the beach. Just last week he had given her a gift, a gorgeous lily pendant. Cass felt its pressure in the hollow of her throat, the lily's diamond center moving in and out with each of her breaths. Luca would make the perfect husband. He was handsome and kind and smart, a good man, from a well-established Venetian family. And he loved her. He loved her so much, he would die for her; he had proven that already. But Falco was . . . Falco. Just the taste of his name on her lips made Cass a little dizzy.

Her situation was hopeless: betrothed to one man, wildly in love with another.

Heavy footsteps outside her room shattered the reverie. Quickly, Cass slipped the letter under her pillow. She tucked an unruly shock of hair back under her sleeping cap as she hurried to her armoire and grabbed a dressing gown from inside. Securing the belt around her waist, she opened her chamber door a crack and peeked out into the hallway. It was dark, but the corridor was full of strange men dressed in scarlet and gold. Men with swords and clubs tucked into leather sheaths.

Soldiers.

"What's going on here?" Cass asked.

The soldiers turned as one, quickly averting their eyes at her state of undress. "We've orders to search Signor da Peraga's chambers," one of them said stiffly. He wore a gold medallion pinned to his doublet. Cass assumed he was the man in charge.

"*Search* his chambers?" she repeated, incredulous. "For what?"

"Best you step aside, Signorina." The soldier waved her out of the way with one of his filthy leather gloves. "These orders come straight from the Senate."

Cass's handmaid, Siena, appeared at her side, dressed but still half drunk with sleep, her blonde hair stuffed loosely under her bonnet. "Signorina Cass," she whispered. "What's happening?"

"I don't know." Cass followed the soldiers to the room where Luca had been staying. Siena trailed behind her. The two girls stood in the doorway as the men converged upon the bed, tearing the pillows and sheets from it and tossing them to the floor. Finding nothing of interest in the linens, they moved to the worn leather trunk that sat against the wall. Horrified, Cass watched as one of the soldiers flung armfuls of books and clothing over his shoulder.

"Where is Luca?" she asked, her voice rising in pitch. "You've no right to go through his belongings without him present."

"I suggest you go speak to Signor da Peraga yourself," the nearest soldier said. "He's in the *portego* with the rest of the brigade."

Rest of the brigade? Pulling Siena behind her, Cass stormed down the hallway and pushed into the main room of the villa. The shutters were still closed, but the cavernous portego was aglow with torchlight. Agnese's harp and the angel statues that stood on either side of it were casting deformed, wavering shadows across the marble floor. Luca stood near a velvet divan, talking to another group of soldiers.

Cass counted seven of them. They smelled of sweat and ale and ashes. Scarlet and gold blurred before her eyes as the soldiers circled her fiancé like lions preparing to pounce.

"Luca! What's happening?" She pushed her way through the sea of red to Luca's side, her forward momentum almost throwing her into his arms. It had been a while since she had been this close to him, close enough to see how his brown eyes faded to honey at the edges, close enough to smell a hint of citrus and cinnamon on his clothing.

"I'm being arrested," he said calmly.

Cass felt as though the ground had opened beneath her feet. "On what charges? Under whose authority?" For a moment, she pressed her face against his broad chest, hiding her skin from the dancing flames of the nearest soldier's torch. The silk of Luca's doublet felt cool against her scorched cheek.

"What is the meaning of all this?"

Cass pulled away at the sound of Narissa's shrill voice. Narissa was Agnese's personal handmaid and the unofficial second-in-command of the villa. The stout, gray-haired woman surveyed the scene with a mix of shock and anger.

A crowd was beginning to gather at the edge of the portego. Siena stood just inside the doorway, her body leaning heavily against the wall as if she might collapse at any moment. She gestured wildly as she murmured to Narissa, but Cass couldn't make out what the women were saying. She felt as though she hadn't yet woken from her dream. Everything was strange and disjointed. Bortolo, Agnese's elderly blind butler, stood behind the handmaids, his grizzled face twisted in confusion. In the other doorway, a trio of serving girls huddled silently together, taking in the scene with wide, frightened eyes.

A large thud made Cass jump. It sounded as if the soldiers were hacking Luca's belongings to pieces with their clubs. With all the noise, Agnese was almost certainly awake now. Cass knew she should go to her aunt's bedside, but she couldn't bring herself to leave Luca.

As Cass watched, Narissa broke away from Siena and strode purposefully toward Luca's chambers, undoubtedly to make sure the soldiers weren't stealing anything or destroying the furniture. Cass knew Agnese would be hobbling her way into the chaos the instant she heard of the transpiring events. Ideally, Narissa could control the soldiers *and* her aunt, who was too weak to deal with something like this. Agnese's latest bout with imbalanced humors had required a large bloodletting, and the doctor had recommended bed rest for a few days.

"On what charges do you arrest my fiancé?" Cass asked again, directing her words to the group. When no one answered, she focused on the nearest soldier. His beard was flecked with gray, and several medallions glimmered on the breast of his doublet. Perhaps he, not the man leading the ransackers, was the leader. "You. Answer me." The soldier looked pityingly at Cass but said nothing.

Cass turned to Luca. "This is madness!"

"They can't tell us the charges." Luca pressed his hands to Cass's shoulders, steadying her. "They probably don't even know. They're just following orders." He touched his lips to her cheek, then angled his mouth toward her ear. "Be strong," he murmured. "And stay away from Signor Dubois."

"Does he have something to do with this?" Cass knew that Luca had been to see Joseph Dubois only yesterday, and every shady dealing in Venice seemed to lead back to the Frenchman. A few weeks ago, he'd ordered Luca's half brother, Cristian, to "dispose" of a maid from his estate. The girl's mutilated body had surfaced in the Grand Canal, and now Siena's sister, Feliciana, another servant at Palazzo Dubois, was missing. Cass prayed to San Antonio every night for Feliciana's safe return, but privately she feared the worst.

Luca didn't respond. The remaining soldiers filed into the portego, having apparently completed their search. Between the two groups there must have been close to twenty men. Did the Senate really think it would take so many soldiers to subdue a single man?

"Did you find anything?" The soldier with the graying beard lifted his torch so that the faces of his companions were illuminated.

"Nothing," one of the soldiers barked in reply.

The brigade surrounded Luca and Cass, separating them from the rest of the household. The heat from their torches made the room go blurry. Cass blinked hard, but golden spots floated in the air, melding with the ocean of scarlet fabric, reflecting off medallions and sword hilts. She braced herself with one hand against Luca, trying to keep her knees from folding beneath her.

"Signor da Peraga must come with us now," a soldier said. He detached a coil of rope from his belt and looped it around Luca's wrists, cinching his hands behind his back.

"No!" Cass threw her hands around Luca's neck, pulling him close. She fought back a sob, but a tear escaped, trickling down her cheek before she could brush it away.

"Everything is going to be fine, Cass," Luca said. He leaned down to brush his lips against the tear. "Don't cry."

One of the men took Cass by the shoulders and wrenched her away. She stumbled backward, unmoored. Siena materialized at her side, reaching out, helping her regain her balance. The soldiers engulfed Luca and dragged him toward the stairs.

The front door of the villa slammed, and Cass ran to the window. The sky had gone from silver to blue. The soldiers doused their torches in the water as they forced Luca aboard the sturdy wooden ship. White sails snapped in the breeze as the boat pulled away from the dock. The waxing daylight wasn't enough to see clearly by, but Cass swore Luca turned to look back at her as the ship bobbed out of sight. She touched one hand to the window, her breath condensing on the glass.

Luca was gone.

"Members of the Order must band
together to vanquish our enemies.
Neither man nor the Church shall be
allowed to jeopardize our higher purpose."

—THE BOOK OF THE ETERNAL ROSE

Cass heard Narissa's voice before she saw the handmaid helping her aunt down the corridor. "One step at a time. Excellent, Signora. Slow and steady," Narissa said, supporting Agnese as the old woman struggled toward the portego.

"Aunt Agnese!" Cass cried out, wiping at her cheek with her hand. She did not want her aunt to know how terrified she was. "You should be in bed."

"Explain to me," Agnese wheezed, "why those savages thought they could destroy my home." She pointed in the direction of Luca's room. "It looks like the End of Days in there."

"They said they had orders to search Luca's chambers," Cass said. *But search for what?*

"*Orders*," Agnese scoffed. "Don't worry, Cassandra. They'll be taking *new* orders soon." She clutched at her chest, as if the mere act of speaking were taxing. "Narissa, I'd like to return to my room. Bring me wax and parchment. I'll be sending several letters immediately." As she tottered back down the hallway on her handmaid's arm, she added, "And someone put that room back together immediately—there's nothing more debased than an overturned armchair."

Siena touched Cass on the shoulder. "I'll go straighten in there."

A strange protective feeling welled up inside Cass. She didn't want anyone else going through Luca's private things. "I can take care of it," she said quickly. "You go to the market. Keep your ears open. Maybe you'll hear someone talking about the arrest."

Siena curtsied. "Whatever you think is best, Signorina Cass."

Cass had already turned away. She held her breath as she crossed the threshold into Luca's room, afraid of what she might find. The four-poster bed was still standing, but barely. The armoire and washing table were also whole, but overturned. All of Luca's fine clothing had been yanked from the armoire's shelves and dumped in a heap on the floor. Books and stockings were strewn about in front of his trunk.

Cass's cat, Slipper, was pawing at a fur-lined collar that protruded from the mess of clothes. "Shoo," Cass said, bending down in front of the armoire.

Slipper bounded off to explore the tangle of stockings. Cass began to refold Luca's breeches and doublets, placing each piece of clothing back onto the shelves. She caught a whiff of his scent—citrus and cinnamon—from a tailored gray doublet and had to restrain herself from beginning to cry.

She reminded herself that crying would help no one.

Next, she went to work on his chemises. The linen fabric had creases at the chest and shoulders. Luca even folded his underclothes. Cass took her time, matching her folds to the creases, trying to put everything back just as it had been. She told herself that it was all a mistake, that he would soon be home, that he would want his clothes as he had left them.

Slipper had found a scrap of lilac ribbon from somewhere and was parading around the room with the treasure hanging from his teeth. Cass watched him for a moment and then moved to the mess outside of the trunk.

She paired the long stockings as best she could and placed them gently into the back of the trunk. She stacked the books into a pile, scanning each cover as she did so. Most of them were related to law and government—subjects Luca had been studying at university—but one of the leather-bound volumes was the same Shakespeare story that Cass had been reading when he had first returned to Venice several weeks earlier. Luca had never been one for stories, especially love stories. Cass couldn't help but wonder if she had changed him the way that Falco had changed her.

Already, the room was looking better. *If only people, and lives, were as easy to fix,* she thought. What was Luca doing right now? Was he scared? Where had he ended up? Was he being held somewhere clean and well lit, with hot water and fine food, or in a rat-infested, watery prison? She hoped Siena's errands would be speedy. Surely some of the servants at the market would be gossiping about the arrest of a nobleman. Once Cass knew more about the charges, she would go to the Palazzo Ducale and demand to speak on Luca's behalf. While she was there, perhaps she could bribe a guard to let her see her fiancé for a minute or two.

She placed the stack of books into Luca's trunk and rose to her feet. As she headed for the door, her lily pendant came unclasped and slipped down inside her bodice.

Cass fished it out, pausing for a moment to admire its beauty. Four silver flower petals framed a circular diamond in the center. She held the pendant up to the light and watched the way the diamond bent and reflected the daylight, scattering sunbeams across Luca's room.

Slipper abandoned his ribbon and threw his tiny body at one of the dancing streaks of light, colliding instead with the wall.

"Slipper!" Cass said, nearly dropping the necklace. "Are you all right?"

As if he understood her words, the cat walked dazedly in a circle and then licked one paw and rubbed his face before launching himself at another rogue ball of light.

Cass returned her attention to the pendant. As she struggled to work the tiny clasp behind her neck, she thought about the day Luca had given it to her. She'd been in the garden, reading, when he had come around the front of the house, a pale lily cradled in his hands.

"*Grazie*," she'd said when he rested the lily next to her on the bench. Her eyes had flipped back to her book. She didn't mean to ignore him, but she was at a good part in her story.

"Cass." He'd angled his head toward the back of the garden, where roses bloomed in the wooden trellis. Stuck among them was another pale pink lily.

Cass had arched an eyebrow, but then given in and closed her book. She and Luca had played this game when she was younger, both at his family palazzo and at Agnese's. Luca used to hide little presents for her and mark the hiding spots with lilies.

A smile playing across her lips, Cass got up to look at the second pink lily that he had poked into the trellis. Behind the delicate petals, a gold box was tied to the wood. Inside it, this necklace. Cass remembered the soft touch of Luca's hands and the tickle of his breath on her skin as he bent low to work the tiny clasp.

The wall clock chimed, and Cass was shocked to discover that she had been in Luca's room nearly two hours. She slipped down the hallway and knocked quietly at her aunt's door. No answer. She peeked in to find that Agnese was sleeping, her body propped up awkwardly in her bed with several embroidered pillows.

Agnese's health had taken a turn for the worse after Madalena's wedding. Sometimes Cass could hear her coughing well into the night. She watched Agnese's chest rise and fall beneath the fabric of her dressing gown. Her breathing seemed labored, her exhalations shallow and raspy. One gnarled hand, fingers twisted and swollen, dangled off the edge of the bed.

Crossing the room to her aunt's side, Cass knelt down and folded Agnese's arm so that her hand now rested on her lap. The old woman didn't even stir, and Cass couldn't bring herself to disturb her.

As Cass retreated into the hall and closed the door to her aunt's chamber, she saw Siena hurrying down the corridor. They both opened their mouths to speak at the same time, but Siena spoke first. "You have to come quickly, Signorina Cass," she said, her eyes wide.

"What is it?" Cass asked. "What's happened?"

Siena struggled to catch her breath. She tucked her trembling fingers into the folds of her dress. "It's my sister," she said, her voice catching. "I found her."

"The Order's existence
must remain a secret,
and new members selected
prudently and sparingly."

—THE BOOK OF THE ETERNAL ROSE

three

Siena took Cass's gloved hand to help steady her in her chopines as they threaded their way through the narrow streets of the Rialto, the main island of Venice. They emerged from an alleyway onto the wide path that ran alongside the Grand Canal. The area was crowded with peasants carrying paper-wrapped packages and sacks of vegetables. Siena headed for the arches of the Mercato di Rialto, where almost everyone went to buy food and herbs.

Peasant women and older children jockeyed for position in front of the stalls. Cass was reminded of the busy alleyway in Fondamenta delle Tette where she and Falco had gone to search for the identity of the dead body Cass had found in the contessa Liviana's tomb a few weeks earlier.

That area had been full of brothels. To Cass, the marketplace seemed almost as bad, with Gypsies pushing trinkets outside the arches and fishermen hawking their catches inside. Anyone could be roaming within that crowd—con artists, pickpockets. Cristian.

"She's waiting *here*?" Cass asked.

"Yes." Siena yanked her forward impatiently.

Cass eyed the crush of people again. The back of a blond man, the ends of his hair reaching almost to his shoulders, melted into a cluster of brightly clothed peasant boys pushing and shoving each other as they headed toward the arches. *Cristian.* She stopped quickly, nearly pitching forward onto the damp, garbage-slicked cobblestones. "I'll wait here while you go get her."

Siena gave Cass a strange look. "She won't come out, of course. She's afraid someone will see her and report to Signor Dubois."

Cass cursed herself for being such a coward. According to Luca, Cristian had left Venice for good. There was no reason for her to be seeing him in every crowd. "Lead the way, then," she said.

Cass followed Siena into the market, her head pounding from the cacophony of vendors and customers trying to outshout each other. Her stomach churned from the stink of fish and sweat. She wished she could fetch her fan out from her pocket, but the peasants were packed arm to arm, as tightly as the seafood they were bidding on. Cass paused for a moment, covering her mouth with a gloved hand, trying not to retch.

Siena flicked a quick glance over her shoulder. "I almost forgot." She pulled a tiny cloth bag from her pocket and handed it to Cass. "Breathe through this."

Cass took the sachet of herbs gratefully. Pressing the small bag up to her mouth and nose, she inhaled mint and rosemary. She skimmed the sea of faces for the blond man. Suddenly he was right in front of them, bidding on a fish. Up close he looked nothing like Cristian. *Idiota*, she thought. Still, she couldn't make her heart stop racing.

Siena led her down the main row of stalls, slipping effortlessly through the minuscule spaces between other people. Cass felt huge and clunky trying to do the same, excusing herself repeatedly as she wobbled in her chopines and stepped on the occasional toe. She pressed one hand tightly to the fabric of her dress, imagining that each accidental touch belonged to quick fingers trying to extract the leather pouch of coins from deep inside her pocket.

A peasant woman dressed in plain muslin squeezed past her, adeptly leading her three daughters through the fray. The smallest girl reached out to stroke the soft fabric of Cass's skirts as she wandered by. Again, Cass felt silly. Why was she afraid of a place where Siena came almost every day?

As Cass and Siena weaved their way deeper into the market, some of the vendors called out excitedly, holding up gutted fish or giant squid for Cass's approval. It was rare, she supposed, to see a well-dressed noblewoman wriggling her way through the masses. She quickly averted her eyes from what Siena told her was a sea bass, filleted down the middle and folded open to display its slick white interior. Cass had never seen the inside of a raw fish up close. She hoped the cook was fixing chicken for dinner.

Siena pulled her past a stall where shrimp and clams were piled high in woven baskets. Cass swore she felt a hand close around one of her ankles. She lurched forward, knocking a few of the shellfish onto the ground. A plaintive yowl came from the direction of her chopines. Looking down, she saw an emaciated black cat flick its tail against her leg again before pouncing on one of the fallen shrimp. Cass muttered an apology and tossed a copper coin at the scowling vendor.

Finally, they were past all the seafood and into the far side of the market where the produce was sold. The smell here was almost as bad, but at least Cass was no longer in danger of being assaulted by the sight of a gutted fish. She had seen plenty of rotting fruit before. The servants would sometimes buy it just before it turned. Agnese did love a good deal.

Siena pulled Cass behind a stall selling grapes and pears. A beggar in a brown wool dress and a black cloak knelt next to a stack of empty wooden crates, her hood pulled low to hide her face. She had her hands clasped around a half-rotten pear that she had no doubt fished out of the bottom of one of the crates.

"I've brought Cass," Siena whispered.

The beggar looked up at her, and Cass immediately recognized Feliciana's bright blue eyes. She swallowed back an exclamation of joy and relief so as not to call attention to Feliciana's presence. She could hardly believe it. There were so many things she wanted to tell her. So many things she wanted to *ask* her.

But then Cass took a closer look. The left side of Feliciana's face was colored yellow with the remnants of a welt, and her lips were swollen and marred by black blood, having split open and scabbed over. How could Siena's vibrant older sister have become this skeletal, bruised woman?

Feliciana ducked her head again as the pear vendor, an older woman with deep lines etched into her tan face, stacked another empty crate behind the stall. "You should find refuge at a convent," the woman said. "It's hard for the good Lord to take care of you out here in the streets." Feliciana nodded without lifting her chin. Someone hollered from the front of the stall, and the vendor disappeared.

Cass fumbled in her pockets as if she were searching for a few coins, talking low under her breath as she did. "You'll come back to the villa with us, of course. We can get everything sorted out once you're safe."

Feliciana nodded again. "But what will you tell your gondolier?" she whispered. "If anyone were to recognize me—"

"I'll get rid of Giuseppe," Siena said. "I'll say we're going to walk across the way to the weaver's to order some cloth and then take a stroll down to Piazza San Marco. I'll tell him he should return to the villa, that we'll find our own way home."

"Good idea, Siena." Cass turned back to Feliciana. "No one will recognize you." Even if she hadn't been emaciated and bruised, in the hooded cloak and rough woolen dress, Feliciana could have just as easily been her aunt Agnese as a runaway servant.

"Stay with her, Signorina Cass," Siena said, as if she were afraid her sister was a ghost who might vanish if they both turned their backs. "I'll find us passage home." Siena disappeared in the direction of the Grand Canal.

Cass knew it must look strange to the people passing by, a noblewoman bent down over a beggar, but she didn't care. "Are you sick?" she asked, kneeling to get a better look at Feliciana. The skin under her eyes was purple, and the fingers that protruded from the oversized sleeves of her cloak looked like twigs.

"Just sick of hiding," Feliciana said with a wan smile. "And hungry." She bit into the good side of the pear. She chewed slowly, as if it had been a while since she had eaten solid food.

"Of course. What's the matter with me?" Cass made her way to the front of the stall, where she purchased a second pear and a cluster of grapes.

"Cass—Signorina Cass," Feliciana corrected herself, when Cass returned. "I didn't mean for you to—"

"I know," Cass said, handing the fruit to Feliciana. "I wanted to."

Feliciana finished the good part of her scavenged pear before beginning on the grapes. Each one brought a smile to her discolored face, as if they were the most exquisite food in all of Venice.

Siena returned, and Cass was overjoyed to learn they wouldn't have to backtrack through the crowded marketplace to get to their ride. "I had to offer the return fare too, Signorina Cass," Siena said apologetically. "You know how the gondoliers hate going all the way out to the islands."

"That's fine." Cass would have offered her entire purse just to spirit her former lady's maid to safety.

Feliciana kept her hood low as the three girls squeezed out the back of the market and headed for a gondola moored at the edge of the Grand Canal. An elderly gondolier helped them aboard. Cass instinctively checked his hands to see if he wore a ring with a six-petaled flower design. She didn't know what the symbol meant, but she had seen it on a ring that Falco found in Liviana's tomb and then again on the outside of Angelo de Gradi's workshop full of body parts. Later, she had noticed Donna Domacetti, Venice's biggest gossip, wearing a similar ring. Cass knew that the symbol heralded dark things—bad things.

It would look highly suspicious if they arrived home too soon after Giuseppe, so Cass commanded the gondolier to go slowly, saying she felt ill. The old man scowled, but slowed the rate at which he moved the long flexible oar through the canal water.

Cass reclined on the bench inside the *felze*, and Siena and Feliciana knelt on the boat's stamped leather base, facing her. The three girls tucked their heads tightly together, speaking in hushed tones.

"What happened?" Siena asked, reaching out to push her sister's hood back just far enough so she could see her eyes. "Did he hurt you?" Cass knew that Siena was referring to Dubois.

Feliciana shook her head and bit her lip. "No. Not like that. Joseph was . . . fond of me." She avoided her sister's eyes, and Cass wondered what Joseph Dubois had done to show his affection, and how Feliciana had grown so familiar with him that she would use his given name. "All the girls had whispered that he was fond of Sophia, too, and that she might be with child." Feliciana faltered slightly over the words. "When she disappeared, I figured she had run away. Maybe gone to the Chiesa to live until the baby was born."

Cass watched as the gondola passed the Chiesa delle Zitelle, which sat on the island of Giudecca, almost directly across from the entrance to the Grand Canal. It functioned as both a house of worship and a refuge for single women. Whether healthy or infirm, unmarried girls and prostitutes often sought shelter there.

Feliciana shuddered. "But then I overheard him speaking to a man I'd seen around the estate—another Frenchman—about what needed to be done about Sophia. Joseph told this man to make the problem go away."

Cass's throat squeezed shut. Cristian.

"Then I heard that her body was pulled from the Grand Canal. After that day, I began to cross paths with this man more and more. I was afraid maybe he'd seen me the day I heard him speaking to Joseph." Feliciana's eyes went dark. "I didn't want to be next."

Cass reached out and gave Feliciana's hand a quick squeeze. "You're safe now," she said, hoping it was true. Once Feliciana was inside the villa, Cass would inform her about what had happened over the past few weeks. It wasn't safe to talk about it further here. In Venice, even the water had ears.

Siena was staring at Feliciana. "So you and Signor Dubois were—"

Feliciana shook her head forcefully. "No. But it would have come to that." And then, seeing Siena's look of shock, she added, "Oh, don't be naïve. No woman refuses that kind of request from her master, not if she wants to stay employed."

Cass twisted around the edge of the felze to sneak a glance at their gondolier. The man was staring down at the lagoon, watching his oar move through the water.

Feliciana laughed bitterly. "Poor Sophia. One of her roommates told me that Sophia believed she was going to be transferred to Dubois's mainland estate, into her own set of chambers. Instead she was transferred into the ground."

"Why didn't you come directly to San Domenico?" Cass asked. "Siena and I would have helped you. We would have protected you."

Feliciana scoffed. "But what about your aunt? Was I to just show up and say, 'Scusi, Signora Querini, will you take me on again?' The old woman might have sent me directly back to Joseph. Even if she didn't, how was I to know I wouldn't be bringing danger to the villa?"

"You still should have gotten a message to me," Siena said accusingly. "I thought you were dead. We both did."

Feliciana reached out and gripped her sister's arm. "I never should have left you. I thought if I did well at Palazzo Dubois, I could persuade the master to hire you on as well. I never meant for us to stay apart."

The gondolier had crossed the lagoon and was now cutting between the Giudecca and San Giorgio Maggiore. They'd be at the northern shore of San Domenico in just a few minutes. "He said he would take us around to Agnese's private dock," Siena said.

"And then what?" Feliciana asked, dropping her hood low once more.

"Siena will enter the servants' door while we wait on the side lawn," Cass said. "We'll keep ourselves tight against the villa so we won't be visible from any of the windows. Siena can come get us once she thinks it's safe to sneak you inside."

After the gondolier had moored at Agnese's dock, the three girls disembarked. Siena disappeared inside while Cass and Feliciana skirted the edge of Agnese's property, staying out of view of the windows. After a few minutes, Siena returned, and the three girls crept in the main door of the villa and quietly up the stairs. The portego was empty except for Agnese's butler, Bortolo, who was napping as usual. The girls proceeded quickly to the back of the villa, where Cass and Agnese had their bedchambers. The three of them squeezed through the doorway to Cass's room all at once, and she closed the door with a click.

Feliciana shocked everyone by dropping her hood to reveal an almost-bald head. Siena whimpered, and Feliciana patted her sister on the hand. "It's just hair. It'll grow back. Though the sister who razored it all off did seem to take a cruel pleasure in the task."

"So you actually joined a convent?" Cass asked incredulously. The vibrant Feliciana in a nunnery made about as much sense as quiet Siena becoming a courtesan.

"My options were limited," Feliciana said. "I went to the Chiesa delle Zitelle and they found me a spot in a nunnery on San Giorgio Maggiore. But the nuns were hateful. They were always waking me up at all hours of the night to pray. Each time I was late or 'insolent,' they forced me to wear a garment woven out of goat's hair under my habit. It rubbed my skin raw and kept me from sleeping. They also made me empty the chamber pots for the whole convent and scrub the floors until my fingers bled." She glanced down at her cracked and swollen fingertips and winced. "And then last week I saw one of the Sisters speaking to a man who looked familiar. I was afraid Joseph had sent his men to find me. I escaped the convent after dark, and returned to the city. I passed the days at the Mercato di Rialto and spent my nights locked inside the Ghetto with the Jews, hiding in the back room of a butcher's shop. I knew eventually I would find someone I could trust at the marketplace."

Siena reached out to touch the fuzz of blonde hair that was left on Feliciana's scalp. "I still can't believe you're here," she whispered.

"Believe it." Feliciana wrapped her bony arms around Siena's neck, and the two sisters embraced. Feliciana turned to Cass next, gripping both of her hands and leaning in to kiss her on the cheek. "You saved me," she said. "Both of you."

Cass tried not to flinch. Siena's sister smelled almost as bad as the marketplace.

Feliciana pulled back and held the end of her sleeve up to her face. "Ugh, I smell like rotten squid." She looked pleadingly at Cass. "For the good of everyone here, would it be possible to wash up?" She turned her eyes on Siena.

"Absolutely," Cass said. "Siena will get you anything you need." She cleared her throat meaningfully. "Just be discreet."

Siena scampered off. Cass still hadn't worked out exactly where she could hide Feliciana. The servants were notorious gossips, and all of Venice would know of her reappearance by the end of the week if any of them spotted her. Cass wished she could stash her former handmaid in the butler's quarters; she was in no danger of being spotted there. Bortolo was so blind that if spindly Feliciana stood holding out her arms, he'd probably mistake the girl for a coatrack.

That gave Cass an idea. Just across from the butler's office was Agnese's storage area. If Cass could manage to sneak the key,

Feliciana could hide out on the villa's lower level with minimal danger of being discovered. It would be much safer than if Siena tried to hide her away in the servants' quarters.

Siena returned with two clay jugs of warm water and a bundle of clothing tucked under her arm. She poured the water into the basin that sat in Cass's tiny bathroom. Stripping out of her cloak and dress, Feliciana stepped into the bathroom in just her chemise. She had grown so thin over the past month that Cass could see her ribs through the thin garment. "Burn those clothes, will you?" Feliciana said.

Siena gathered her plain skirts and sat daintily on the bed next to Cass. Her eyes flicked back and forth from the doorway to the bathroom to the tiny prayer alcove just outside. Below the crucifix mounted on the wall, a small statue of Cass's favorite saint sat on a marble pedestal. San Antonio. Cass often prayed to him about things that were lost. Now she thanked him for things that were found. Warmth bloomed inside of her as she heard Feliciana singing to herself as she washed up. She might be thin and bruised and bald, but Feliciana was still the same vivacious girl who had been Cass's handmaid for the better part of four years. At least her ordeal had not dampened her spirits.

"I think we should hide her downstairs for the time being," Cass said quietly, knowing this would disappoint Siena. "Agnese's storage."

"I was hoping she might stay with me." Siena picked at her skirts.

"It's too dangerous," Cass said. "Someone will see her, and then the whole marketplace will be buzzing with the news that she's been found."

Siena nodded slowly. "You're right." She shot Cass a weak smile.

"And I suppose your aunt's storage room is better than the nunnery or the Ghetto. At least we can bring her food. And visit her whenever we want."

Feliciana emerged from the bathroom wearing a plain white bonnet and Siena's newest servant's outfit, a royal-blue-and-gray ankle-length dress that hung loosely on her gaunt frame. She flounced down on the bed between Cass and Siena. "Are you discussing what to do with me?" she asked.

"We'll keep you in my room until everyone falls asleep," Cass said firmly. "Then we'll sneak you downstairs. The servants don't even dust some of those rooms, so at least we know you'll have privacy." Still, Cass didn't know how long they could stash Feliciana down there before someone noticed Siena's visits—or before Feliciana went crazy from boredom. But she wouldn't worry about that now.

A stern rapping sounded at the door. Cass froze. Siena let out a yelp. Feliciana sprang up from her seat on the coverlet and crawled beneath the bed, disappearing just as the door to Cass's bedchamber flew open.

"The Church foolishly equates
the victimless act of heresy with the
crimes of robbery and murder.
It is an easy way to remove those
who stand in our path."

—THE BOOK OF THE ETERNAL ROSE

four

C ome in," Cass said innocently. "Oh, look, you already have."

Agnese's handmaid, Narissa, stood in the doorway. Her arms were folded across her ample belly, and her eyes narrowed disapprovingly at the sight of both Cass and Siena sitting on the bed. Siena jumped up immediately so as not to provoke a scolding about where servants should and should not sit.

"Come along, Siena," Narissa said, "or you'll miss out on supper." She raised an eyebrow at Cass, her gaze lingering on the sagging folds of Cass's dress. "Will you be dining this evening, Signorina Cassandra? Or have you given up on eating altogether?"

Cass was about to tell Narissa that she wasn't hungry, but then remembered she had Feliciana to feed. "Actually I'm famished," Cass said. "Can you ask the cook to prepare a full tray for me tonight?"

Narissa nodded curtly before excusing herself and turning toward the door. Siena trailed behind the older handmaid, looking penitent.

Cass counted to thirty before dropping her head over the edge of her bed and peeking underneath it. Feliciana looked almost comfortable stretched out on her back in the thin black space. Slipper lay nuzzled against her side.

"Traitor," Cass whispered at the cat. He gazed back at her with wide green eyes.

"I probably still smell like squid," Feliciana said, crawling out from under the bed and dusting off the front of her dress. "It'll take me another bath and then some to get rid of that odor."

"I can't believe you're really here," Cass said. She couldn't wait to tell Feliciana about everything that had happened: the murdered courtesan, Falco, Madalena's wedding, Luca's arrest. But she didn't want to start now, while she might be interrupted. "And just in time. Your sister almost went crazy with worry."

"Poor thing," Feliciana said. "She's always been the nervous one. Remember back when she worked in the kitchen and broke one of your aunt's teacups? I found her up in our room, crying her eyes out, positive she'd be sent away."

"And the time that boy from the gardening crew flirted with her?" Cass said. "I thought she might faint right into the rosebushes."

Feliciana laughed. She asked Cass about each of the longtime servants, happy that so many of them were still working for the estate and doing well. "I never should have left," she said. "Everyone here is so kind." She rolled her eyes. "Well, everyone except for Narissa, of course." Someone else knocked at the door and Feliciana sighed. She started to duck back under the bed.

"Don't worry, it's just me." Siena slipped into the room with a dinner tray laden with sliced chicken, herbed potatoes, cheeses, breads, and bowls of creamy soup. Cass and Narissa obviously had different ideas about what constituted a full tray. There was more than enough food for two famished people.

Siena set the tray in the middle of Cass's bed. "It's for *the two of us.*" She winked at Feliciana before turning to Cass. "Your aunt said it would be fine if I dined in your chamber tonight since you've had a difficult day."

"She didn't happen to mention if there had been any further news, did she?" Cass asked hopefully. Siena had been so stunned to discover her sister at the marketplace that she hadn't thought to ask around about Luca's arrest before hurrying back to San Domenico. Cass didn't blame her, but she was dying to know what Luca had been charged with, and it was too late to go to the Palazzo Ducale today. She'd go first thing in the morning. By then, perhaps the misunderstanding would have been cleared up and Luca freed.

Siena dropped her eyes to the floor. "She didn't, but Narissa would have mentioned if a message had been received . . ."

Feliciana looked from Cass to Siena. "News about what?"

"Luca," Cass admitted. "There's been some trouble."

Feliciana's eyes gleamed. "Is he still painfully short?"

Cass smiled. The question was completely inappropriate, but coming from Feliciana she didn't mind. "He's actually grown about a foot," Cass said. "And according to Madalena he's become quite handsome."

"That doesn't sound like trouble."

"It's a long story," Cass said. "We can talk about it tomorrow." She couldn't bring herself to discuss Luca's arrest. Not tonight. Siena seemed to understand, because she stayed quiet as well.

The three girls clustered around the tray, sharing the silverware and the food. The sun painted the sky outside the window a rainbow of oranges and pinks as it began to set. Slipper bounded up on the bed and sniffed eagerly at the tray. Cass tossed a small chunk of chicken in the direction of the armoire. The cat leapt from the bed and pounced on the hunk of meat, devouring it eagerly.

"Quite the hunter," Feliciana remarked. "I remember when he was just a tiny baby."

"He's still a baby," Cass said, thinking of all the trouble Slipper managed to get into. "He's just bigger now."

"Oh, I almost forgot." Siena held up a tarnished key: it was the key to Agnese's storage room. "I managed to swipe it when I delivered her dinner tray," she said proudly. "I already unlocked the door. I'll replace the key after Signora Querini falls asleep."

"Thank you, Siena," Cass said.

The sun disappeared below the horizon and the stars began to appear. Siena clasped her older sister's hands in her own, giving Feliciana a fierce hug before retiring to the servants' quarters. Feliciana went to the window and inhaled deeply.

"I've missed this sky," she said. "There's so much haze over the Rialto, you never get to see stars."

Cass thought about how she used to feel the same way, before her friend Liviana's body had disappeared and set into motion a series of events that ended with Cass being attacked. Outside the window, the spikes of the graveyard fence glittered in the moonlight, the high grass beckoning to her like skeletal fingers. No one knew where Livi's body had ended up, but Cass suspected it lay piecemeal in Angelo de Gradi's workshop. The courtesan Mariabella's body still lay in Liviana's tomb.

And what of Sophia's body, which had floated to the surface of the Grand Canal? She hoped Dubois had had the decency to bury her, so that her soul could ascend to heaven.

But it was unlikely.

"I'm sure you're ready to get some sleep," Cass said. She didn't want to think of dead bodies or Joseph Dubois anymore tonight.

Feliciana ran a hand over her bonnet, smiling once again at the night sky. "I'm just happy to be here," she said. "It has been forever since I've felt safe. But I do, now."

Cass wished it were that easy. She didn't feel safe anywhere. But she just smiled and nodded. Grabbing a folded blanket from the bottom shelf of her armoire and a pillow off her bed, she opened the door of her bedroom just a crack. The villa was dark and silent.

She lit a candle that sat on her washing table and motioned to Feliciana. The two girls crept through the portego and into the dining room, where they descended the narrow servants' staircase. San Domenico was built up slightly higher than the Rialto, so there wasn't any standing water in the hallways, but the stone floor was damp and the air smelled moldy.

"Sorry," Cass whispered. "It's probably not too much of an improvement from your previous accommodations."

"If you're not going to wake me in the middle of the night and command me to pray, I'll consider it an improvement," Feliciana whispered back.

Cass led Feliciana past the butler's office to the far corner of the villa's first floor, where an arched doorway was cut into the stone. She pushed on the wooden door and it creaked inward. Unlocked, just as Siena had promised. Cass held her candle high in the dark space. She had no idea what her aunt was storing down here.

Neat stacks of evenly spaced wooden crates filled most of the low-ceilinged rectangular room. Some of the piles were covered with canvas sheets. All of the stacks were balanced on platforms made from stucco bricks, which kept the lowest boxes from being damaged by occasional flooding and the near-constant dampness.

"What is all this?" Feliciana asked, peeking beneath one of the sheets. "Your parents' things?"

Cass shook her head. "I don't think so. My parents' belongings were sold with the estate." She tried to remove the top of the crate nearest to her, but it was nailed shut.

"Who knew Signora Querini had so much?" Feliciana asked.

"Feel free to nose through it," Cass said, handing Feliciana the candle. "Maybe you'll find some additional clothing that fits. Siena or I will do our best to sneak you some breakfast in the morning."

Feliciana dragged two wooden crates together and laid Cass's blanket down on top of them. "Pleasant dreams, Signorina Cass," she said. "Are you sure you won't need the candle to get back to your room?"

"I'll be fine." Cass had navigated the darkened villa so many times, she could do it blindfolded and in her sleep. "Good night, Feliciana."

Back upstairs, Cass crawled beneath her covers. She had feared she wouldn't be able to sleep, but the events of the day had exhausted her. She dreamed of a tossing black sea and voices calling to her from the dark, and then she didn't dream at all.

Loud voices from the portego woke Cass the next morning. She slipped on a dressing gown and stepped out into the hallway. Agnese was sitting on the divan, clutching a teacup in one hand and a roll of vellum in the other. Siena hovered close by, a basket of mending perched on one slender hip. Cass couldn't remember the last time she had seen her aunt up so early.

"What is it?" Cass asked, praying someone hadn't already discovered Feliciana. She held a hand in front of her eyes to block out the harsh daylight streaming through the open shutters.

Agnese shook the roll of parchment. "Heresy," she said. "Luca's been imprisoned for speaking out against the Church."

"*What?*" Cass grabbed the letter out of Agnese's swollen fingers and scanned the swirly handwriting. The message was from Donna Domacetti. Of course. She would be the first to know—and spread the news—about any tawdry gossip. Apparently, the donna had seen soldiers escorting Luca toward the Palazzo Ducale the day before and had asked her husband, a senator, why Luca was being arrested.

"That's madness," Cass said. Luca was a good man. He had never spoken out against the Church, she was certain of it. If anyone deserved to be accused of heresy, it was Falco, who wandered around saying science was his religion and that bodies ought to be torn apart in the name of research. "On what evidence?"

"We'll know more soon," Agnese said. "Donna Domacetti is on her way over. You'd better make yourself presentable."

Cass allowed a pale and trembling Siena to tow her in the direction of her bedchamber.

"Heresy," Siena croaked out. "It's such a serious crime, Signorina Cass. What are you going to do? What *can* you do?"

"Have you seen your sister today?" Cass asked impatiently. She was quite certain she had not moped around the house like a shivery, wilting flower whenever anything bad had happened to Falco. Siena needed to pull herself together, immediately. "Luca is a man who can take care of himself. Feliciana is depending on us, for the time being. Try to remember that."

Siena hung her head. "I was sneaking her a bit of breakfast when I saw the messenger approaching. She's fine. Bored, but fine."

"Good. Now help me get dressed before Donna Domacetti arrives and starts telling lurid tales without me."

Siena pulled a cream-colored garment from Cass's armoire.

"Not those," Cass said. "My other stays." Ever since Cristian's dagger had narrowly missed her heart by embedding itself in the whalebone ribbing of her ivory stays, she had considered the undergarment lucky. With a runaway servant hidden in the storage room and Luca in prison, Cass would take all the luck she could get.

She slid her arms into the armholes, and Siena began to thread the laces from behind, her obvious distress causing her to cinch them even tighter than usual.

"Ouch," Cass said. "Remember, I have to be able to breathe when you're finished."

Siena loosened the laces slightly and then began searching through Cass's armoire for skirts and a bodice. She came back with a set of emerald-green skirts and a gray bodice with long silvery sleeves already attached.

Cass slipped the skirts over her slim hips while Siena went to work on the laces of the bodice. "Once I hear what the donna has to say, I plan to go to the Palazzo Ducale, to speak on Luca's behalf."

It was unlikely that the Senate would let her speak to Luca, but Cass was going to try. She couldn't help him without more information, and she wasn't sure she could trust a single word that came from the mouth of that gossiping crone Donna Domacetti. It couldn't hurt to *ask* for a meeting. Maybe a little extra gold would open doors, literally.

Siena grabbed the silver-plated hairbrush from the dressing table and motioned for Cass to sit. Cass waved her away. "I'll just twist it all under a hat," she said, grabbing one made of gray velvet from a shelf in her armoire. "I don't want to miss a moment of the donna's visit."

Donna Domacetti was just settling herself in a velvet chair when Cass returned to the portego. The woman lurched back to her feet, putting a dangerous amount of weight on the wooden frame of Agnese's chair as she did so.

"Cassandra, you poor dear." She leaned in and grasped Cass's bare hands in her own. "My heart goes out to you." Dressed all in red with her gray-streaked hair twisted into a high pair of horns, the donna looked more like an obese devil than Venetian nobility.

"Grazie." Cass curtsied stiffly. Her eyes dropped to the donna's fingers. In addition to a fat ruby and a diamond-encrusted circle of gold, the woman still wore the ring with the six-petaled flower design.

The donna gathered her wide skirts around her as she took her seat on the chair again. Cass noticed the scarlet gown was embossed with shiny metallic threads—gold, undoubtedly. Agnese was still seated stiffly on the divan, a blanket covering her legs and waist. As a kitchen servant appeared with a pot of tea and several cups, Cass realized she was the only one still standing. She pulled a chair over from the far side of the portego, passing by the life-sized depiction of *The Last Supper* as she did so. Cass shivered. She liked the work of da Vinci, but she always felt like the figures in the giant mosaic were watching her.

"We're so grateful you took the time to come," Agnese said. "A dreadful, dreadful business."

"Indeed." Donna Domacetti drained her tea in a single drink, leaving a smear of blood-red lip stain on the rim. "I was shocked. Luca da Peraga, taken to the Doge's prison by order of the Senate. My husband and I could hardly believe it." She lifted her hand and twisted her wrist at one of the serving boys. The boy hurried over and refilled her cup.

Cass set her cup gingerly on the table and glanced over at her aunt. She had plenty of questions for the donna, but it would have been rude for her to speak before Agnese.

"It's absolutely absurd." Agnese clucked her tongue. "Trumping up some charges against a good Venetian man who's returned home for a betrothal ceremony? Exactly how do we go about getting him released?"

Donna Domacetti shook her head sadly, her multiple chins jiggling back and forth. "I wish it were that simple, Agnese. Not only was Signor da Peraga implicated through the *bocca di lione—*"

"The bocca di lione?" Cass nearly upset her cup. "They're holding him based on anonymous accusations tossed into the mouth of a sculpture? I've seen children throw parchment in there as a joke."

"You didn't let me finish, dear." Donna Domacetti took a long drink, swallowing slowly and dabbing at her crimson mouth with one of Agnese's good napkins before continuing. "It seems there are also eyewitnesses to your fiancé's heresy. Nobles who came forth to give testimony." She said this with such undisguised enthusiasm that it took all of Cass's self-control to keep from flinging her untouched cup of tea at the woman's smug face.

"And who exactly are these confused nobles?" Agnese asked,

shooting Cass a warning glance. Cass knew she was one comment away from being ordered to her room. She reclined in her chair and gave Donna Domacetti her most daggerlike scowl.

"I really shouldn't say anything," the donna demurred, "but rumor has it Don Zanotta's own wife is one of the accusers."

"Hortensa Zanotta?" Cass had met her when she visited Palazzo Domacetti for tea. What she remembered most was the deep gouge of smallpox scars on the donna's cheek. That and how she had spoken so cruelly about the murdered women, as if they had deserved their fates. Scarred or not, a wealthy donna with a powerful husband could have whatever she wanted. Why in the world would she condemn an innocent man to die?

"Will there be a trial?" Agnese asked. Her swollen hands dropped to her lap. Cass realized her aunt was working the beads of her rosary. She watched Agnese's fingers push a bead along the golden chain.

"I'm afraid not," Donna Domacetti said. "That is why I came immediately, so that you both would know the gravity of the situation. The Senate has ordered Signor da Peraga to be executed, exactly one month from today."

For a second, no one spoke. The room started to dissolve before Cass's eyes, individual tiles of the da Vinci mosaic winking out like candles that had been extinguished. She fanned herself with one hand. Her bones felt weak, slippery. She had the strangest sensation that she might slide right out of the cushioned chair and onto the floor. When she opened her mouth to speak, her voice was that of a stranger, tiny and timid. "Executed?" she managed to squeak out. "What—what do you mean?"

Donna Domacetti cleared her throat to say more, but Agnese cut her off. "That's preposterous." She reached out to pat Cass on the arm. "Luca is an innocent man, a devout Catholic. Once the Senate has ample time to contemplate the facts, I'm sure they'll reconsider."

Cass inhaled sharply, and then again. It felt like someone had stabbed her in the chest. "But if there's to be no trial, when will anyone contemplate anything?" she asked. The room started to come back into focus, but things were still a little off, like she was viewing everything through a smudged wineglass.

She watched her aunt struggle to her feet and motion to the donna. The two women slowly crossed the portego and hovered at the top of the spiral staircase. Their lips were moving, but Cass couldn't hear their words. She wanted to get up and move closer, but her bones still felt soft, her muscles useless. She rested her head in her hands and tried to replay the parts of the conversation she remembered. *Luca da Peraga . . . Doge's prison . . . order of the Senate . . . eyewitnesses . . . heresy . . . executed . . .*

Executed.

Luca had gone to meet with Joseph Dubois and now he was in prison. *Executed.* It couldn't possibly be a coincidence. If he was arrested because of something he'd said to Dubois, it probably had something to do with Cristian. Which meant it had something to do with her. *Executed.* Cass touched the lily necklace through the fabric of her bodice. Luca had saved her once. Now it was up to her to save him.

"Applied properly,

the rope or the blade

will break all men."

—THE BOOK OF THE ETERNAL ROSE

five

Cass and Siena left for the Rialto just moments after Donna Domacetti waddled down to the dock and disappeared into her own boat.

Summer was preparing for its arrival in Venice. Despite the breeze off the water, the late-spring air was still muggy and thick, the high sun obscured by a ribbon of clouds. Cass fanned herself with her favorite ostrich-feather fan as she settled in beneath the felze of Agnese's gondola.

Siena gathered her muslin skirt around her as she scooted next to Cass. Behind them, Giuseppe—her aunt's gardener and personal gondolier—hummed an unfamiliar tune as he expertly navigated the coastline of San Domenico north toward the lagoon that separated the Rialto from the outlying southern islands.

Cass fiddled with the rosary that hung from the waistline of her skirt. Her mind was whirling as she tried to remember all of Agnese's instructions. *Be polite. Stand up straight. Inquire about the possibility of a trial, but don't be demanding.*

"Are you all right?" Siena asked.

"Fine," Cass said tightly. It couldn't have been further from the truth. If only her aunt had felt well enough to accompany her.

"I wish I was up for the journey," Agnese had declared as she told Cass what to say. "It's a grim business for a girl your age."

Murderers. Grave robbers. Cass was more familiar with grim business than her aunt ever would have guessed.

A fish jumped in the nearby water, sending a spray of droplets cascading through the air. Cass looked up. Stonemasons dangled from the roof of San Giorgio Maggiore, chipping and carving details into the façade of the grand church, while a flurry of men hollered instructions to them from the ground. The gondola bobbed slowly past San Giorgio Island, and she turned her attention to the tiny waves of the lagoon that sloshed back and forth against the boat.

Giuseppe docked the gondola just south of the Palazzo Ducale. The enormous palazzo loomed over the Piazza San Marco, bridging the gap between the basilica and the edge of the lagoon. Bricks in shades of brown and bronze glittered in the daylight. Elaborate friezes and bas-reliefs adorned the larger arched windows. A breezeway ringed the building's perimeter, supported by Gothic columns, each topped with a clover-shaped cutout.

Cass had passed the Palazzo Ducale many times in her life and always thought of the building as a magical place where the Doge and Dogaressa lived and threw spectacular parties. She knew the palazzo was also home to Senate meetings and other official government functions, but she had never thought of the gleaming U-shaped building as a prison. Somewhere in the back of her mind, she must have always known about the *pozzi*, the tiny dank cells on the palazzo's first floor, and the scorching-hot *piombi*, additional cells for "special" prisoners beneath the lead-plated roof of the building, but she had never *really* thought about it.

Until now.

She imagined the worst: Luca buried in blackness, locked away among dark and creeping things. Foul canal water rising up, threatening to drown him while he slept. Rats scrabbling through the bars, sinking their teeth into his flesh. She felt a sharp pain in her chest. It was hopeless. She was one girl against Dubois, against the Senate, against all of Venice. Would anyone even agree to see her?

She took Giuseppe's hand as she alighted from the gondola. Siena followed her. Striding forward as if she clearly belonged there, Cass considered the Palazzo Ducale's many doors and made for the *porta della carta*, the main entrance.

The wooden door was at least ten feet tall, with flower designs carved into the wood at regular intervals. A sculpture of a previous Doge facing a winged lion decorated the top of the door, an elaborate arched window above that. Towers of additional sculpture work flanked each side of the entrance. Cass recognized the figures of Charity, Fortitude, Temperance, and Prudence, their flowing gowns painted in brilliant blues and yellows. Where had those virtues been when someone was dragging an innocent man to prison?

Two soldiers dressed in scarlet and gold were standing guard. "What is your business today, Signorina?" the taller soldier asked gruffly.

"I wish to speak to the Doge," Cass said, raising her chin. "Or to a member of the Senate." In her chopines, she stood slightly taller than the soldiers, and for once her height didn't feel like a liability.

The other soldier grunted with laughter. "Don't they all," he said. "Do you have an appointment?"

The lie was on the tip of her tongue—of *course* she had an appointment—but she couldn't manage to spit it out. She swore under her breath. Falco would have coughed up a lie without hesitation. "No, I don't," Cass admitted. "But I will wait as long as necessary."

The soldiers laughed again, their tan faces turning pink with amusement. "We'll send someone to fetch a chair," the shorter one said. "It might be a couple of fortnights."

Cass was tired of being laughed at. "Listen," she started, trying her best to look menacing. "It's imperative that I speak to someone, so if it cannot be the Doge, then let me speak to one of his associates. I'm here to discuss Signor Luca da Peraga. I believe he has been imprisoned on false charges."

"Ah." The taller soldier ran a finger through his beard. "Signora da Peraga."

Behind her, Siena coughed. Cass started to correct the men that she and Luca were not yet married, but thought better of it. "That's right," she said smoothly.

The guards exchanged a look. Now she could tell that they pitied her. "I suppose we can find *someone* who can better explain to you the charges." The guard motioned, and the girls followed him inside the Palazzo Ducale. Cass slipped out of her chopines and left them just inside the door. She and Siena were ushered up a staircase covered in gold leaf. Servants passed them on the way down, their chins tucked low, eyes toward the ground. The guard led Cass and Siena across a square vestibule to a large room with four doors.

The room was supported by black marble columns, with threads of white running through them like veins. The long walls were paneled in dark wood and embossed with gold. Paintings of religious figures adorned the ceiling: images of God and his angels.

"Wait here," the guard instructed her, and then retreated back the way he had come.

Cass wondered where the other three doors led. Was Luca somewhere nearby? Would he hear her if she called out to him? She went to each door in turn, pressing her ear to the wood. She couldn't hear anything. Did she dare open the door a crack? She tried the first one. Locked. She tried the others. Also locked.

Cass sighed. A hard wooden bench ran along one side of the room. She gathered her skirts and took a seat. Siena paced back and forth, wringing her hands. Cass watched her handmaid's plain leather shoes cross the room, her worn soles temporarily obscuring shining specks of pink and gold embedded in the marble floor.

After what felt like an eternity, a short man dressed in black breeches and a bright purple doublet skittered out from one of the doors. He was about Luca's age, with wire-framed spectacles and a hooked nose that made him look more like a bird than a person. "Signora da Peraga?"

"Yes?" Cass stood up. Siena stopped pacing and stood stiffly next to her.

"I am Giovanni da Riga, aide to the Senate. You will follow me, please."

Cass followed Giovanni into an even larger room. Quickly she realized she was in the Hall of the Senate. If there were to be a trial, it would be here, with the room full of politicians and bloodthirsty citizens who were always eager to see a man condemned to die. The chamber was empty, but Cass could imagine how it must look when occupied—the elevated platform with ornate wooden seats for the Doge and the Council of Ten, the velvet cordoned-off chairs for other high-ranking Senate members, wooden booths for those in attendance but not part of the official proceedings.

Giovanni motioned for Cass to sit in the first wooden booth. Siena sat next to her, and Cass could feel her trembling. Giovanni stood in front of the girls, pacing back and forth, peering down at a half-unrolled parchment as he spoke. "Signor da Peraga's situation is quite grave. The signore has been indicted and imprisoned on the charge of heresy, as accused by parties both anonymous and in person."

Cass felt rage seething in her veins. "And who are these parties who have accused him in person?" Her voice came out hot and tight.

"I'm not at liberty to give out that information," Giovanni said haltingly.

Cass couldn't help it. She jumped up and ripped the parchment from the aide's hands. She would see for herself just what kind of *witnesses* Signor Dubois had managed to buy. A bunch of starving lepers and mercenary prostitutes, undoubtedly.

Hortensa Zanotta's name was on the list, as were several other names Cass didn't recognize. She gasped. "All of these people accused Luca?"

"Signora!" Giovanni seized the list from her trembling fingers. "You must maintain order."

Cass inhaled deeply, trying to cool the heat that threatened to boil out through her skin. She changed her tactics, forcing a demure smile as she returned to her seat, adjusting her skirts to show just a hint of her stocking. "*Mi dispiace*, Signore. I'm just afraid that my fia—my husband has been the victim of a terrible crime, and that unsavory people were paid in exchange for their testimony." She arched her eyebrows meaningfully.

"You—you're not suggesting—"

"Surely those who are desperate for a little gold might be persuaded to remember events in a certain way, don't you think?"

"I understand your concerns, Signora, but Signor da Peraga's accusers are from noble families. Well-known, God-fearing members of the community." Giovanni's spectacles started to fog over, as if his face had begun to sweat. "You can understand why the Senate took the accusations quite seriously."

"Is there any chance at all of a trial?"

"My understanding is that Signor da Peraga has already been sentenced," Giovanni said.

Siena made a tiny whimpering noise. Cass shot her a sharp look and she ducked her head, focusing her attention on the floor. Cass turned back to Giovanni and nodded. "I don't suppose I can visit Signor da Peraga? Even to lay eyes on him just for a moment would be such a relief."

Giovanni shook his head vigorously. "It is never permitted. Only his legal counsel is allowed to see him."

Did Luca even have legal counsel? Perhaps Cass should send a message to his mother on the mainland just in case. No. He had mentioned that his mother was unwell. This was the sort of news that could kill a woman. Luca was industrious and prepared. Undoubtedly, he had gotten word to an attorney.

Cass shook a few gold pieces out of her purse. She transferred them from one hand to the other. "There is absolutely *no* way I can see my husband, not even for a moment? Not even from a distance?" She dabbed at her eyes with the back of a gloved hand, trying to squeeze out a couple of tears for the aide's benefit.

Giovanni stared at the gold. "I would like to assist you, Signora, but it would be a grave risk for *both* myself and the jailer." He licked his lips.

Cass doubled the amount of coins in her hands. Behind her, Siena inhaled sharply. It was probably more gold than she had ever seen all at once.

Giovanni removed his spectacles and polished them on his shirt. He glanced around the Senate Hall warily, as if he thought maybe the paintings were spying on him. "Return to the antechamber." He gestured toward the door they had come through. "Let me see if there's any possible way I can help you." His voice wavered slightly.

He disappeared, only to return a few minutes later. "Exchange your cloak and shoes with your maidservant and put up your hood," he said. "Someone will come for you." He skittered back through the door like a nervous rat before Cass could ask who, exactly, was coming for her.

Probably someone to arrest me, she thought as she slipped out of her cloak and shoes. She secured Siena's plain muslin cloak around her gown and lifted the hood so that it obscured her face and hair. She settled back in on the bench, watching with amusement as Siena awkwardly fastened Cass's embroidered silk cloak around her neck and slipped her feet into Cass's velvet slippers.

A different door creaked open, and a stumpy bald man shuffled through. He was almost as old as Agnese, with yellowing skin and a hump on his back that made him walk stooped over. He looked up at

Cass with a pair of beady eyes that were set close to his crooked nose. He had the look of a man who had lost one too many tavern brawls.

"You." He pointed at Cass and then rotated his hand until the palm of his dirty leather glove faced up. It took her a moment to realize he was waiting for payment. She deposited the gold coins into his hand. "Follow me," he said.

Cass gave Siena's hand a quick squeeze and then wordlessly rose from the bench. She nodded at the man, who did not respond except to turn his back and mutter under his breath. She followed him back through the door, across a gallery, up two narrow flights of stairs, and down a dingy passageway lit only by minuscule openings carved straight into the marble walls. The heat was unbearable, the sun on the lead-plated roof turning the entire corridor into an oven. The passage ended at a thick metal door. A tarnished ring of keys hung on a hook just outside.

"Keep your head down," the jailer muttered as he reached up and grasped the set of keys. He shoved one in the lock and jiggled it. The door swung open with a groan.

Cass raised one of her gloved hands to her mouth, willing herself not to vomit from the overpowering scent of urine and feces that wafted into the hallway. Holding her breath, she ducked her head low to enter the room. *No wonder the jailer walks hunched over,* she thought. The ceiling couldn't have been higher than five feet.

She stood inside a garret, the roof of the Palazzo Ducale just above her head. A single high window cast a beam of scattered light across the dusty enclosure. A row of thick iron doors with circular vents cut in the middle ran along the edge of the room. So these were the infamous piombi—cells so cramped and sweltering that men sometimes went mad from being imprisoned in them.

Cass tried not to look at the dark holes centered in each of the cell doors. She didn't want to make eye contact with any of the prisoners, at least one of whom was moaning. Instead, she focused her attention on a long wooden table that ran against the far wall of the room. On it sat coils of rope and scattered pieces of silver that reflected the scant light. Cass squinted. Were those . . . knives? She took a tentative step forward, and then another. Sure enough, an assortment of daggers was displayed on the table, their tips smeared with rust.

Or blood.

Horrified, Cass spun around to glare at the jailer.

He ignored her accusing look. "Last one." He pointed toward the corner of the room. "You have five minutes."

Cass gathered Siena's cloak around her body and strode toward the cell at the end, slouching low to account for the sloping roof. Mindless of the grimy floor, she crouched down and peered through the circular grate, into the cell beyond. "Luca?" she whispered.

The blackness seemed to recede into forever, as if Cass were staring at a pit that went all the way to hell. A blurry figure materialized from the dark.

Luca knelt before the grate, his soft eyes peeking out at her with surprise. His beard was a little unkempt and there were bluish circles under his eyes, but otherwise he looked unharmed. His hair glistened with sweat, and the fabric of his doublet clung fast to his chest. "You shouldn't be here," he whispered. "They'll kill you if you get caught. Besides, there's nothing you can do."

Cass pressed one hand against the grate. She cast a glance back over her shoulder at the wooden table. "Are they hurting you?"

"No," he said.

Not yet. Cass couldn't shake the feeling that his predicament was her fault. "There has to be something. You're innocent. Tell me how I can prove it."

Luca shook his head. "You can't, Cass. The testimony has been bought and paid for. No one will go against Dubois. He owns half of the Council of Ten."

The Council of Ten was a group of senators elected from within the general council. Hortensa's husband, Don Zanotta, sat among them. They were some of the most powerful men in all of Venice. They and Joseph Dubois.

"But I know the names of your accusers," Cass said, fanning herself with her free hand. Rivulets of sweat were beginning to trickle down the sides of her neck. "Donna Hortensa Zanotta, for one."

Luca frowned. "I've never even met her."

"If I could persuade her to recant her statement, do you suppose you might go free?" She let the tips of her fingers curl their way through the grate.

"Unlikely," he said. "It's my understanding she is one of several accusers, all of whom probably gave false testimony at the behest of Dubois." Luca reached his own hand up so that his fingertips met Cass's. "Promise me you won't go threatening Dubois. There's no point in both of us dying."

Cass twined her fingers through Luca's, their hands separated only by the network of steel bars. She leaned forward until her forehead rested against the grate. "But I don't understand," she whispered. "What did you do to make him so angry?"

Luca lowered his voice to a whisper. "Dubois is a member of a group called the Order of the Eternal Rose. When my father died, he gave me a key that unlocked a hiding place to certain papers relating to this Order. I told Dubois I would make these pages public unless he sent Cristian away, but then Dubois demanded I relinquish the papers to him. I told him I had burned the papers, but he didn't believe me."

"What's so special about these papers?" Cass's eyelashes flicked against the metal grate as she blinked.

"Dubois thinks the papers incriminate him in crimes perpetrated by the Order."

"What crimes?"

"That's exactly it. I have no idea," Luca said, shaking his head. "I only know the Order must be involved in something terrible. Unfortunately the papers aren't quite as incriminating as I let on."

"It was all a bluff," Cass said, starting to understand.

Luca sighed. "Dubois's name *is* on them, but there are no crimes mentioned. They're largely chemical formulas and research notes. They're part of a larger book—the Book of the Eternal Rose. That's what he's really looking for. According to my father, the complete set of pages describes enough atrocities committed by Dubois and the other members to have them executed several times over."

"So this book is the only way to fight Dubois? Do you know where it is? I'll bring it to you. I'll . . . ," she trailed off.

"Cass." Luca squeezed her fingers, and her insides went a little weak. "You owe no debt to me. Have your aunt arrange another match, perhaps with someone of your own choosing. Go be happy. It's what I want for you."

"Luca!" Her voice rose in pitch. "Don't even speak like that." Once upon a time she'd dreamed of those words. *Go be happy.* Luca releasing her so she could be with Falco. But she hadn't meant for it to come to this. It couldn't come to this. She could never be happy with someone else, knowing that only Luca's execution had made it possible. And what exactly did he mean, *someone of her own choosing*?

"Quiet," the jailer growled. "You have one more minute."

"Tell me more about the book," Cass begged. "I can find it."

Luca exhaled deeply, touching his forehead to hers. "I don't want you to get hurt, Cass." His voice threatened to break apart on the last word. He reached his other hand up to stroke Cass's cheek with a single fingertip.

"*I* don't want you to die," Cass whispered. A droplet of sweat fell from her chin and landed on the dusty floor in front of the cell. Inside of her, a wound opened, spilling sadness and rage throughout her body. Luca was brave. Luca was innocent. Luca would never let her rot away in a prison cell.

Their fingers were still intertwined, their foreheads touching. Connected. So close. Their eyelashes practically weaving together.

Cass realized she could kiss him. She could just tilt her head slightly and their lips would meet. For the first time she wanted to. She wanted to show him that she cared for him, that she was a good and decent woman, not the kind of person who would just let him die because it was convenient to do so.

Luca reached up with his free hand again. Cass felt certain he was going to angle her mouth toward his. Her eyelids started to flutter closed, but then stopped when she felt a point of pressure against her throat. She realized her cloak had fallen open, and that her lily pendant was exposed. Luca was touching it.

"I'm so glad you're wearing it," he whispered, his voice growing hoarse. "It'll be something for you to remember me by."

Cass swallowed down a lump in her throat. She touched her lips to the corner of his jaw, exhaling hard against his skin. "Stop it this instant. I will not give up on you, Luca da Peraga."

Luca turned his mouth so his lips just barely brushed against hers, so quickly her mouth formed an O of surprise. Her legs wavered and her body threatened to crumple to the floor. She didn't know if it was the unbearable heat or her uncomfortable position. Or the kiss. She closed her eyes for a second, holding fast to Luca's hand until her bones went steady again.

He chuckled, an actual laugh. "Now, no matter what happens, I'll have that to remember you by."

Cass leaned forward and felt the metal bars of the grate digging into her skin. She didn't care. Suddenly she wanted to be as close as she could to Luca. Luca, who now wanted her to forget his death and find someone else with whom she could be happy. Cass had never known such selflessness before. She pressed her mouth hard against his, ignoring his sweat and the stubble of his beard digging into her skin. His whole body tensed in response. For one sweet moment, the filth and the stench and the grimness of the situation dissipated. All Cass felt was herself and Luca, connected.

When they broke apart, she struggled to catch her breath. "Now stop talking of remembrances and tell me where to find this book."

Luca touched his free hand to his lips. His face was flushed and his eyes were bright. "My father believed the book was in Florence, the birthplace of the Order." He dropped his voice. "But I can tell you for certain where to find the pages."

"Where?" Cass asked. Around her, the prisoners' moaning seemed to fade; the whole room fell quiet.

"Locked inside your family tomb."

"What?" Cass wasn't quite sure she'd heard him right. "The Caravello tomb?"

"Yes."

"But why would your father put them *there*?" Cass asked.

"He didn't," Luca said. "Your mother did."

"The truth is often
different from what is perceived
as truth, but only the latter
is of any consequence."

—THE BOOK OF THE ETERNAL ROSE

"The truth is often
different from what is perceived
as truth, but only the latter
is of any consequence."

—THE BOOK OF THE ETERNAL ROSE

six

W hat? Why would my mother—"

Heavy boot steps sounded behind her. The jailer was coming. Cass was out of time.

"The key is in the study at my family palazzo," Luca whispered. "Hidden in the fireplace."

Before Luca could explain further, the jailer took hold of Cass's arm and hauled her back to her feet. "You must go now," he said, prodding her roughly through the door that led back into the passageway.

Wiping the perspiration from her brow, Cass retraced her steps to the room with four doors, where she quickly exchanged her shoes and cloak with Siena.

"Let's go," Cass said. "I'll explain on the way." She towed Siena across the vestibule and down the stairs. A pair of noblewomen stood just inside the porta della carta, their handmaids hovering dutifully at their sides. Cass could feel all four sets of eyes burning into her back as she passed.

"Get everything you came for?" the shorter soldier asked as Cass slipped back into her chopines. She ignored him, heading quickly across the smaller part of the piazza to the lagoon, where Giuseppe and their gondola bobbed in the quay.

For one brief second, Cass allowed herself to replay the kiss, the prickle of Luca's beard against her chin, his lips on hers. Softness. Pressure. How could he just tell her to forget him and find someone else if he loved her? Even if Cass were to be executed, she would want her husband to weep over her corpse, to declare her the great love of his life.

Without waiting for Giuseppe's assistance, she wobbled her way into the boat. She instructed him to take them down the Grand Canal.

"Where are we going?" Siena asked, taking Giuseppe's gnarled hand in her own as she lifted her skirt over the side of the gondola.

Cass yanked open the slats on the felze. "We have to go to Palazzo da Peraga, but first we're going to pay a little visit to Donna Zanotta."

Giuseppe obeyed wordlessly. He had been working for Agnese's estate for more than thirty years and had learned not to question the whims of Cass or her aunt. It occurred to Cass for the first time that he must know many secrets about Agnese. She wondered what sort of stories he might be able to tell.

As they passed into the wealthiest part of the San Polo district, Cass balled her fists tightly in her lap. Hortensa had everything. What could Dubois possibly have promised her in exchange for her testimony? Had she done it just to be cruel, to be hurtful? Or had he threatened her to get her to comply?

Giuseppe slowed the boat to a stop in front of Palazzo Zanotta, a vast and ostentatious building with a façade made of brick and brightly painted marble trimming. Don Zanotta's private dock featured a pair of mooring posts carved in the shape of knights wielding broadswords. Giuseppe tied up the gondola and helped Cass and Siena from the boat.

Cass glanced up as she stepped onto the dock. The sun had made its way across the sky. It must be late afternoon already. She adjusted her lace collar, which seemed intent on strangling her.

The front door of Palazzo Zanotta was made of carved wood and gold filigree. An ornate bronze doorknocker in the shape of a wreath was mounted at eye level. Cass reached up and knocked the circle of metal leaves, wincing when the foliage's sharp edges pricked the skin of her hand.

No one answered. She knocked again, this time more insistently. Louder. More knocks. "It appears no one is home," Siena ventured.

"Of course someone is home," Cass said crossly. "Don Zanotta wouldn't just let his palazzo sit empty, not even if he and the donna were away."

Eventually the front door opened a crack and a wrinkled, pasty face appeared. "The don and donna are away in Florence," the servant rasped.

Cass wasn't even sure if she was speaking to a man or a woman. The door started to close and Cass jammed her foot in the crack. "When will Donna Zanotta be back?" she asked. "It's important that I speak to her as soon as possible."

"Not until the end of summer. They left yesterday at daybreak. You just missed her."

How convenient. Hortensa Zanotta had given false testimony and then immediately fled the city. And to Florence of all places, where Luca believed the Book of the Eternal Rose to be. Could it be a coincidence? Or was everything somehow connected?

Cass nodded at the servant, and then she and Siena returned to the gondola. Giuseppe made quick work of rowing them through the network of smaller canals to Palazzo da Peraga. The whole place looked a little worn, as if even the servants were neglecting it. The shutters were fastened tightly and the mooring post was in bad need of a repainting.

It had been years since Cass had last visited Luca's family home. Back then, her parents would always speak quietly to his parents in the study while she and Luca were either abandoned in the portego or ushered out into the tiny courtyard to "play." For Luca this usually meant time to read. Sometimes he would pick out a book for Cass too. Then they would sit curled up in garden chairs for hours. Cass had found it dull, and even a little rude, that Luca spent so much time reading around her. Now she thought perhaps it had just been his shyness that kept him from speaking more.

The girls exited the gondola, and Cass stepped up to Palazzo da Peraga's door and rapped sharply. Siena stood next to her, worry manifested in her posture, in the way she kept threading and unthreading her fingers.

Cass knew it should bother her—really bother her—that Siena was in love with Luca, especially if she was going to continue serving her after Cass and Luca got married. But right now, Cass was just grateful to have such a staunch ally.

"What exactly are we looking for?" Siena asked.

"A key." Cass didn't explain further, that the key unlocked her family tomb. She was still struggling to wrap her mind around that fact. Surely her parents hadn't been members of any Order that included Joseph Dubois, but then how had her mother come into possession of the documents Dubois was so desperate to acquire?

The da Peragas' butler, a tall lanky man with silvery hair and piercing brown eyes, opened the door. Though she had been just a child when she had last visited, he recognized Cass immediately. "Signorinas, do come in," he said.

"Signore," Cass said, trying to recall the man's name, but failing. "I wish we were meeting under better circumstances."

Two men were sitting in the portego, sorting through stacks of crumbling parchment.

The butler noticed Cass staring. "They're looking through the estate's finances. We are trying everything we can to help Signor da Peraga during this difficult time." The butler stumbled over the last couple of words.

"Do you believe he is innocent?" Cass said.

"Of course," the butler said, looking shocked. "But sometimes it isn't the truth that matters. It's what other people think is true." He sighed. "What can I do for you, Signorina?"

"I was hoping to look around," she said. She tried to make her voice wistful, as if she were merely interested in acquiring a few tokens to remind her of her fiancé. She didn't want to tell the men she had spoken to Luca earlier. They would not approve of her bribing the Palazzo Ducale jailer.

"Go ahead. The soldiers came to search the place this morning. We've done our best to return everything to its place."

Cass's stomach tightened. So the soldiers had been here. She could only hope they had not discovered the key.

Siena trailed behind her as Cass pushed open the thick wooden door to the study. It swung inward, creaking on its rusted hinges. She went immediately to the fireplace. Kneeling on the tile floor, she peered up into the darkness of the chimney. She reached a gloved hand into the flue. Soot rained down, blackening her glove and making her cough. She examined the entire fireplace, running her hands across the bricks, wondering if maybe she'd misunderstood Luca's words.

Then her fingers skimmed a rough edge. She paused and peered closer. Once again, she traced a finger of her dirty glove over the thin strip of mortar between two of the bricks at the back of the fireplace.

One of the bricks was definitely loose. She jiggled it, biting her lip to keep from crying out as the brick fell into her hand, exposing a hollow space at the back of the fireplace. Cass reached back into the dark opening. Her fingers closed around something wrapped in fabric. She pulled it out for examination. It was a bright red bundle. Inside it was a key.

Siena sucked in a breath. "Whose crest is that?" She pointed at the carving of a lion holding a shield. "The da Peraga family?"

Cass shook her head. Her mouth was dry. "It's mine," she croaked out. "It's the Caravello crest." She had seen the emblem on sashes and wall hangings and even some of the dinner napkins she had used as a child.

Turning the key over in her hands, she ran one finger along the dulled edges of its teeth. How did her mother come to possess documents from a mysterious Order? Why had she hidden them among the dead?

When Cass and Siena arrived back at the villa, there was another surprise waiting for them: a wide blue boat with long leather privacy curtains was tied up at Agnese's splintering dock. A black silk banner emblazoned with a gold griffin holding a flaming sword was mounted on the stern of the boat. The word *victory* was splashed across the sword's blade.

The rage that Cass had been fighting all day threatened to overwhelm her. She knew that crest. She had seen the blue boat before. "What is Joseph Dubois doing here?" she spat out.

She didn't even wait for Siena to exit the gondola behind her. She kicked off her chopines as she ran across the damp lawn, sprinting up the stairs and into the portego. Dubois was sitting across the table from her aunt Agnese, sipping from one of Agnese's painted teacups. They both looked up at Cass in surprise.

"Haven't you done enough?" Cass burst out. Blades of wet grass fell from the hem of her skirts onto the clean portego floor. "Letting thieves and murderers go free while sending an innocent man to the gallows? Now you've come all the way out here to revel in our misery? Is that it?"

"Cassandra!" Agnese cried out, shocked.

Dubois looked unfazed. "Signorina Caravello," he said, rising from his seat to bow. "Your passion is so like your mother's."

"You have no right to speak of my mother," Cass said, wishing her voice wouldn't shake.

Agnese looked as though her eyes were about to pop out of her head. "I apologize, Signore," she said quickly. "I can't imagine what has made my niece behave in such a fashion." She turned back to Cass, scowling so deeply that her silvery eyebrows met in the middle of her forehead.

"It's all right, Signora Querini," Dubois said. "Young Signorina Caravello is under a great deal of stress. Perhaps, Signorina, it will please you to know that we have apprehended the man responsible for Sophia Garzolo's death. He is scheduled to be hanged at sunset exactly a fortnight from now."

Footsteps sounded on the main staircase. Siena burst into the portego with Cass's chopines dangling from one hand. She froze when she saw Dubois. Dropping her eyes to the floor, she backed quickly against the wall.

"And what man is that?" Cass asked, raising her chin and meeting Dubois's stare. What other poor unfortunate soul had crossed the Frenchman and ended up sentenced to death?

"Signor Carmino, the estate butler. I was very surprised to find out he had been . . . harassing several female members of my staff. I assume he was trying to court Signorina Garzolo." Dubois examined his nails. "Things must not have gone his way."

Cass fought a feeling of revulsion. She did not believe a single word that came out of Dubois's mouth. "And did this man explain why he took the time to carve an X in the poor girl's chest?" she challenged. If Dubois was going to send another innocent man to die, Cass wanted him to understand that she knew it.

Dubois raised his shoulders slightly. He managed to make even a shrug look regal. "Who can understand the mind of a criminal?" He sipped from his teacup. "The important thing is that Signor Carmino is going to hang for his crime. Justice will be served." He set his cup down onto the gold-rimmed saucer with a delicate clink.

"Speaking of justice," Cass said, her voice turning to acid, "perhaps you can explain to me why my fiancé was carted off to the Doge's prisons the day after seeking an audience with you."

Signor Dubois tilted his head just slightly. "Signorina Caravello," he said piteously, reaching out toward her, "I can assure you I was as stunned to hear about his arrest as you were."

Cass pulled her hand out of Dubois's reach. "And are you also stunned to hear of his impending execution, just a month from today? Certainly you must not have known or you wouldn't have been so cruel as to pay us a visit and speak so cavalierly of a hanging."

"I apologize. I was unaware a sentence had already been handed down." Dubois's eyes flicked around the room. They landed on Siena, who was still pressed against the corner. She appeared to be growing paler with each breath. Soon she would fade completely into the white marble. "But actually I came here because I heard rumor that you or your lady's maid might have heard from Feliciana Minorita, my missing servant." Signor Dubois's eyes went dark for a second; his voice dropped in pitch. "You see, I would do almost anything to have her back."

"The crypts of Venice are
overrun with willing corpses
waiting to be harvested for
the good of science."

—THE BOOK OF THE ETERNAL ROSE

seven

nything, including lie or kill, Cass thought.

"Cassandra, is this true?" Agnese asked. "Has Feliciana been found?"

Cass shook her head quickly, praying that Siena wouldn't collapse on the floor in a heap. "No, Aunt Agnese. Most likely, someone saw me talking to Siena and mistook her for her sister."

The sisters looked alike from the back, or had anyway, before Feliciana's hair had been shorn from her scalp. It was a plausible story, and Agnese seemed convinced. But Dubois was staring hard at Siena, as if he thought she might shatter under his gaze.

"Is there anything else we can help you with, Signor Dubois?" Cass asked quickly.

Dubois stood up, running a hand through his gray-streaked hair. "It is I who should be offering my assistance to you in this time of crisis," he murmured. "Do contact me if you hear from Signorina Minorita. And of course, I am at your disposal if you think of anything I can do for you."

Cass could think of several things she'd like Dubois to do, like stick his head in a canal and leave it there, but she kept quiet. After he left, she quickly filled her aunt in on what she had learned at Palazzo Ducale, leaving out the part about bribing Giovanni and the jailer. Agnese gave Cass a soft look. "Try not to worry. Truth is a pesky rodent. No matter how deeply it is buried, it will dig its way to the surface eventually."

Cass sighed. Truth. No one seemed to care much about that.

She couldn't bear the thought of Luca in prison. Who knew what might happen to him there? They could starve him or worse: torture him. She tried not to think of the table laden with coils of rope and blood-smeared daggers.

Instead, she forced down a quick supper and then returned to her bedroom, where she sat at her dressing table, staring at the tomb key. She had strung it onto the silver chain with her pendant, worried that it might simply vanish otherwise. Her fingers traced the outline of the lion figure, the swirls of its mane, the sharp points at the tip of each paw.

She flicked her eyes toward her bedroom window. Only blackness peeked back at her through the broken shutter. What she ought to do was just wait until tomorrow, to find the pages in the light of day. But Cass couldn't stop thinking about them. Was there a side to her mother that she didn't know about? Secrets hidden within the folds of parchment? Cass had to know.

The wall clock said it was almost nine. Was it late enough to sneak out of the villa undetected? She got up from the dressing table and went to the doorway. A soft glow of light came from the direction of the portego. Agnese didn't spend much time out of her bedroom after dinner. It was probably Narissa or one of the other servants, doing some mending.

Cass decided to pay a visit to Feliciana before venturing out into the graveyard. If anyone caught her sneaking out, Agnese would have her head. Besides, Feliciana was probably hungry.

Concealing a small bundle of meat and cheese she had saved from dinner, Cass lit a candle and made her way to the portego. Sure enough, Narissa sat in a chair by the window, her knobby fingers working a needle and thread through one of Agnese's fraying chemises.

"I'm just going down to the kitchen for a snack." Cass held her arm tightly to her side, hoping Narissa would assume she was carrying her journal, as always. That would be a difficult trick to pull off if the napkin decided to unfold and spill food scraps all over the floor.

In the bobbing candlelight, Narissa's face was a mix of sharp angles and deep lines. "All right, but stay inside." Her voice softened. "I understand why you can't sleep, Signorina Cass, but remember your aunt doesn't like you wandering by yourself at night."

Finally: something Cass and Agnese could agree on. Just the thought of venturing out into the quiet blackness made her heart start thrumming in her chest. She couldn't believe some of the wild adventures she'd had with Falco. Traipsing around the Rialto in the dead of night unarmed—they were lucky they hadn't ended up stabbed or worse.

It occurred to her that in only a few short weeks she'd become someone different, someone who wouldn't even walk the grounds of her family's private estate after sunset anymore. What would Falco think of the Cass who jumped at shadows and was afraid to venture beyond her villa door?

She reminded herself that he wasn't there, to witness or to judge—he had chosen to leave. She knew it was selfish, almost outrageously so, for her to wish Falco had stayed in Venice to fight for her. Still, wasn't love about sacrifice? Luca had put his studies on hold to spend time with her, after all.

Did that mean Luca loved her more than Falco did? It didn't matter. Falco made her come alive in a way she didn't think Luca ever would. But there was that moment at the Palazzo Ducale, when she had felt compelled to kiss Luca. It was just the drama, she decided. The clandestine meeting. The swell of emotions. Plus, Luca had risked his life for her, repeatedly. Even as he sat in prison awaiting his execution, his main concern was still for Cass's safety and happiness. She loved him for that, but not in the way she loved Falco. Still, Luca had saved her, and now she had to save him. Everything else would come later, in time.

Glancing back over her shoulder to make sure Narissa wasn't eyeing her, Cass crept down the shadowy first-floor hallway that led to the storage area where Feliciana was hiding.

She knocked twice, so softly that she figured it was unlikely that Feliciana even heard her, but the door creaked open and Siena's sister peeked out warily. She'd been at the villa for only two days, but already her face seemed less hollow, her eyes less sunken, as though she were a corpse that Cass and Siena were slowly bringing back from the dead.

"I brought you dinner." Cass slipped inside and closed the door behind her. She handed the wrapped bundle of food to Feliciana, who unfolded it carefully.

"Thank you, Signorina Cass." Feliciana crossed the damp stone floor and sat on her makeshift bed. "I didn't know if I'd see you or Siena tonight."

"We spent all day in the city." Cass quickly relayed the story of

Luca's imprisonment and the trip to the Palazzo Ducale to speak on his behalf. Finally there was someone she could tell everything to. Feliciana wouldn't lecture her about bribery. She'd be impressed.

And she was. Feliciana's eyes got wider and wider as Cass spoke. "Luca da Peraga? A heretic? It's laughable." She ran a hand over the fuzz of blonde hair on her scalp. "Next they'll be saying he's the one who killed Sophia."

Cass couldn't help but notice how when Feliciana spoke Luca's name, it felt completely different from when Siena did. She wondered whether Feliciana knew of her sister's feelings for Cass's fiancé. "Actually, a Signor Carmino has been found guilty of Sophia's murder. Dubois took great pleasure in informing me of his execution."

"What?" Feliciana practically screeched. "Signor Carmino may have been a flirt, but he was no murderer."

Cass put a finger to her lips. "I know he didn't do it. It was Dubois and his henchmen. And Dubois is also the reason Luca ended up in prison."

Feliciana's eyes narrowed. "How does your fiancé even know Joseph? Hasn't Luca been living abroad for years?"

"He's met with Dubois several times since he returned to town," Cass said. "Including the day before he was arrested."

"But why?" Feliciana asked. "Why would Luca meet with him? What aren't you telling me?" She patted the crate next to her.

Cass lowered herself to the blanket-covered wood, wincing slightly. She hated the thought that Feliciana was forced to sleep on the rough crate, but she supposed it was better than directly on the damp floor, as nuns often did.

"It's a long story." Cass took a deep breath and then exhaled slowly. "A few weeks ago, my friend Liviana passed away. Do you remember her?"

Feliciana nodded. "She was always such a frail girl."

"She was interred in the graveyard right outside the villa," Cass continued. "When I went to visit her tomb, I noticed the door was open. I went inside and saw that the cover to her coffin was askew." Cass looked down at her hands. She could feel her throat constricting, her voice tightening as she thought about Mariabella. "As I struggled to replace the lid, I couldn't keep from glancing down at the body. It wasn't Livi. It was a girl I'd never seen before, a girl with an X carved over her heart." Slowly, the rest of the story spilled out. Cass running into Falco in the graveyard. Their murder investigation. How it led them to Angelo de Gradi's workshop full of body parts in neatly arranged tin basins and Sophia's body floating in the Grand Canal.

Cass's throat grew dry as she spoke. "Falco and I, we—" She blushed.

Feliciana's eyebrows shot up. "Signorina Cassandra! You're telling me . . ." She trailed off, but the implication was obvious.

"No," Cass said quickly. "But we kissed, and sometimes I think . . . I think I love him. *Loved* him," she corrected. She continued her story before Feliciana could press for the intimate details. "At Madalena's wedding I was lured into the wine room by a friend of Signor Rambaldo's. His name is Cristian, and I believe he is the same Frenchman you saw at Palazzo Dubois. I didn't know it at the time, but he's actually Luca's half brother. He tried to—" Cass swallowed hard. "I think he meant to kill me." She finished by telling Feliciana about the deal Luca had struck with Dubois.

"The Order of the Eternal Rose. I may have heard that name mentioned by visitors to Palazzo Dubois." Feliciana frowned. "How much does your aunt know?"

"Very little."

Feliciana arched an eyebrow.

"Almost nothing," Cass admitted. "She knows I was attacked at Madalena's wedding, but she believes it was by a random thief. She knows nothing of the Order or Dubois's involvement in the murders."

"It's quite a sordid tale." Feliciana struggled to conceal a yawn.

"You're tired," Cass said, straightening up. Her knees ached, and her hands were covered with dust. "I should let you rest." It was getting to be late enough that she could safely sneak outside. She could no longer put off venturing out into the graveyard in search of the sheaf of papers.

"I am tired," Feliciana said. She blinked hard. After a moment she added, "Thank you for saving me. You and my sister. I don't know what I would do without you."

"We're glad you're here." Grabbing her lantern, Cass slipped out of the room and closed the door behind her.

Cass passed back through the portego, noting with satisfaction that Narissa had retired for the night. The crypt key hung around Cass's neck, cold against her flushed skin. All she needed was her cloak, she decided, heading for her bedroom. *That and a little courage.*

Just as she slipped back into her chamber, something slammed against the glass of her window. Cass's heart leapt into her throat. Was someone prowling the grounds of the villa? Falco had thrown rocks at her window once, but the pebbles had sounded like fingers snapping, rattling the panes ever so slightly. This was more like someone pounding on the glass with a fist.

Cass approached the window from an angle, as if she thought something might reach straight through it and grab her. She squinted at the grainy glass. Could a bird have flown straight into the windowpane? Or a bat?

She could just barely make out the fence of the graveyard and the rows of crypts behind. A chill crept up her spine. She hadn't been to the graveyard since before Madalena's wedding. Just the thought of the mist-shrouded air, the looming crypts, filled her head with horrible images. Cristian and the dead Mariabella sharing a deep kiss beneath the sliver of moon while Cass watched, terrified, unable to look away.

She wrapped her hand around the key, feeling its edges dig into her skin. She had to try. For Luca.

Throwing her cloak around her shoulders, Cass made her way downstairs, grabbed a lantern from the kitchen, and headed for the front door. Outside, a steady stream of mist was blowing in from the Adriatic. The sharp, salty air bit into her skin, stinging her eyes and stealing her breath away.

The moon hung low and heavy in the sky. It peeked through the fog, bathing the estate in muted yellow light. Tufts of damp grass snatched at her ankles. Cass swore she saw bats winging their way through the haze. She kept her fingers tight around the handle of the door for a moment, reluctant to give herself up to the night, to the horrors it might be hiding.

Each step she took toward the graveyard was another weight crushing her chest. She struggled to breathe. No matter how tightly she hugged the cloak to her, she couldn't get warm. Twice she stopped, certain that if she moved forward, she would faint onto the damp grass.

The gate clanked in the breeze. Cass watched the kiss of metal on metal, and then finally, feeling as though her feet were turning to stone, she threw herself beyond the threshold—straight into the graveyard.

She craned her neck in all directions and then let out a long sigh. She had made it past the gate, and nothing bad had happened. She could do this. Luca needed her to do this. He trusted that she was strong enough.

And she was.

She headed for the northeast corner, to the small plot of overgrown land where the Caravello family tomb had sat, undisturbed, for years.

The grass rustled sharply and Cass almost dropped her lantern. She whirled around, her eyes combing the outlines of the nearby headstones and shrubbery. Nothing. Overhead a bat soared, a sharp black shadow across the hazy moon. Something tickled her ankle. Cass gripped the lantern tightly and stepped back instinctively.

A ghost-white cat yowled as her foot landed on its tail.

"Sorry," she said, expecting the cat to scoot off into the bushes. Instead, it looked up at her, its yellow eyes bright with hope. She ducked down with her lantern. She could see each individual bump on the animal's spine. Reaching out, she stroked the cat's back gently. It nuzzled its forehead against her leg.

"I have no food," Cass whispered regretfully. The cat lay down on its side, rolling in the dirt.

Cass was sorry when it didn't follow her. Even the company of an animal was infinitely preferable to being out here alone. Maybe she'd ask the cook if he needed another mouser for the kitchen. It did seem to be a friendly sort of cat.

Holding her breath, Cass approached the door of the Caravello tomb. Even back when she had wandered the graveyard day and night, she had not come to this corner in years—not since she found Slipper sleeping just outside her family crypt. With the kitten's arrival, her mother's spirit had gone elsewhere, or at least that was how Cass felt. What had once welcomed her began to repel her. Warmth faded. Vines overtook the tomb, obscuring the engraved lion crest and the name Caravello.

Cass pushed the prickly vines away from the padlock, hand trembling. She stared at the lock for a moment. Would it open? She pulled the chain with the key over her head and slid the key into the lock.

It fit, but it didn't turn. She felt both relieved and disappointed. Perhaps Luca had been confused about the location of the mysterious papers. Then the key shifted slightly. Cass pushed harder and the metal groaned. The lock was rusted inside too, perhaps full of debris.

But the key was turning.

"The Ancients believed in
the existence of a fifth humor
within the body, a mystical
substance of uncharted power."

—THE BOOK OF THE ETERNAL ROSE

C ass felt as though she were moving underwater, simultaneously weightless and weighted down. The lock clicked open. She removed the key and slipped it back around her neck as the door leaned inward. Holding her lantern high, she stepped forward.

The thick, musty odor of the crypt nearly made her gag. She leaned back, waving a hand in front of her face to dissipate the smell and dislodge the glimmering silver threads of a giant spiderweb.

Slowly, her eyes began to adjust to the dark. The Caravello tomb was smaller than Liviana's, with four shelves on each side and just enough space in between for Cass to stand. She edged farther inside, bringing the hem of her cloak to her mouth, breathing through it.

The dead bodies of her ancestors crowded around her. Cass noted with relief that all of the stone coffin lids were secured in place. But beneath the lids . . .

She knew it was irrational, but she was gripped by the idea that her relatives had been taken, like Liviana. What if all the coffins were empty, or worse, filled with bodies that did not belong there?

The thought possessed her, consumed her; she had to check. She set down the lantern and tugged on the nearest stone lid with both hands, pulling back with all her strength. The cover slid back to reveal a slender bundle wrapped in white shrouds. Cass pushed apart the gauzy layers to reveal a grinning skull. Shuddering, she dragged the stone lid back in place.

That was enough of that. Time to stop being foolish and find the papers. She wished Luca had been more specific. Were the pages tucked inside one of the heavy stone sarcophagi? It took all of Cass's strength just to pull back each lid and peek inside. More corpses. No papers. She examined the floor of the tomb and the dusty rafters above her head. Nothing. Stretching up onto her tiptoes, she reached a hand between the highest coffin and the wall of the tomb. Her bare fingers grazed soft fabric. No, leather. She pulled out a rectangular bundle, wrapped in well-worn suede. Undoing the cord and folding back one of the corners, Cass saw a thick sheaf of parchment tucked inside.

Suddenly the night, the dead bodies, all of her fear melted away.

She held the lantern close to the papers and saw that they were bound together with crude twine. She wanted to read them right away, but there was no place for her to rest the pages except for the damp floor of the crypt, and she wasn't going to risk getting the papers wet or damaged.

Rewrapping the leather around the parchment, Cass tucked the bundle under one arm. She ducked out of the crypt, sucking in deep breaths of fresh air as she relocked the door. Then she hurried back through the graveyard, crossing the estate's side lawn and heading back to the front of the villa. Slowly opening the door, she peeked inside to make sure no one was up waiting for her.

Hurrying up the stairs, she tossed her cloak over the back of her dressing table chair. She sat down at the table and eagerly unwrapped the pages.

Her stomach lurched. She recognized some of the writing: it was her mother's long flowy script. She skimmed the lines.

> *We have learned that the head of the Florentine chapter*
> *is attempting to isolate the fifth humor solely from blood.*
> *We plan to travel to Florence to observe his methods,*
> *and to adjust our own process accordingly . . .*

Cass frowned. She knew all about humors from her father, and she had heard stories of physicians who claimed they were selling healing tonics full of fifth humor. But everyone knew they were charlatans. There were only four main humors within the body—blood, phlegm, black bile, and yellow bile. Physicians believed that an imbalance of these humors caused various infirmities. Only by bleeding certain vessels that connected to certain organs could the balance be restored.

Perhaps her parents had been trying to create a medicine? Her mother described, in the next passage, that her attempts to make an elixir had been unsuccessful. But why did she speak of the fifth humor as if it were real?

Next there were some notations in someone else's handwriting. Cass flipped through snippets of notes from what seemed to be a scientist's journal. Subjects. Trial numbers. She didn't understand a lot of it, didn't even know what some of the hastily drawn symbols meant. Most of the entries were dated 1594, just one year before her parents had passed away. There were repeated references to Florence and to the Order of the Eternal Rose.

Cass carefully turned another page. At the top of a yellowed and crumbling piece of parchment, someone had scrawled a six-petaled flower inside of a circle. It was the symbol from Angelo de Gradi's workshop, the symbol Donna Domacetti wore on her ring. The flower inside the circle must be the symbol for the Order of the Eternal Rose.

But what were her mother's notes doing mixed in with papers pertaining to some mysterious society? It was inconceivable that her parents would have been involved in grave robbing and sacrilege.

Cass felt her throat closing up. She continued turning pages, this time frantically, searching for some explanation. On the next page, a list of names and cities was scrawled in different handwritings beneath yet another symbol of the Order. Cass guessed it was some kind of attendance list.

She traced one trembling finger down the first column. Her parents' names were on the list, midway down the page, and below theirs was the name Joseph Dubois.

She quickly scanned the other names. Luca's father was on the list. Also Angelo de Gradi and Don Zanotta, husband of Hortensa Zanotta, who had accused Luca. Cristian's name was not on the list. Most names Cass didn't recognize at all—the vast majority of the signatures were listed as being from Florence. The name at the very top of the list was written larger than most of the others, but at some point the parchment had gotten wet and the letters had faded into a smear of black across the page. Cass could read the city on the right, though: Florence.

If all of these papers mentioned Florence, surely Luca was right and the book was there. *As well as Hortensa Zanotta.* Cass had never been to Florence, but suddenly the city was calling to her.

"Living burial usually
results in death caused
by suffocation or sheer terror."

—THE BOOK OF THE ETERNAL ROSE

Cass had the nightmare about Cristian again—only this time, when his hands started to tear away the fabric of her gown, the scene began to ripple and distort. When the wavering stopped, Cass realized she wasn't in the wine room anymore. She was somewhere else dark and damp. And she wasn't alone.

"Hello," she said, but the word came out muffled. Her mouth filled with something wet. Mud. She spat fiercely, trying to clear out the muck, but it was raining down on her now, a storm of moist dirt falling from above. She was in an open grave. Someone was burying her alive.

Cass screamed, and her mouth began to fill again. She coughed, writhing in the mud, trying to stand. She couldn't. Two other bodies were packed in next to her—one on each side. They were just fragmented skeletons, pieces of charred black bone, but somehow Cass knew they were her parents. She was horrified to see that her own arms and legs were bound to the skeletons. She turned to the remains she knew belonged to her mother. The skeleton was wearing a pendant—a flower inscribed in a circle: the symbol of the Order of the Eternal Rose.

Cass tried to rip the pendant from her mother's neck, but the metal was so hot, it seared a six-petaled insignia into Cass's palm. She screamed again.

"Help me!" she cried.

Her father's skull seemed to move. Cass thought it was going to speak to her, but when the jaws creaked open, a thick cloud of spiders crawled out. Ripping herself loose from her bonds, she wrestled her way onto her knees, digging her fingernails into the damp side of the pit.

As she struggled to her feet, something heavy fell from above—a body wrapped in white burial shrouds, a shock of blonde hair protruding from within the folds. Liviana's half-decomposed face grinned at her through the thin fabric. "Where's my necklace?" the corpse hissed.

Another body fell, slamming hard into Cass, stealing the breath from her chest and driving her back to her hands and knees. Cass didn't want to peer beneath the shrouds, but she did.

Luca looked back at her. "Why did you forsake me?" he asked. His eyes glimmered, but when he started to cry, it was blood, not tears, that flowed down his cheeks.

Cass awoke with his name on her lips.

Luca.

He would die if she couldn't free him, and the only way to do that was to find the Book of the Eternal Rose.

But how was she supposed to get to Florence? Aunt Agnese would never let her go on a trip by herself. Cass wasn't even sure how to get there. Madalena's father, Signor Rambaldo, made frequent visits to

Florence for work. Maybe there was a chance Cass could tag along with him if he was going soon.

It was a long shot, but it was the only shot Cass had. She summoned Siena to assist her in dressing. She planned to go to Madalena's palazzo immediately.

Mada's new home with Marco was just a few blocks from her father's palazzo, down one of the main side canals. The cream-colored building had red clay roof tiles and thick glass windows outlined in gold leaf.

Giuseppe anchored the gondola and helped Cass and Siena alight from the boat. He then settled back on the baseboards, covering his face with his wide-brimmed gardening hat. Apparently, he was planning on a nap.

Siena held a parasol above Cass's head in one hand while she rapped the ring-shaped bronze doorknocker with her other. Cass waved her fan in front of her face as she watched a flat-bottomed *peàta* loaded down with sacks of fruits and vegetables float by.

The butler opened the door and ushered the girls inside. Madalena floated into view at the top of the stairs. She wore her favorite crimson bodice, which was fitted with a pair of long gossamer sleeves that hung down past the end of her fingertips. Her entire ensemble was blood-red—the skirts, the sleeves, even the high satin collar. It must have taken hundreds of kermes beetles to dye so much lush fabric. But that didn't matter; Mada had been spoiled by her father, and now she would be spoiled by her doting husband. It was only fair. She had lost her mother and her younger brother years ago. She deserved her happiness.

"Cass." Her whole face brightened as she glided down the stairs.

"This is a surprise. If I'd known you were coming, I would have held breakfast."

"Some tea would be lovely," Cass said. Siena excused herself and went to find Mada's handmaid, Eva, a friend of hers.

"Tea it is, then." Madalena led Cass through the palazzo and out back to a small courtyard not unlike the one at her old home, Palazzo Rambaldo. The two girls sat across from each other at a small stone table that was shaded by the overhang of the palazzo's roof.

Madalena reached out for Cass's hand. "You poor thing. I was just composing a letter to you. I only found out this morning and simply cannot believe it." She shook her head. "Luca da Peraga arrested."

Cass nodded mutely. She had passed a small pile of messages sitting on the side table as she left her aunt's villa. It had taken only a couple of days for the news to spread all across the city, and Agnese's acquaintances had begun expressing their condolences.

A serving girl arrived with two teacups, two teaspoons, and a small plate of sugar. Cass waited for her to return with a steaming kettle of tea before she started speaking. "I was wondering if your father would travel to Florence soon," she began slowly.

"Funny you should ask," Mada said. "He's been there for a couple of weeks. He left not too long after my wedding. Why do you ask?"

After a quick glance to make sure they were alone, Cass quickly recounted the story of Luca's arrest, Feliciana, the trip to Palazzo Ducale, and the Book of the Eternal Rose.

"You've had a busy couple of days," Madalena said, frowning. For a second she was quiet.

Cass leaned over and grasped Madalena's hand. "I know it all sounds like madness, but I must get to Florence as quickly as possible," she said.

"What does old Agnese think of all this?" Mada asked.

"I haven't told her," Cass confessed. "She's been so weak. Just the soldiers ransacking the place looking for evidence of heresy took a lot out of her."

"Evidence of heresy." Madalena shook her head. "Ridiculous."

"I know. But I have to prove he's innocent somehow." Cass had twisted her napkin into a coiled rope. "Or else they're saying he's going to *hang*."

Mada's dark eyes widened. "Of course we'll get you to Florence." She sipped her tea again. "Marco is supposed to meet my father there next week. He is scheduled to leave in two days. I can just arrange for us to accompany him. We'll all stay with my aunt Stella. I haven't seen her since I was a child."

"And Feliciana?" Cass asked hopefully. "She doesn't want to go back to Palazzo Dubois."

"I'm sure we can squeeze in one more," Mada said. "Perhaps Stella is looking for another maid."

Excitement stirred within Cass. If she could get to Florence, she could find Hortensa Zanotta, and the Book of the Eternal Rose. Ideally, Hortensa would recant her testimony and the book would show Dubois for what he was—a monster. If Cass threatened to expose him, he would use his shadowy power to set Luca free.

Luca had done so much for her. This would be her way of beginning, slowly, to repay him.

Back at the villa, Siena paced Cass's room like a caged animal. "I still don't see how we can just leave," she burst out. "With Luca rotting in prison."

Cass cleared her throat meaningfully.

"*Mi dispiace,*" Siena mumbled immediately.

"I'm not leaving him to rot," Cass said. "My only chance to free him is to find the Book of the Eternal Rose, and Luca believes it to be in Florence. Not to mention one of his accusers is hiding out there. Besides," she added, "we can finally get your sister far away from Dubois."

"I know it's the right thing to do, but . . ." Siena shook her head as she stared down at the floor.

"And after we free Luca, I'm sure he'll be more than happy to bring Feliciana into his employ." Cass forced herself to speak with a cheery confidence she didn't feel. There was one more obstacle standing between her and Florence: she had to persuade her aunt to let her go.

Fortunately, Agnese didn't require as much convincing as expected. Cass let her aunt lead the conversation through dinner, doing her best to appear attentive but remaining uncharacteristically quiet. When Agnese finally asked her what was wrong, Cass sighed dramatically.

"I just can't stop worrying about Luca," she admitted. That much was true. "And every time I leave the house . . . ." she trailed off.

"Yes?" Agnese coughed into her dinner napkin.

"I feel like everyone is staring at me, and saying horrible things." Cass looked up at her aunt for just a second before dropping her eyes back to the tray balanced on her lap. "Mada thinks I should get away for a while. She and Marco are going to Florence in a couple of days. She keeps insisting that I join her." Cass sighed again. "I keep telling her that I should stay. I can't just run away because the entire city seems to be mocking me, or worse—pitying me. What do I care what other people think?"

Agnese swallowed hard, placing her fork down next to her plate of roasted duck. She cared greatly what other people thought. "I do worry about whether Matteo has heard of Luca's predicament," she said. Matteo was Agnese's nephew by marriage. He would come of age soon and inherit the estate, and Agnese fretted obsessively about her stature in his eyes because she didn't want him to toss out Cass and the serving staff if he chose to come live in the villa. "Maybe a short trip would do you some good," Agnese continued. "Florence *is* lovely this time of year."

"But I can't leave you here alone, Aunt Agnese," Cass said, knowing this would further convince her aunt that she should leave. She picked listlessly at a greasy slab of duck, hoping she wasn't overdoing it. Agnese was no fool. If she figured out Cass was trying to con her, Cass would end up locked inside the villa again while Narissa watched her every move.

"Alone? I wish I could have a moment alone in this house," her aunt grumbled. "Narissa checks on me nine times a day, and that foul doctor shows up at all hours with his bloodsucking pets, not to mention the serving staff—I hardly think you'd be leaving me alone."

Cass formed her face into a hopeful expression. "Really? It *would* be nice to get away for a bit . . ."

Agnese nodded. "And Madalena's mere presence is a tonic for you."

Cass leaned forward and kissed her aunt on the cheek. "You've convinced me," she said. "I'll send word to Mada immediately, if you're sure you don't mind being without me."

"Of course I don't mind. It was my idea. I only wish you would listen to me more often," Agnese huffed.

Cass had to lift her napkin to her mouth to conceal a smile.

"The church believes the 'Devil's children'

should be interred near a crossroads,

so that the power of Christ might prevent

the evil from rising from their graves."

—THE BOOK OF THE ETERNAL ROSE

Cass spent the entire trip to the mainland thinking about the papers she had found in her parents' tomb. What kind of elixir was the Order trying to create, and when had her parents become involved? Was that why they had never been home?

She couldn't help but feel a wave of anger. How could her own parents have willingly associated with Joseph Dubois? How could they have felt a greater allegiance to a secret society than to their own daughter? These same thoughts tumbled relentlessly through her head as their ship approached land.

Men with carriages were waiting for the party as they docked at Mestre, the main connecting point between the Rialto and the mainland. The carriages were made of sturdy wood with big metal wheels, each pulled by a single horse.

Cass stared in fascination. The last horses she'd seen had belonged to the Doge—great glossy black things that were draped in gold and velvet and stood almost twice as tall as she did. These were shorter, with wide furry legs and bare backs. Cass approached the nearest horse, reaching out a hand toward its muzzle.

The horse raised one of its forefeet and stamped it on the ground. Cass hesitated. The driver laughed. "Go on then. He won't bite you."

She reached out to stroke the horse's forehead and it nickered softly. Suddenly, she missed Slipper terribly.

"He likes you," the driver said. "He always likes the pretty girls."

Cass blushed. She patted the horse again. It made a chuffing sound as it studied her with its big black eyes.

The party split into two groups. The servants and the men hired to tend to the horses rode in one carriage, and Cass, Madalena, and Marco rode in another. Cass hadn't ridden in a carriage since she was a little girl. Back then it had seemed fun, the rhythmic clip-clopping of hooves as the carriage skipped along. Now she felt like her head might bounce right off her neck. She clutched the side of the bench for support while Marco wrapped his arms around Mada to steady her. When the path flattened out, Marco and Madalena remained twined around each other, trading occasional quick kisses when they thought Cass wasn't looking. Cass swallowed a sigh. She wished she were riding in the servants' carriage with Feliciana and Siena. They were probably gossiping and giggling.

"Are you all right, Cass?" Marco asked. "You've got a funny look on your face."

Cass blurted out the first words that came to mind. "I was just wondering how long it will take to get to Florence." She glanced out the window. The sun had already fallen below the tree line. She couldn't believe how many trees there were. Ribbons of pines and firs snaked out in all directions, twisted gray trunks crowned with feathery branches. The air smelled fresh, like a fire at Christmastime. Completely different from the moldy, fetid odors of Venice.

"About a week," Marco answered.

A week! Cass tried not to imagine how sore she'd be after an entire week of being jostled around the tiny carriage compartment. And worse, she quickly did the math in her head. That would leave only two and a half weeks for her to find the Book of the Eternal Rose and return to Venice before Luca's execution.

As she adjusted to the roiling, jerking motion, she distracted herself with the stunning and unfamiliar views that rolled past her window: more and more forests, a multitude of green patches, and far in the distance, a line of mountain peaks jutting high above the trees.

"The Apennines," Marco said, following her gaze. "Lovely, aren't they?"

It took three days to reach the base of the Apennines. The surface of a turquoise lake shimmered in the moonlight, and the dark shadows of the mountain peaks loomed all around them. Cass couldn't help but think of Falco. He would love this beauty; he would know how to draw it.

One day turned into another. And then another. They traded the mountains for wild open meadows, for tall wet grass and soft dirt roads. The sun rose and set again. Twice during the journey, Cass's carriage got stuck in the mud. The male servants and the carriage attendants had to push and pull the giant wagons to get them through the murky soft spots and back onto the path. Cass began to wonder if they would ever reach Florence.

Finally, the carriage driver announced they were nearing their destination. Cass hung her head out the window, eager for a view of the city.

But she didn't see any buildings or people, not even way off on the horizon. All she saw were more fields, great grassy meadows that stretched out for miles, with rolling hills beyond them. She pulled her head back inside, intending to check the view from the other side of the compartment.

Suddenly, the carriage lurched violently to the left, throwing her and Madalena against the edge of the window. Cass heard the shrill whinny of the horse, followed by swearing. Metal shrieked on metal. The carriage tilted at a strange angle, leaving the window pointing toward the ground.

"Mada, are you all right?" Cass and Marco reached for Madalena simultaneously.

Madalena nodded, rubbing her side and wincing. "What happened?"

The driver's head appeared in the window. "Is everyone all right?" he asked, red-faced. One at a time, he helped the girls crawl out through the small opening.

Cass wriggled awkwardly through the window, tugging her skirts behind her. She landed on the dusty ground, where Siena immediately helped her to her feet. One of the front wheels of the carriage had hit something—the wooden axle was broken clear through.

"What now?" Cass asked. The servants and carriage attendants were all milling around, muttering. They had broken down near a crossroads, but both streets were completely bare of traffic. Open meadows stretched around them, with tree-covered hills off in the distance.

Marco cursed. "And only an hour outside of Florence."

The driver knelt beside the fallen axle. "We can't move on until the damage is repaired."

Just then, Cass heard a howl from the trees. She turned toward the noise and saw a pack of wild dogs across the field—four of them in total, slinking around the periphery of the tall grass.

"Marco," she said, her throat tightening. "Dogs."

Marco turned. "They won't bother us, Signorina Cassandra," he said. "We're too many. Dogs are cowards."

The largest dog lowered its haunches to the ground, and the others followed its lead. But Cass couldn't shake the feeling that they were watching her.

Waiting.

She stared back, not wanting to appear afraid, until the rhythmic drumming of hoofbeats drew her attention. A carriage was approaching from the direction of Florence. She watched the cloud of dust draw near, realizing it wasn't a carriage after all. It was an old wooden cart pulled by a short, squat horse. Two men in leather doublets were perched on the back of the cart, their boots dangling almost to the ground. Another man straddled the horse. When he spotted the disabled carriage, he slowed the horse to a walk and pulled up near the side of the road. Cass headed toward them to see if they could offer assistance. Too late, she realized what the cart was carrying.

Bodies.

She stopped right in the middle of the road, hugging her arms around her waist. The scene brought her back to the night she had discovered Falco's secret. But these men weren't robbing graves. Apparently, they were going to dig them.

The two men in leather doublets jumped off the back of the cart with their shovels and traipsed across the field. One of them pounded a wooden cross into the ground while the other began to dig. The third hovered close to the cart, glancing occasionally at the linen-wrapped bodies, as though he thought they might walk away.

Cass wondered why they would be taken so far outside of the city to be buried. Curiosity outweighed her fear, and she started across the road again. Madalena followed her.

"Be careful." The man—the driver—positioned himself between the girls and the cart.

Cass glanced down at his hands. He wore a plain silver band around his thumb. "Are they . . . infected?" A ripple of fear moved through her. Luca's own father had contracted the plague from one of his servants. He had died in less than a week.

"Oh, they are infected all right," the man said. "With the Devil's own affliction."

Cass struggled to understand his thick Florentine accent, but she was pretty sure she had heard him right. She leaned back from the bundle. With one hand, the man delicately parted the burial shrouds around the first body's face. The dead girl looked like her, with freckled skin and auburn hair.

And she had a brick jammed into her mouth.

"They are vampires," he said grimly.

"The Church decrees that
the undead must be drowned in
holy water, as staking or
burning might free the affliction
from inside their unholy
bodies and spread the scourge of
vampirism across the land."

—THE BOOK OF THE ETERNAL ROSE

eleven

Vampires?" Mada squeaked. Cass could only stare. The brick had been forced so far down the girl's throat that it looked as if her jaw had been dislocated.

"Bitten, anyway," the man said. He let the white shroud fall back over the girl's face. "We bind their hands with silver and put the bricks in their mouths so that they cannot escape their shrouds if they turn." He looked Cass and Madalena up and down with his dark, sharp eyes. "You'd best be careful if you stop in Florence. There's been a run of vampire attacks recently, mostly on young women."

"A girl is attacked by a vampire and your solution is to kill her and dump her body in the countryside?" Cass asked, her voice rising in pitch.

The man glanced over at the two men digging. The pile of soil at the edge of the trench was growing in size. "There is no cure once you've had the bite. You'll either die or become a vampire yourself. We've started drowning them." He spat on the ground. "The magistrate won't allow us to stake them or burn them because he thinks the blood and ashes might spread the affliction. The way I see it, no matter what, we are doing them a *favor*."

Cass looked toward the trench and felt nausea welling in her chest. "But what if they *do* wake up in there? They'll be trapped underground, for eternity." Before anyone could stop her, she headed across the high grass toward the wooden cross and the hole in the ground beside it. Mada hurried after her, and the maidservants followed.

The girls stood around the open grave. Cass couldn't help but remember the nightmare she'd had before she left Venice. The one of herself stretched out beneath the ground, bound to the bones of her parents. As she and the others watched, the two men flung shovel after shovel of dirt onto a pile. The hole grew deeper and wider, like a mouth waiting to swallow them whole.

The men ignored the girls completely. When they were satisfied with their work, they dropped their shovels and went to retrieve one of the bundles from the cart. Madalena looked positively horrified as the men carried over the first girl.

The first body.

The first vampire.

Cass took a step back from the edge of the grave, again envisioning herself encased in dirt, white-wrapped bodies falling from the sky, as they had in her dream. She couldn't help but wonder what Falco would have thought of this scene. He didn't believe in vampires. To him this would be madness. Paranoia. Murder sanctioned by the Church.

For the thousandth time, she was struck by the differences between herself and Falco. The two of them had lived in the same city, but in completely different worlds. Cass was foolish to ever dream they could be together. Her parents and Aunt Agnese, they had been right all along. Luca da Peraga was the proper man for her. Regardless of whatever charges Dubois had trumped up against him, Luca was a good man who believed in the Church. In right and wrong. Luca was the same as she was, when it came to the things that mattered.

A second white-wrapped body went into the hole, sending up a sudden draft from deep beneath the ground. Cass shivered. She wished Feliciana and Siena would step back from the edge of the grave.

A clap of thunder sounded. Cass glanced up at the sky. Billowing gray clouds were rolling in. She could just barely make out the hazy tips of the Apennines behind them. The third body landed with a soft thud.

A guttural wail broke the grim silence. Cass snapped her head around to where the pack of dogs had been. They were scattering into the trees, as though even they could not bear to stand witness to this. The two men with shovels began to replace the dirt over the white-wrapped corpses. There was no funeral, no priest. There were not even any words spoken.

"What of their families?" Cass asked, her voice trembling. "Is there no one here who will speak over their bodies?"

"They don't have families anymore," one of the men said. He pulled a dirty handkerchief from his pocket and mopped the sweat from his brow. "They are not human. No priest will speak for their souls."

The sky rumbled again. The air was still dry, but the wind had picked up. "What proof was there that they were bitten by vampires?" Cass crossed her arms, warming herself.

"They have all the symptoms," the man said grimly. "Weakness, pale skin, delirium."

"But that is nothing," Cass protested. "Maybe they just fell ill. Maybe they succumbed to a new strain of plague."

The man shook his head. "They had the marks too. Puncture wounds on the neck, all identical." He looked back at Cass. "Fangs," he said, as if she hadn't understood.

Marco had stayed near the wagons this whole time, overseeing the men struggling to fix the broken axle. Now he strode across the grass and joined the girls by the freshly dug grave.

"This is far too gruesome a scene to attract the attention of ladies so lovely." His voice was light, but he drew Cass and Mada firmly away from the gravesite. "The axle is almost fixed and a storm is brewing. We should be under way shortly."

"But Marco," Mada protested. "These men say that Florence is overrun with vampires."

Marco touched his hand to Madalena's lower back and steered her across the grass. "Come, my goddess. You'll have nightmares." A gust of wind stole away part of his next words. ". . . die before I let anyone hurt you, right?"

Mada rotated her face in toward Marco's chest. "But you're going to be so busy." She sounded childlike, honestly afraid.

Marco kissed the top of her head. "Not too busy to protect my beautiful wife." He led her back toward the carriage, and the rest of the girls turned away from the grave as a group.

The driver took the repaired carriage for a short test loop around the uneven ground of the field and then declared it fit for travel. Cass hopped back into the travel compartment and pulled the curtains closed across the window. Within moments, the group was heading toward Florence again.

A clap of thunder made the seat beneath Cass tremble. Parting the curtains with her fingers, she peeked out, expecting to be pelted with cold rain. But the air was dark and dry. The storm was chasing them, but it hadn't yet caught up.

They left the field and the graves behind, passing through a series of rolling green hills. A sharp breeze tickled her skin as Cass leaned slightly out the window. She could just barely make out a jagged skyline in the distance. Florence. After a grueling week of travel, they were finally there.

By the time the carriages reached the outskirts of the city, the storm had blown past and night was beginning to fall. Again, Cass peeked out through the curtains.

Her first thought of Florence was that it was heavy and deserted. Large, hulking palazzos made of red and tan brick lined both sides of the cobblestoned streets. Elaborately painted chimeras loomed from the rooftops like hideous protectors. Most of the houses looked abandoned, their shutters pulled tight against the gathering dusk. The streets were mostly empty; there were no merchants returning home from a long day at the market, no peasant boys prowling for women and wine.

Cass inhaled deeply. The air was different, sharp and crisp, with only the faintest tinge of stale water from the Arno River, which cut through the city. She had grown used to the sweet moldy smell of Venice, to the low-hanging fog that blanketed everything. The air of Florence was a welcome change, clear and fresh.

Cass heard the crescendo of angry voices as the carriages rolled past a large, open piazza with a statue at its center. Here was where all the people were gathered, apparently. Peasants in brightly colored breeches and doublets stood in a throng around a statue. One of them was waving a piece of parchment.

"What are they doing?" Cass asked.

Marco leaned over to look out the window. "This is the Piazza del Mercato Vecchio, where the townspeople shop and gossip. It looks like they're posting pasquinades."

"Pasquinades?" Mada repeated, wrinkling her nose.

Marco gave her a squeeze. "Complaints against the church, public statements, and pronouncements. Nonsense, mostly. The citizens are always complaining about *something*." He frowned. "The place where we'll be staying is just off the piazza. I knew the square was always full of people, but I hope we won't have to suffer their constant noise."

"Here?" Mada squealed, wrinkling her nose. "This isn't how I remember Palazzo Alioni at all. This whole neighborhood looks so run-down. So old."

Marco nodded grimly as the driver slowed the horses to a stop. "Your father sent word to warn me that your aunt's living conditions had deteriorated, but I had hoped for better than this."

They had pulled over in front of a three-story palazzo made of red stucco and trimmed with marble. The chipped roof tiles and peeling paint made Cass think of Agnese's villa. "It's not so bad," she said, with forced cheerfulness. "It looks lived-in."

The carriage driver opened the wooden double doors that led into the palazzo's courtyard. Mada's face fell even further. Up close, the house looked even older than Agnese's villa, and the only thing growing in the garden was weeds. A rusty bucket sat on the edge of a well. Mada turned to Cass incredulously. "It looks like no one's lived here for a hundred years," she insisted. "There's no one outside to greet us and not even a candle burning in the window. Did they forget we were arriving today?"

The driver had returned to the carriage and prepared to help the ladies out. He caught Mada's last few words. "Many are afraid to be out on the streets after sunset," he explained as he helped Cass step down from the high carriage. "Because of the vampires."

Cass and Madalena exchanged a look. Mada reached down, her fingers finding the crucifix that dangled from her belt.

They made their way across the uneven stone courtyard. Each side of the palazzo's wooden door was flanked with a faded banner emblazoned with a pair of white unicorns, their horns crossed as if in battle. Marco reached out and rapped sternly on the wood. A stooped and sagging butler opened the door after a few moments. He ushered them into the house and up into the portego.

The inside of the palazzo was a slight improvement over its exterior. The portego was wide and airy with high, vaulted ceilings and solid, if slightly worn, furniture. Giant murals decorated each wall, though the paint was faded in places, revealing the cracked plaster underneath. The candlelight illuminated only portions of the murals, so it took Cass a moment to realize she was standing next to a giant nude Eve holding an apple. She flinched slightly and turned away, but not before her eyes traced the Serpent's coils all the way out to the forked tongue that was flicking in the direction of Eve's exposed breasts.

The far wall was even worse: a white-wrapped Lazarus emerging from his tomb. It made Cass think of Liviana and the vampire girls and her dream of being buried alive. She shivered. The butler had disappeared into the bowels of the house. Cass hoped he was alerting the kitchen staff as well as the mistress about their arrival. She needed a cup of tea and something to eat.

Feliciana came up behind Cass. "*This* is where you expect me to find employment?" she whispered. "They don't look like they are able to feed the staff they already have."

"Don't worry," Cass whispered back. "If they can't use you, we'll find someone else here who can. At least you're safe now."

Madalena's father emerged from the back of the house, his brilliant green-and-gold breeches lighting up the dingy room. A plump older woman in a lilac gown trailed behind him. Cass assumed this was Madalena's aunt.

The woman smoothed the front of her bodice. "I'm Signora Stella Alioni."

The signora had grown up on the Rialto with Mada's father, and remnants of her Venetian accent still lingered. Cass found her speech easier to understand than that of the men outside the city.

"My husband is already asleep," Signora Alioni continued. "He's leaving for Padua in the morning on business. I'm so glad I'll have a full house to keep me company while he's away." But as she looked over the group, her lower lip twisted into a frown. Perhaps she hadn't anticipated hosting so many people. "The servants can double up with some of my staff, and I have a pair of empty bedrooms, one on this level and one upstairs. I do hope the noise from the piazza won't keep you awake. This district has gotten a bit rough. All day I get to listen to angry peasants. At night, the square fills up with drunks and revelers."

Cass was given the smaller room on the upper level of the house. Unlike parts of Venice, where first floors were unlivable because of the moisture that seeped up through the rock, the palazzos in Florence had actual cellars, which housed the wine and foodstuffs along with most of the serving staff. The upper level was usually for the senior staff: the butler, the head gardener, and the ladies' maids.

Cass's chamber was empty except for a bed, a washing table, a ratty old chair behind the door, and a dusty painting of the Virgin Mary on the wall. The floor was in need of a good sweeping, but otherwise the room was satisfactory, though it lacked an armoire, meaning Cass would have to live out of her trunk. As she perched on the edge of the small bed, she again felt a pang of loneliness for Slipper. Narissa had promised to attend to him while Cass was gone, but he was used to being spoiled, and Narissa would put a stop to that immediately. She had probably already put him to work in the butler's pantry as a mouser. Cass smiled to herself. If Slipper did manage to catch a mouse, he'd be more likely to play with it than eat it.

Someone knocked loudly at her door and she jumped up, hoping it would be a servant offering her something warm to eat or drink. No such luck. It was the driver of the carriage, with her trunk. He dragged it unceremoniously into her room and left it sitting by the wall.

Cass pulled out her journal and checked to be sure the leather bundle of parchment was still hidden at the very bottom of her trunk, beneath her skirts and stays. It was. She dragged the old chair over to her washing table and pushed the basin for soaking collars and chemises back toward the wall. This would work just fine for writing in her journal. Now to find some ink.

She wandered back down to the *piano nobile*, the main floor of the palazzo, where she saw that the carriage drivers had just finished unloading the servants' small trunks. Marco's attendant, Rocco, was offering to carry Feliciana's to her room for her. Cass raised a hand to her mouth to stifle a smile. Even skinny and bald, Feliciana managed to attract the attention of every man she met. A servant hurried by, and Cass asked for a pot of ink.

Ink in hand, she returned to her small room and sat down at her makeshift desk. She turned to a blank page and began to write.

The trip to Florence was long and bumpy, but breathtaking in places. It's been so long since I've seen a forest, so many giant trees reaching for the heavens, with feathery green needles flaring out like fans. Even the air feels different here. Like for the first time in my life I'm able to breathe deeply, completely.

Our carriage broke an axle just outside of Florence. We came across a trio of men. They were digging a mass grave for a group of women who had been bitten by vampires; they are apparently running loose in the city of Florence. It was horrible. The men used bricks to—

The tip of her quill punctured the parchment. Cass realized her hands were trembling. She was thinking of the dream again, of being buried alive. It was almost worse than the dream of being attacked by Cristian. She wondered why she was being plagued with nightmares every time she closed her eyes. She laid the quill down on the washing table.

The letter from Falco poked out of the back of her journal. Cass resisted the urge to unfold it and read it for the thousandth time. His soft words would soothe her, but she was here to save Luca. He had led Cass here, to Florence. Now she just had to find the Book of the Eternal Rose, or at least Hortensa. Cass didn't know if the donna was a member of the Order, but her husband was. Even if Hortensa refused to recant her testimony, she might say something useful. Something that could give Cass a place to start looking for the book.

Hooves thundered just outside her window. Cass peeked out, surprised to see not only a carriage passing by, but also seven or eight men mounted on horseback—servants, from the looks of their simple attire—riding alongside it. Silver bells hung from each horse's bridle, jangling loudly as the group rode by. The handful of peasants still gathered around the statue in the piazza turned to watch the procession before returning to their conversation.

A boy wearing a leather doublet and a hat pulled low over his face appeared at the far side of the piazza. Cass watched him stumble across the cobblestones, a canteen dangling from one hand and a roll of parchment from the other. He could have been anyone—a student, a messenger—but Cass saw the parchment and could think only of artists, and of Falco. Midway across the piazza, the boy weaved dangerously and nearly bumped into one of the peasants.

Another carriage rolled by, horses whinnying sharply as whips cracked down on their hindquarters. Four men on horseback followed the carriage. One hollered a greeting to the peasants as he rode past.

Cass sat on the windowsill and gathered her skirts around her. She might not get much rest here, but at least Florence was more interesting than being isolated out on San Domenico Island. And the signora was right. The streets might be bare, but the piazza seemed to be full of traffic at all hours of the day.

Someone out there would be able to help her in her quest. Cass was certain of it. Hortensa Zanotta and the Book of the Eternal Rose were both in Florence, and Cass was determined to find them.

"It is easier to blame
the undead than it is the living for
the evils that pervade society."

—THE BOOK OF THE ETERNAL ROSE

T he next morning, Cass awoke with the lily necklace tangled in her hair. As she gently unsnarled the tendrils that had wrapped themselves around the clasp, she realized Luca's execution was less than three weeks away.

After a quick breakfast, she persuaded Madalena to go to the giant square behind Palazzo Alioni with her. Surely in the Piazza del Mercato Vecchio she would find someone who knew Hortensa Zanotta. It wouldn't be safe to just go asking about the Book of the Eternal Rose, not if the Florentine members were anything like Dubois, but that didn't mean she couldn't keep her eyes open for any sign of the Order.

Cass haunted the piazza all morning, interviewing merchants and scanning the crowds for a glimpse of Hortensa or the six-petaled flower symbol. At first, Madalena didn't mind accompanying her. There were plenty of shops and stalls for her to frequent, all the while lamenting Marco's absence.

"He told me he wanted a child. How are we supposed to do that if he doesn't spend any time with me?" Mada wailed. She waved an onyx fan embellished with amethyst in front of her face.

Behind Madalena, her maidservant, Eva, rolled her eyes.

Cass stifled a smile. "It's not as if he won't return to the palazzo later," she said soothingly.

"Later after I'm fast asleep." Madalena snapped the fan shut and scrunched her face into a pout. "Why doesn't he want to be with me? Is it so terrible?"

"Of course not," Cass said. She was only partially listening. She had just caught sight of a tall blonde woman who reminded her of Hortensa. The woman was crossing in front of a stall selling jewelry from the Orient. "He's probably just trying to impress your father by working so hard."

Madalena sighed deeply but let herself get distracted by one of the storefront displays—a string of tiny pearls displayed on a bed of crushed velvet. "Let's go in here," she said.

"You go ahead," Cass said. The blonde woman was nearly to the other side of the piazza. "I'll be back. I thought I saw someone I know."

Madalena shrugged but signaled for Eva to follow her into the jewelry store. Siena hurried across the square alongside Cass, expertly weaving her way through the crowded piazza like she was at the Mercato di Rialto. "Was it Hortensa?" she asked eagerly.

"Perhaps." Cass wasn't certain which of the shops the woman had gone inside. There was a bakery, a butcher shop, and a tailor all in the same area of the piazza. A donna would send her servants to buy meat or bread, Cass decided. She headed for the tailor. Maybe Hortensa was doing like Madalena and passing her time in Florence by seeing how much of her husband's gold she could spend.

But the tailor's shop was empty, except for a boy Cass's age who looked up from the fabric he was cutting to give her an appraising glance. He had bright green eyes and wheat-colored hair that fell to his shoulders.

"*Scusi,*" Cass said. "I was looking for a blonde woman. Did she come in here?"

"Many blonde women come in here," the boy said. "Personally, I like dark hair." He winked and held up a bolt of satin. "Would you like to be fitted for a gown?"

Cass blushed. She stepped backward and nearly knocked a cloth-draped wooden form from its pedestal. Siena had been hovering just inside the door, fingering a display of lace cuffs and collars. She looked up in time to see Cass stumble, and tittered quietly.

"Perhaps another time," Cass said. She could feel the boy's eyes on her as she hurried back out to the piazza with Siena in tow.

"I think he liked you," Siena teased.

Cass gave her a dark look. That was the last thing she needed—another boy to add to the mix. "I think he just liked my gold," she said.

They tried the bakery next. The walls were painted a soothing pink, and the whole place smelled of olive oil and freshly baked bread. A three-tiered pastry platter sat on the countertop, each level filled with a different flavor of tart. The shop was empty except for the baker, who was wrapping up a purchase, and a woman who was arranging her coins on the counter, her back facing the door. She was tall and blonde, with an elaborately braided hairdo.

Cass froze for a second. Her heart pounded in double time as she approached the woman.

"Signorina Cass—" Siena had wandered up to the counter to admire the selection of pastries.

Cass held up a hand and Siena fell quiet. "Excuse me." Cass gently touched the woman's shoulder.

The woman looked up from the counter. "Yes?" she asked with a curious smile.

Cass's heart plummeted into her stomach. It wasn't Hortensa.

"*Mi dispiace*," Cass murmured. "I thought you were someone else."

The woman took her purchase from the baker and smiled again as she left the shop. Reluctantly, Siena turned away from the platter of tarts.

Cass pulled a copper coin from her leather pouch. "Let's get a couple of pastries, shall we?" she said. "Then the morning won't be a total loss."

She paid the baker, who unfortunately had not heard of the Zanottas, for two pastries and handed the larger one to Siena. They returned to the square to find Madalena clutching a shiny golden box with a scarlet ribbon. "I bought the pearls," she gushed. "Marco won't mind. He's been saying he wanted to take me shopping. This way I did all the work for him."

Cass sighed. At least someone was getting something accomplished.

After dinner, Madalena frowned when Cass said she was heading to the piazza. "Again, Cass? I was hoping you might want to come with me to tea," she said. "Stella's gotten us an invitation to Palazzo di Alighieri. The signora is descended from the writer Dante."

Cass had thoroughly enjoyed *La Davina Commedia* and would have loved to go to tea with Signora di Alighieri, but Luca had less than three weeks to live. "I really have to go back, Mada," Cass said. "Luca is depending on me."

Madalena frowned, and Cass could tell she wanted to say more.

Mada probably thought Cass's quest to save Luca was insane, and that Cass should just start to accept the reality that her fiancé would be executed.

She wasn't ready to do that. She would never be ready.

So the two girls went their separate ways. Siena dutifully followed Cass out to the square and walked beside her as she continued going from shop to shop, asking the shopkeepers if they knew of Donna Hortensa Zanotta. Both a jeweler and a weaver were familiar with the name, but neither could tell Cass where she lived.

Feliciana found them at the hottest point of the afternoon. The sun shined down on the dark stones of the piazza, making the heat radiate up through the soles of Cass's shoes. She fanned herself desperately, almost as warm as she had been the day she visited Luca in the Doge's prison.

"The mistress and Madalena have returned from tea and want to know if you'll be joining us for the evening meal," Feliciana said. Turning to her sister, she added, "Signora Alioni thought maybe we could help her get caught up on washing the linens. Her washwoman is ill."

Cass was starving, but she'd questioned only three-quarters of the shop owners and wanted to speak with all of them before the sun went down. She felt like if she left the piazza, she'd miss her one chance to find out something that could help Luca. Someone had to have seen the donna. "I'm just going to buy some bread from a vendor," Cass said. "But go ahead, Siena. I'll be all right." She didn't want to keep Siena from a chance to spend time with her sister.

"But Signorina Cass . . ." Siena flicked her eyes from Feliciana to Cass, her lips twisting into a frown. Finally she followed her sister back toward Palazzo Alioni.

Cass watched her leave and then returned to the bakery, where she bought a fresh loaf of bread and a crock of honey. Spreading her skirts around her, she sat on the low wall that ran around the periphery of the piazza and watched the people pass before her in all directions. Many of the women wore gloves, but Cass checked all the uncovered hands for rings with the flower insignia. When she finished eating, she tossed the remnants of her crust of bread to the cobblestones for the birds to pick at and resumed quizzing anyone who would listen to her about Hortensa. The sun passed across the sky and started to set, and still, Cass had learned nothing.

"The name Zanotta sounds familiar . . ." A tall woman with her hair wrapped into a high cone on her head fiddled with one of her lace cuffs. "A donna, you say? Is she related to the Padua Zanottas?"

"I'm not certain," Cass said. "But thank you for your time." She had just caught sight of a boy with a thick leather sack slung across his chest. A messenger! If anyone knew where to find Hortensa, he would.

The boy wore a black cap pulled low over his ears and a thin chemise covered by only a doublet hanging open. He pulled a small canteen from his satchel and took a long gulp, wiping his mouth with one hand as he recapped the bottle.

"Excuse me," Cass called as she hurried across the piazza. She waved one of her gloved hands in the messenger's direction, but he didn't seem to notice her. He turned and headed toward the corner of the piazza.

Cass swore under her breath. She ran after him, clumsily cutting between the throngs of people. She pushed past a man with a long braided beard who was peddling necklaces made of dark green stones and nearly tripped over a peasant woman who had bent down to tend to her child. Luckily, the messenger stopped to take another swig from his canteen and Cass managed to catch up. She reached out and clamped a hand down on his shoulder.

He looked up in surprise. "*Bongiorno.* Do you have a letter you wish to be delivered?"

Cass paused for a moment to catch her breath. "Actually, I'm looking for someone. Donna Hortensa Zanotta. A Venetian."

The messenger frowned. "Palazzo Zanotta. I know it. It is south of the Piazza della Signoria, just north of the Arno. Down one of the side streets. A bit tricky to locate."

Cass was so excited, she could have kissed him. She repeated the directions to herself so that she wouldn't forget. Casting a quick glance back at Palazzo Alioni, Cass decided to pay a visit to Hortensa immediately. She wasn't convinced she could get the donna to admit to lying, but knew there was a greater chance Hortensa would tell her the truth if Cass went to see her alone. Besides, Siena was probably still doing chores with Feliciana, and Cass didn't want to steal away her handmaid's limited time with her sister.

Don Zanotta's Florentine palazzo wasn't quite as majestic as his home in Venice, but the walls were painted a smooth gray, and carved stonework decorated the façade. Cass felt her heart start thrumming as she knocked boldly on the front door. What if Hortensa refused to receive her?

The butler, an older man with gray hair, opened the door. "Yes?" he asked.

"I am looking for Hortensa Zanotta," Cass said firmly.

"The mistress has gone to Santo Stefano," the butler said, as if Cass were daft and quite possibly a heretic for not being in church herself. He started to close the door.

Cass quickly put a hand against the door frame. "But there's no Mass tonight," she said. If there had been, Madalena likely would have insisted on their attending. She glanced past the butler, but all she could see was a hallway receding into darkness and a set of white marble stairs that led up to the portego. If Hortensa was hiding in the palazzo, Cass would never be able to tell.

"The mistress and some of the local parishioners have come to-gether to sew banners for the altars and the baptistery," the butler said. "She's very pious."

Right, Cass thought, *when she isn't lying and sending innocent men to their deaths.* She smiled demurely. "I do appreciate your time. And sewing banners sounds lovely. I may have to pass by the church and see if they can use another pair of hands. Which church did you say again?"

"Santo Stefano, just east of the Ponte Vecchio."

Cass knew of the Ponte Vecchio, the long enclosed bridge over the Arno, lined on both sides with food stalls and butcher shops. She was only a couple of blocks north of the river—she could smell it. "*Grazie,*" she called over her shoulder as she returned to the street. She headed toward the water and had no trouble locating the small gray-and-tan church with three sets of wooden doors built into its façade.

And sure enough, when Cass slipped quietly inside the entrance hall and peeked into the main room of Santo Stefano, she saw three women gathered in the front of the church, one of them holding up a swatch of fabric. Maybe there was more to Hortensa's story. Maybe Dubois had coerced her into giving false testimony and she was working through her guilt by spending extra time in church.

If that were the case, Cass might have a real chance at getting her to confess. The donna had left Venice so quickly, she probably didn't even know that her words were going to send Luca to the gallows. Cass felt her pulse quicken at her throat. Hortensa wouldn't want an innocent man to die, would she?

One of the girls suddenly burst into laughter, and Cass watched as Hortensa flung the swatch of fabric around her waist. Cass's eyes widened. It wasn't fabric to cut and sew for banners—it was a skirt. A brilliant, scarlet top skirt.

She crept a little closer and realized that the women weren't sewing at all. They had taken refuge inside the little church to change their clothing. Their gowns hadn't initially seemed out of place, but that was because Cass was from Venice, where jewel-toned fabrics and scandalously plunging necklines were the fashion. Here in Florence, Hortensa and her friends were going to raise many an eyebrow in their low-cut bodices.

What were they getting so dressed up for? Where were they going?

Hortensa pulled a tiny pot of lip stain out of her pocket while her friends arranged her cloak so that it covered her dress. She rubbed some on her lips and turned to one of the other women.

The woman dabbed at Hortensa's mouth with one finger and then nodded her approval. She tossed her hair, glancing toward the back of the church at the same time. Cass quickly let the door fall shut.

Ducking around the side of the church, she secured her own cloak and waited for the main portal of Santo Stefano to swing open.

The women emerged a few minutes later, their vibrant gowns tucked safely beneath black cloaks. Cass followed them across the far side of the church *campo*.

The donna and her friends walked west along the Arno River. The water was flowing quickly, the moonlight reflecting off pockets of white-tipped current. Cass hurried after the women. They moved almost as if they were a single entity, navigating the darkened streets without a lantern or a candle. A right, and then a left. Then another right. Cass tried to remember the turns so she'd be able to find her way home. The women passed through a narrow alley and then paused in front of a palazzo made of black marble with threads of white stone running through it. The green-shuttered windows were all pulled closed, except for a single second-floor window where six tiny candle flames danced in the night.

Cass ducked between two buildings, watching as the trio of women went around the side of the palazzo, toward the servants' entrance in back. She pulled her bonnet low. She didn't want Hortensa to recognize her. Not yet. Not while they were in the streets and the donna could escape.

She followed the path Hortensa and her friends had taken. As she came around the house, she saw the back door shutting, and a brief burst of laughter was quickly quelled as the door clicked once again into place.

She approached the door and paused with her hand on the knob. It was made of bronze and shaped like a coiled serpent, with two bright green stones for eyes. Had the women knocked to gain admittance? Cass wasn't certain. Just as she was going to try the door, the knob turned beneath her fingers. A blonde woman a few years older than her pulled open the door.

The woman wore a plain white dress and had her hair fashioned into a high bun. "Are you just going to stand there?" she asked crossly. "Or are you going to come in and join the party?"

"The art of coercion lies not
in seizing control, but in determining
a person's needs and sating them."

—THE BOOK OF THE ETERNAL ROSE

thirteen

S-sorry," Cass stuttered, but the woman had already faded into the dark. As she closed the door behind her, Cass realized she was in a small kitchen. The room was bare except for an oven and a long wooden table. Masks of various sizes littered the table. Apparently she had stumbled into a masquerade party. What luck! Cass could sneak up on Hortensa without any danger of being recognized. She chose a mask at random, turning the strip of velvet over in her hands. It was simple and unadorned, different from the style she was accustomed to in Venice.

Readjusting her bonnet, Cass tied the mask securely over her eyes, feeling slightly braver now that her face was partially concealed.

Past the kitchen was a dark corridor. The air smelled sweet, like rosewater and lilies mixed with some type of smoke. A pair of flickering candles sat on a side table, casting undulating shadows upon the wall.

A stone staircase spiraled upward into the piano nobile. Cass heard laughter from above as she crept quietly up the steps. The room was dimly lit, its crimson walls pulsing with darkness. Everyone's face was hidden: the women in half masks, the men in smaller ones that obscured only their eyes. Most of the guests had shucked off their cloaks. Cass unfastened hers and added it to a stack of outergarments piled on a divan in the corner.

Serving women dressed in simple white chemises moved through the crowd with trays of wine goblets. Someone was playing a harp, and masked figures swayed to the music. A few appeared to be dancing all alone, their bodies moving strangely, like puppets on strings.

Cass could no longer see Hortensa and her friends. She stood and made her way into the portego. Thin fingers of smoke, emanating from a ring of red and black candles that lined the perimeter of the room, wafted through the air. It made her think of Venice, of the lacy mists that coated everything.

A man caught her eye from the far side of the portego. Cass's heart leapt into her throat when she saw his dark hair—almost the color of Falco's. He moved like a cat, coming toward her stealthily. But it wasn't Falco, of course not. She turned away, pushing through the crowd, determined to find Hortensa. Unfortunately, several of the women wore scarlet dresses. With her distinctive scarred cheek covered by a mask, the donna could be anywhere. Or anyone.

The dark-haired man reached her side. "Bella," he said, slightly out of breath. His hand grazed her lower back. "It is poor form to make a man chase after you, do you not know that?"

Cass moved just out of his reach. "*Mi dispiace*," she said coolly. "I am looking for someone."

"I, too, have been looking for someone." He tossed a curtain of hair back from his face. "And I have found her."

"You must be mistaken," Cass said, taking another step back. "I don't know you." There was something disconcerting about the man's piercing gaze. His eyes were too big, too dark.

He reached out toward her, and Cass's whole body went rigid. "I wasn't looking for a friend. I was looking for the most beautiful woman in the room."

Cass began to turn away from him when she noticed he was wearing a ring—a six-petaled flower inscribed in a circle. Blood began to pound in her ears. Finally: the symbol of the Order of the Eternal Rose.

She tucked her shaking hands into the folds of her gown. She couldn't just ask about the ring. It might make the man suspicious. She cleared her throat and forced a smile. "My friends dragged me along tonight," she said. It was, to a certain extent, true, although Donna Zanotta was certainly not a friend. "I do not even know who is hosting this party."

His eyes lit up. "You're not familiar with Palazzo della Notte? Then perhaps you will let me show you around, Signorina . . . ?"

"Livi," Cass said. Her dead friend's name had just come to her. She wasn't even sure why she had lied. "And your name is?"

"Piero Basso." The way he smiled, and the clump of dark hair that fell forward over his masked eyes, once again reminded Cass of Falco. An ache bloomed inside of her.

"I know that look," Piero said.

"Oh?" Cass scanned the room behind Piero, studying each masked woman in an attempt to locate Hortensa.

"It is the face of a woman who deeply desires something." He moved closer to let a pair of guests slide behind him, his hand reaching out to casually touch her arm. "Something I can give to you."

Cass wished it were that easy, that Piero could become Falco just because she wanted him to. She imagined his hand moving from her arm to her waist to her back, his other hand ripping off her bonnet and twining itself in her hair.

Piero's lips twitched, like he could read her mind. He signaled a woman in white. The woman floated over and curtsied. She handed him two glasses of a dark muddy liquid. Piero offered one to Cass.

"I insist," he said, pressing the glass into her hand. "It helps with the anxiety."

"Do I seem anxious?" Cass asked. She sampled the liquid hesitantly. It had a surprisingly sweet taste.

Piero tucked a tendril of hair behind her left ear. "You seem enchanting." His hand lingered at the area where her jaw became her neck. His fingertips were points of cool pressure against her flushed skin.

"But you can't even see my face," Cass protested. She wanted to turn the conversation away from herself and onto Piero's ring, but she couldn't. She couldn't think. She was losing control.

Piero caressed the back of her neck. "Beauty isn't simply one's face. It's much more than that." He leaned in close to whisper in her ear. "I see all of you." His lips grazed her earlobe and she trembled.

For a second, the portego blurred before her eyes. The other guests melted into the wisps of smoke, and the room went dead quiet. For a second the whole world was her and Piero, with only the sound of their breaths whispering between them.

Cass blinked hard and the room returned to normal. She took a step back from his touch and blurted out the first words that came to mind. "What do you do here in Florence?"

"I'm a physician," he replied. "A doctor in residence for a woman who lives just outside of town." Piero's pupils widened, and for a second Cass thought she might pitch forward right into his eyes.

The wineglass trembled in her hand. "Is she quite ill," Cass asked, thinking of Agnese, "to require a full-time physician?"

"She is"—Piero paused—"a woman most concerned with staying well."

Before Cass could ask what *that* meant, she caught a glimpse of who she thought was Hortensa moving through the crowd. She was on the arm of a tall, broad-shouldered man with silky blond hair. He was definitely not her husband, Don Zanotta. Cass was torn. Piero was wearing the ring of the Order, but she couldn't figure out how to subtly probe him for more information, especially when he seemed more interested in seducing her than talking. Hortensa, however, had most certainly lied in accusing Luca. And Cass would have no problem asking about *that*.

"I'm sorry," she said abruptly. "I must go."

"But—" Piero began to protest.

"*Mi dispiace,*" Cass apologized again. She made her way across the room and followed Hortensa up another winding staircase.

At the top of the stairs, Cass hung back behind a large potted plant. She quickly dumped the remainder of her drink into the soft soil, and then set the empty glass on the floor. The hallway was narrow, lined with three doors on each side. Cass watched as Hortensa and the man entered one of the far rooms.

She inched her way down the hall. The door to the room remained open a crack. Cass pressed her face to the opening. Someone had lit the fireplace, even though the air was warm. Dancing orange flames illuminated the outline of two bodies in the dark. They stood in a loose embrace in the middle of the room, almost as if they were dancing.

The man bowed, pressing his lips lightly to Hortensa's wrist. She turned her back to him. Cass watched with fascination as the man reached out and began to undo the laces of Hortensa's bodice. Hortensa held her hands out in front of her, and the man slipped the satin garment over her arms. His hands went to her waist, and Hortensa's vivid scarlet skirts landed on the floor with a dull thud. The donna stood there in just her stays and her chemise.

Cass felt a sudden surge of fear. She told herself she was over-reacting. Hortensa was an adult, fully capable of deciding who she did and didn't want undressing her. Cass couldn't see the look on the donna's face, but her body seemed relaxed, completely willing. As the man began to unlace Hortensa's stays, Cass couldn't help but think of the couple she'd seen at the brothel back in Venice.

She'd been investigating with Falco, looking for the identity of a missing courtesan. Falco had left her alone for a moment, and Cass had gone exploring the dark hallways of the brothel. She'd stumbled into a room where a prostitute and a patron lay naked on a mattress. Cass had stood, frozen, watching their figures twist and rock together until eventually the prostitute had caught her spying and invited her to join them.

Cass's face burned. She shouldn't be watching this moment, just as she shouldn't have watched back then, but she couldn't help it. The brothel in Venice had seemed so wild, so savage. Hortensa and the man here were different. Controlled, almost formal, as if they were strangers instead of lovers.

Hortensa stood frozen in the center of the room, as if she were a doll someone had posed. She stared straight ahead as the man disappeared from view. He reappeared with a glass of the same muddy liquid Piero had offered Cass. The donna raised the glass to her lips and drained it. Her arm dropped to her side. The man's hands had returned to her back. Cass held her breath as Hortensa's stays fell to the floor.

The man stroked Hortensa's chin and jaw with one hand. As he tilted her head to expose her throat, he turned the donna slightly toward the door. She stared straight at Cass without seeing her. Her eyes were glassy, thick, as if she were drunk. Or drugged. Hortensa's eyelids fluttered closed as the man kissed the side of her neck. As he caressed her, her lips parted and she sighed.

Suddenly the donna's body seemed to fold in on itself. She crumpled against the man. He steadied her on her feet, whispering something into her ear. Hortensa smiled dreamily. The wineglass fell from her fingers, shattering on the stone floor.

Cass gasped. The man looked up and saw her standing outside the door. Lightning-quick, he lowered Hortensa to the floor and headed straight for Cass.

She turned and fled, racing back down the hallway, making her way down the staircase in a couple of leaps, thrusting herself into the throng of masked revelers. She pushed her way roughly through the gyrating bodies and headed back toward the kitchen. The crowd had thinned somewhat, easing Cass's escape. Were there others tucked away in rooms, doing whatever Hortensa was doing? Cass's heart battered itself against her rib cage. What *had* Hortensa been doing?

"Signorina Livi." Piero spotted her and called out, pushing his own way through the masked revelers.

She didn't stop. She made her way down the second staircase, tearing through the hallway and into the kitchen. She hit the back door running, the nighttime shadows reaching out for her as she fled into the street.

Flinging her mask to the ground, Cass ducked immediately around the corner, heading toward the front of the house, toward the Arno, the direction from which she had arrived. She stopped. What if the man from upstairs was waiting for her there? She spun around, retraced her steps, and thrust herself into the alley that ran behind the mysterious palazzo instead. She'd cut back over to the main street in a couple of blocks, when she was a safe distance away from the blond man, and from *whatever* it was she'd witnessed.

The darkness seemed both wide enough to swallow her up and heavy enough to crush her, but Cass was more afraid of what she knew might be behind her than of the unknown lurking ahead. She squeezed herself into the inky space between a pale gray palazzo and its red brick neighbor, pausing for a moment to catch her breath.

Leaves skittered past her ankles as she inched her way between the two buildings. She emerged onto a larger street and turned north toward the Piazza del Mercato Vecchio and Palazzo Alioni. She walked slowly, practically without breathing, praying that Falco was right and there were no such things as vampires.

The thought of Falco calmed her, but just for a second. She knew that even if no one was waiting to drink her blood, plenty might be waiting to spill it. Thieves, or worse. The image of Cristian flashed before her. What had she been thinking, following Hortensa into that place all by herself?

She *hadn't* been thinking. She had just been so desperate to speak to Hortensa that she would have followed her straight into the mouth of hell if it had come to that. And for what? A lot of good it had done.

Cass shook her head. She had been stupid, and reckless. Agnese would have a fit if she knew. Then she'd ask Cass the same thing she always did: *What would Matteo say?* Agnese was rather single-minded when it came to how she and Cass appeared to her late husband's heir, even though Cass doubted the two of them ever crossed the boy's mind. Under other circumstances, the thought might have made her smile.

The southern entrance to the piazza should have been straight ahead, but instead Cass ran directly into a blacksmith's shop. Fear bubbled up inside her. Suddenly, nothing looked familiar. The sharp angles of shops and palazzos cut into the night sky, stealing the bulk of the moonlight. Her blood began to pound in her ears. No. She needed to stay calm. Perhaps she had turned too soon. Cass continued along in the same direction, and a couple of blocks later she saw the piazza off to her right. She was relieved to see the statue papered with pasquinades and the peeling paint of the back of Palazzo Alioni.

A burst of laughter from across the square made her jump. She went to flip the hood up on her cloak to hide her face and then realized she'd left it at the Palazzo della Notte. Swearing under her breath, she tucked her chin low, and then snuck a glance toward the laughter. A trio of boys were weaving drunkenly across the square.

Cass was hoping they wouldn't notice her walking all by herself. She must act confident. That's what Falco would do.

As soon as she thought of Falco, Cass realized one of the boys had dark hair that curled toward his chin. Hair that looked identical to Falco's. It was as if Cass's mere thoughts had conjured him from the air. She blinked, then rubbed her eyes, expecting him to transform into a university student, or for the whole piazza to become her dusty little room at Palazzo Alioni.

But she wasn't dreaming. There, just a few feet away from her, unmistakably, was Falco.

"Lust, love, madness:

the holiest

trilogy of all."

—THE BOOK OF THE ETERNAL ROSE

fourteen

Cass couldn't move. She stood there, transfixed, speechless, letting her eyes wander over his whole body. The moonlight outlined his broad shoulders and the dark brown hair that had grown even longer since she'd last seen him, the ends of it brushing against his cheekbones and dangling below his square jaw. He broke away from his friends with a wave and began to cross the piazza toward her, the collar of his shirt flopping open to expose a triangle of muscular chest. Warmth bloomed in Cass's cheeks. Her hands had been all over those muscles just a few weeks earlier.

Falco's jaw dropped slightly as he approached, his lips curving into the lopsided smile she had missed so much.

"Starling," he said. "I cannot believe it. Are you the product of too much wine or too many wishes?" He reached out, taking one of her hands in his own. "You feel real enough."

"Hello, Falco," she managed to say. She felt as if she might explode. Only now did she let herself realize how she had missed every tiny detail of him. More than anything, she wanted to pull him into her arms, to press her lips to the tiny scar beneath his right eye, to bury her face in the warmth of his hair.

Falco lifted her hand to his mouth, brushing his lips gently across her soft skin. It was an innocent gesture, but Cass could sense the urgency beneath it. He felt exactly the same way she did. She knew it.

Pulling her close and cradling her face in his hands, he said, "I have visited Florence's breathtaking cathedrals and reviewed the works of the masters, but you are the most beautiful thing I've seen since I left Venice."

Heat coursed from his fingers into her skin and the blood and bones beneath it. Falco's hands smelled faintly of paint. Cass smiled. She couldn't help herself. For a second the two of them were back on San Domenico, kissing on a bench in her aunt's garden. For a second, desire budded and bloomed inside of her, as scarlet and fragrant as Agnese's roses. Intoxicating. For a second nothing had changed.

Only everything had changed.

She stepped back from his touch, but the wanting didn't fade. The air had grown warm, too warm. "I thought I might never see you again," she said.

"Here I am." If Falco was dismayed by the fact that she had pulled away from him, he didn't show it. "And what about you? What can you possibly be doing here?" He raised his eyebrows and held up a hand. "Let me guess. You've gotten yourself into more trouble." Before she could respond, he continued. "Come with me. I know somewhere we can talk."

"Somewhere" turned out to be the local *taverna*, a ramshackle building with candles burning behind thick panes of distorted window glass. Above the door, a wooden sign shaped like a wine goblet groaned as a slight breeze teased it back and forth. Cass couldn't read the faded words until they were standing on the threshold. *I Sette Dolori.* The Seven Sorrows.

"You'll love this place," Falco promised.

She was a little surprised, but she didn't know why. Did she think Falco was going to take her to his studio, or perhaps his home? Did she *want* that? She forced the memory of his kisses from her mind. She was here for Luca. Luca, who would die if she couldn't find the Book of the Eternal Rose.

Ignoring the leering glances from a group of men hovering just inside the door, Cass let Falco lead her to a table in the corner of the taverna.

"So what are you doing in Florence?" Falco asked.

Cass fumbled for a reply. She almost spilled the story of what she had seen at Palazzo della Notte, but suddenly she felt ashamed. Perhaps she had stumbled into a fancy brothel. She didn't want to tell Falco what she'd been doing, and what she'd seen.

He grinned. "Lured here by a dead body or a devastatingly handsome artist?" He pulled a dusty wooden chair from beneath the table. "Sit down. Have a drink. I promise to escort you safely back to your satin sheets once we've gotten reacquainted."

Before she could speak, Falco's eyes settled on the diamond pendant that had worked its way out from beneath her bodice. His face tightened. He reached toward Cass's throat, but stopped just short of making contact. "Or maybe your husband is expecting you home," he said, bringing his hand quickly to his side. "Enjoying all the trappings of married life, are you?"

"I'm not married," Cass said sharply, tucking the lily safely away beneath her high lace collar. "And Luca's not in Florence with me."

Falco relaxed visibly, although he didn't smile. "Then I insist on buying the beautiful signor*ina* a drink."

Cass realized she shouldn't have accompanied Falco to the taverna. Every second she spent alone with him, well . . . *complicated* matters. And Cass's life was already complicated. Then again, what harm would one drink do? She had a thousand questions for Falco: how he came to be in Florence, and what he thought about the threats of vampirism. Perhaps he had seen Hortensa around the city, or had heard of the Order of the Eternal Rose. Freeing Luca was going to require all the help she could get.

"Just one drink," Cass relented. She tried to keep her face neutral so Falco wouldn't know how happy she was just to be in his company.

Falco signaled the barkeep, who brought over two mugs of ale. He dropped a pair of copper pieces in the man's hand.

Cass sat down, trying not to notice the way Falco's hair fell perfectly over one of his brilliant blue eyes. "What are *you* doing here?" she asked.

"Remember how I told you I was hired on by a wealthy patron? She lives here, on the outskirts of Florence. She has commissioned me to do a piece of art for every room in her palazzo." He smiled. "The work is mundane—portraits, rolling hills, more portraits—but she pays well and she knows everyone. I'm hoping that her friends will see my work and want to hire me on as well."

Cass could hardly believe she and Falco had ended up in the same place by sheer accident. *Fate,* a voice whispered in her head. She ignored it. Her fate was to marry Luca.

"What is it, my starling?" Falco asked. "You look so worried."

Cass spun her mug between two hands, watching as the froth clung to the side of the glass. "It's Luca," she confessed. "He's in trouble."

Falco's eyes darkened at the mention of Cass's fiancé, but he said nothing. Bit by bit, he coaxed the story out of her.

"Do you remember the flower from the ring outside Liviana's tomb, the symbol from Angelo de Gradi's workshop in the Castello district?" Cass asked. Of course he would. That horrid workshop. Dissected dogs pinned to tabletops. Body parts in neatly arranged tin basins. She would never forget a single detail of what was the most terrifying place she had ever encountered. "It's scrawled all over the papers I found. I think Dubois is the head of a group called the Order of the Eternal Rose. There's a book with records of things they've done. A book that will prove Dubois is evil. Luca believes it's here in Florence, and that perhaps if I can find it, I can use it to procure his release from prison."

Falco shrugged. "Well, you're wrong about the head, unless there are multiple leaders. Signorina Briani, my patroness, is actually the head of a group called the Order of the Eternal Rose. I gather from her conversations that it's a scientific society, a group for those who dare to oppose the teachings of the church." He smiled wryly. "But Signorina Briani is no murderer, Cass. And from what I can tell, neither are any of the other members."

Cass sucked in a sharp breath. Falco's patroness was the head of the Order? If it were true, it would only make sense for Signorina Briani to have the book in her possession. Cass couldn't believe her luck. *Fate.* Once again, the entire universe seemed to be aligning in a manner that brought her and Falco together. Either that or he had an uncanny ability to find his way straight to the heart of everything evil.

"Have you ever seen anything called the Book of the Eternal Rose?" she asked.

Falco drained his glass of ale and signaled for a refill. In the back of her mind, Cass knew she should be getting home, that sunrise was probably only an hour or two away, and that Madalena would assume Cass had been attacked by vampires if she was missing when the household awoke. But Cass needed to hear Falco's answer. He could change everything. He might be the key to saving Luca.

"I'm not one for books," Falco said. "But Signorina Briani must have at least a thousand. Her library is quite impressive, if you like that sort of thing."

"Who are the other members of the Order?" Cass asked.

"I don't know them by name." Falco sipped his mug of ale. "The signorina invited a small group of men to the evening meal a few days ago. I was working close by, and I remember hearing them talk about the future of the Order."

"What did they say?"

"Not much. They discussed some of da Vinci's anatomical findings. I'm fairly certain they're not killing anyone." Falco smirked. "Unlike the Church, which has taken to killing women all over Florence. The priests claim people are being attacked by vampires."

Cass shivered as she thought back to the three bodies lying beneath the unmarked ground just outside the city. She didn't think it was right either, but she knew Falco would go on for hours about the evils of religion if she encouraged him. "It's terrible," she agreed. "But I need to know more about this Order. Do you think it would be possible for me to meet your patroness?" It occurred to her that although she did want to free Luca, Signorina Briani also might have known her parents, a thought that filled Cass with both excitement and dread.

"Are you trying to come home with me, Cassandra?" Falco asked. His smile curled playfully. "My lodgings are meager, but I could certainly find room for you in my bed. I suppose with your fiancé imprisoned you are officially a free woman, no?"

"No on both counts," Cass said quickly, although privately she wasn't sure. Did Luca's sentence nullify their engagement agreement?

Falco pretended to be hurt. "And here I was going to invite you to be my guest at one of Signorina Briani's famous parties," he said. "But if you'd rather I ask another . . ."

"Falco," Cass said, pushing her ale aside. "Stop playing. Luca is innocent of these crimes. If you refuse to help me and he is executed on false charges of heresy, you are no better than the Church you rail against. I need to find the Book of the Eternal Rose. I need your help."

Falco reached out to touch her face again. His fingertips traced their way across the freckles on her cheeks. "All right. Anything for you." He lifted her hands to his lips again, kissing her palms and her wrists. Cass tensed. Falco let her hands fall back to her sides. "I'm sorry, starling, but I haven't seen you in weeks," he said. "I'm trying to control myself. I'd better take you home now."

Cass took Falco's arm as he led her out the door and into the complex network of streets and alleys. She could smell the Arno River, but she couldn't see it. Falco walked briskly. Unburdened by the tall chopines she had to wear in the damp streets of Venice, Cass had no trouble keeping up with him.

This was how they would walk, she thought, if they were husband

and wife. She realized anyone who saw them on the street would assume exactly that. She blushed, feeling guilty for even thinking such a thing. Luca was in prison, his survival depending on her, and she could think of nothing but betraying him yet again.

The jangle of bells and clatter of hooves cut through her thoughts. Falco whisked her sharply out of the street as a carriage clattered by, accompanied by several mounted riders.

"Where are so many people going so late?" she asked.

"I think you mean so *early*," Falco said.

Santo cielo. He was right. The sky had already started to lighten.

She feared Madalena would discover her absence and call the *rettori* before she made it home. They turned a corner, and then another. The area began to look familiar.

Cass pointed toward the entrance to the piazza. "Palazzo Alioni is just across the way." She dropped Falco's arm. "I can make it alone from here."

Falco cocked his head to the side. His eyes sparkled. "Are you afraid of being seen with me?"

"No," Cass said, a little too loudly. He was wearing down her resolve, and that just wouldn't do. Besides, she needed to compose herself before attempting to sneak back in. "I just don't want to wake anyone."

"Fair enough." Falco pulled her closer to him. "But know that I'll be watching you all the way to the door, so there's no danger of you being abducted." He scooped Cass suddenly into his arms and spun both of them around in a circle. "By anyone but me, that is."

Cass gave in to giggling. She couldn't help it. Everything seemed less frightening now that she was home and Falco was with her. "Put me down," she said. "You're going to wake up the entire block."

Falco lowered her to the ground, but he kept his arms around her waist. "I may not be able to give you diamonds yet, Cassandra, but I do have something for you."

"Oh really?" Cass asked, suddenly breathless.

He nodded, his face as serious as stone. "Close your eyes," he commanded.

"Falco," Cass protested. "I really need to—" She knew she should pull away from his touch. But she couldn't.

"Close your eyes or I *will* wake the entire block." He cleared his throat as if to scream.

Cass closed her eyes. It would be fine. What harm could one little . . . ?

Her brain didn't even get to finish the thought. Her body caught fire and her knees buckled as Falco pressed his lips to hers. He lifted her off the ground. She was weightless. She was floating. No, flying. Falco supported her back against the marble wall of the nearest palazzo. A soft sigh escaped his lips. The warm breath tickled Cass's chin. The desire that had bloomed inside of her when she saw him became an entire garden of roses, wild and warm, twining through every part of her soul.

She gave in, pulling him close, tangling her hands in his hair, tasting his skin and his lips and his tongue. She expected him to taste like ale, but he just tasted warm, like summer and sunrise. And happiness. Happiness Cass hadn't felt in weeks. And in that moment she knew that she would go home with him, that she would give in. She would let him return her to his meager lodgings and undress her, and their bodies would flow together like rivers.

But then, out of nowhere, an image flashed: Hortensa Zanotta and the blond man circling each other. Hortensa's knees going weak, her slender frame crumpling to the floor. Cass pulled away. Her mouth, her whole body, was still on fire. "Stop." The word came out choked, like a whisper. "We can't." Cass felt suddenly, inexplicably, like she was going to cry.

"I know," Falco said. "I'm sorry." He raked both hands through his hair in frustration.

Cass shook her head. "I don't understand how you can affect me in such a way." If she hadn't pulled away when she had, she might have let him lay her down right there on the stone walkway. It was madness.

Falco's eyes softened. "I don't understand it either." He shook his head. "Sometimes I think nature is more powerful than I give her credit for. Perhaps the stars brought us back together after we went our separate ways. Like maybe the world has plans for us." He looked down at the ground for a moment.

Cass didn't speak. She was afraid of what she might say.

Falco leaned in and brushed his lips across her cheek. "Go on." He pointed to a glimmer of gold low on the horizon. "The sun will be rising soon."

"Death by drowning occurs when water penetrates the lungs. Fluid displaces the last bits of air and then passes into the vessels, destroying the blood, stopping the heart."

—THE BOOK OF THE ETERNAL ROSE

fifteen

Cass didn't sleep. She couldn't. She just sat at her washing table, journal open in front of her, pages blank. She watched the sun creep through the latched shutters and burn away the darkness. Falco's kiss held fast to her lips. She couldn't stop thinking about it. Guilt gnawed at her. The Virgin Mary stared down from the painting behind the bed. Cass padded across the room and lowered the attached veil over the Virgin's face. It helped somewhat, but not much. There was no veil she could lower over her thoughts of Luca.

Her fiancé had spent the night alone, in a cramped cell, possibly being starved or tortured while Cass had been drinking ale with Falco.

Kissing Falco.

What was the matter with her?

She laid her head down on the table and let the smooth wood cool her flushed cheeks. She didn't know why the mere sight of Falco could cause her to lose track of everything that was important. Was it love or was it madness? Was there any difference between the two?

She thought about what Falco had said, how he thought perhaps the stars had brought the two of them together for a purpose. She'd had the same thoughts herself, about fate, but she knew Falco didn't believe in that.

She wondered what Luca believed. He was a good Catholic. "A good man," Agnese always said. Did Cass affect Luca the way Falco affected her? And if not, would Luca be better off with someone else?

Cass sighed. She was making excuses, trying to justify what had happened. Her head was beginning to throb. She ought to lie down for a few hours, but she could already hear the servants moving throughout the house. She couldn't go to bed now. It would raise questions. Better just to stay up.

Cass opened the shutters. The early-morning sun shone brighter than it ever did on San Domenico.

A group of men were erecting something in the piazza. She watched as they assembled a series of logs and stones into a crude platform. Two priests in black robes and skullcaps stood beneath the archway, observing the proceedings with interest. A pair of men with worn, pockmarked faces carried a large tin basin across the square and hoisted it onto the platform.

Someone knocked on the door. Probably Siena coming to assist her in getting dressed. Cass swore under her breath. How was she supposed to explain still being dressed in yesterday's gown? Another knock. "Come in, Siena," Cass said.

"It's not Siena, silly. It's me." Madalena crept into the room with a tray of cheese and fruit. Luckily, Mada didn't seem to notice that Cass had on the same clothing she had worn the day before.

"I was waiting for Siena," Cass said quickly. "Have you seen her?"

"She and Feliciana are doing some mending upstairs. Do you need her immediately? I thought we could share a bit of breakfast." Mada looked apologetically at the tray. "It isn't much."

"It's fine." Cass picked at a bundle of grapes while Madalena chattered about what she hoped to do later in the day.

"Marco and I spent the whole afternoon and evening together yesterday," Madalena said. "Sorry to abandon you in the piazza. Did you have any luck finding Hortensa?"

"No." Cass didn't elaborate.

"Your skin is glowing," Mada said suddenly. "The air of Florence is already doing wonders for your complexion."

Cass had a feeling it was some combination of guilt and desire, not the air, that was making her glow. She practically smoldered when she thought of Falco's soft touch, of the way his lips felt against hers. How easy it would have been to follow him home and spend the night in his arms.

"What are you thinking?" Mada tilted her head just slightly. "You look as though you might burst out into song."

Cass blushed, debating furiously about whether to tell Madalena about Falco's presence in Florence. If she did, Mada would do her best to discourage her from seeing him. But maybe that was what Cass needed.

Before she could respond, loud voices sounded from outside, in the piazza. Cass glanced up from her breakfast with mild interest. A crowd was forming.

"What's going on?" she asked, grateful for the reprieve from Madalena's questioning.

"I'm not sure." Mada frowned.

Cass stood up and moved to the window. The men who had assembled the platform were now dragging prisoners to the center of the square. Women. Noblewomen, from the looks of their brilliant satin-and-taffeta dresses. The assembled crowd was yelling angrily, and people were pelting the women with pieces of garbage. Cass was so shocked, she could hardly speak. Then she caught a glimpse of the woman at the head of the line.

It was Hortensa Zanotta.

Madalena had come to the window behind her. "Isn't *that* Hortensa?" she asked. "*Santo cielo.* She looks awful. I haven't seen her since the last time she shushed us during Mass."

Cass felt the impulse to turn away from the window. But she couldn't move. "What—what are they going to do to them?" Cass whispered.

Mada just shook her head.

The mob was growing in size. A mix of nobles and peasants, of fine silks and muslins, formed a circle. Hortensa was led to the platform first, and the two other girls followed her. Were these the women Hortensa had been with the previous evening? Cass wasn't sure. All she knew was that they were in some kind of terrible trouble. Their hands were bound, and they were crying.

Where was Don Zanotta? Why would he let this happen?

Feliciana burst into the room without knocking. "One of the servants just told me three more vampires are being put to trial in the piazza," she said, then stopped abruptly when she saw that Cass wasn't alone.

"More vampires!" Madalena exclaimed fearfully. She started to pull the shutters closed, but Cass held out a hand to stop her.

Feliciana looked doubtfully at Cass. "I thought we might try to get closer . . ."

"Are you mad?" Madalena burst out. "If they're really vampires, they might break loose and kill everyone."

Feliciana curtsied slightly. "Begging your pardon, Signora Cavazza," she said. "They don't look very ferocious to me."

Cass thought about the way the masked stranger had stroked Hortensa's neck, about the way the donna had seemed ready to collapse. Could Cass have stumbled into a whole party full of vampires? Her chest tightened, and for a moment she thought she might faint.

One of the women had fallen to her knees and was begging for mercy. Hortensa stood silently in the middle of the group, her chin lowered to her chest, her blonde hair dirty and tangled.

"Hortensa Zanotta," Mada murmured. "I knew she was cold, but a vampire? She and her husband live just down the canal from my father."

"What will they do?" Feliciana asked. A priest all in black was making his way up to the platform.

Cass remembered what the man from the mass gravesite had said. *We've started drowning them . . .*

A tiny part of her felt like Hortensa might deserve this gruesome fate for her accusations against Luca, but if the donna was drowned, Cass would never get a chance to question her about Luca's charges. And Hortensa would never be able to return to Venice and admit that she had lied.

"We have to stop them," Cass burst out. "I have to speak with her."

Mada shook her head. "You're insane. There'll be no stopping anything. Do you see that mob? They're bloodthirsty."

But Cass wasn't listening. She was watching a boy with dark hair struggling to make his way around the mass of people in the piazza. Falco.

"Come on." Cass hurried around the back of the house to where the crowd had doubled in size. Feliciana followed her and so did Madalena, though she continued to protest weakly that Cass had gone mad. Mada hugged the wall of the palazzo as if she thought nothing bad could happen to her as long as she stayed within arm's length of shelter.

The crowd in the piazza continued to swell. Servants peeked out from high windows overlooking the square. A trio of schoolboys climbed the statue to get a better view.

"Falco," Cass called.

He was heading toward the northern side of the piazza, but turned immediately at the sound of her voice. He navigated the swaying mob and met Cass at the back of Palazzo Alioni. He had a thick roll of parchment under his arm. Cass had intercepted him on his way to do some sketching, probably at the nearby Duomo or the Campanile.

Madalena's eyes widened. She had never met Falco. Probably she hadn't expected him to be so handsome. "We should go back, Cass," Mada insisted, tugging at Cass's gown with the hand that wasn't still planted safely on the bricks of the palazzo. "It's dangerous to be here."

Falco's eyes flicked to Mada, then back to Cass. "We meet again," he murmured in a low voice. Then, turning back to the crowd, he raised his voice a little and said, "Why are you ladies bearing witness to this? The Church, executing the infirm." His words were laden with sarcasm. "I suppose it is an excellent way of preventing an outbreak."

"They're not ill," Mada said. "They're vampires."

"There are no such things as vampires," Falco snapped. "The priests would have you fear invisible attacks by monsters, all the better to keep you from fearing what is really threatening Florence—the tyranny of religion."

Feliciana stood behind Madalena, watching the exchange with interest. Or was she just using it as an excuse to stare at Falco? Cass couldn't be sure. It was petty, but she felt a surge of relief that Falco hadn't so much as glanced at Feliciana. He was too busy glowering at Madalena. Cass gave Mada's arm a squeeze.

"Falco has some strong opinions about the church," she said soothingly.

Mada shook off Cass's hand. "I've seen vampires," Mada insisted. "Prowling the streets of Venice."

Falco curled his lip into a sneer. "Sure you have. Perhaps a bat that flew a little too low? A leper who dared to sneak out of the compound in search of an extra crust of bread?"

"You're wrong," Mada said. "The Church says you're wrong."

"The Church is wrong."

Mada gasped. "What sort of man are you?"

"Perhaps you should be up there with them, hmm?" Falco said. "You've seen vampires. How do you know you're not afflicted?"

At this, Feliciana raised a hand to her mouth.

Madalena's eyes flashed. "How dare you speak to me like that? My father could run you out of the city if he chose." She sucked in a deep breath and turned to Cass. "Luca rots in prison an innocent man while this *peasant* gallivants around Florence spewing blasphemy."

"Mada, please!" Cass spoke up. Madalena simply glared at her, then spun around and headed for the safety of her aunt's palazzo.

"You shouldn't have said those things to her," Cass said to Falco. "It was cruel."

"Current circumstances have me far outclassed," Falco snapped, gesturing to the women on the platform. "I've seen enough, and I can't believe you haven't as well. I wish you'd never called me over." He turned to leave.

Cass didn't have time to explain. Her frustration building, she broke away from Falco and Feliciana and pushed her way into the throng. The noise of the crowd swelled to a crescendo as the priest stood in the center of the platform, quoting from a leather-bound Bible. Hortensa stood motionless. The other women cowered before the priest, one crying profusely, the other dry-eyed but sagging against the man who held her silver bindings.

The priest was still quoting Scripture, his booming voice building in intensity to match the roar of the crowd. The piazza was full now, and Cass could see that even the shops and the surrounding alleys were packed with onlookers. The sun cut like a knife. Sweat beaded up on her brow. Cass fumbled in her pocket for a fan or a handkerchief, but she had nothing.

Desperately, she fought to get close to the platform. But she found herself blocked and jostled from all sides. Across the piazza, a man with shoulder-length blond hair caught Cass's eye. Cristian. She fought a wave of panic. *Focus,* she told herself as the man melted into the crowd. It wasn't Cristian. It never was. She turned back to the platform. "Hortensa!" she cried out.

Just as Cass called her name, the priest seized Hortensa by her bound hands and thrust her face down into the tarnished basin. Cass gasped. Hortensa's legs kicked out from her wide skirts. The basin water bubbled and splashed as if the priest were calling out a demon. The mob roared its approval.

"Stop!" Cass screamed. "I must speak with her." But her words were swallowed up by the cheering and chanting of the crowd.

The priest lifted Hortensa's head above the water. "Have you consorted with the undead?" he asked.

"No. No, please." She was begging for the first time. Water dripped from her tangled hair. She coughed, a deep, wracking sound. She reached out toward someone in the crowd.

Cass followed Hortensa's gaze. She couldn't believe it. There, directly in front of the platform, was Don Zanotta. He not only wasn't speaking out to save his wife, but seemed to be finding satisfaction in seeing her tortured.

"Then why do you bear the mark?" the priest demanded.

Hortensa stumbled, almost collapsing to her knees. "I don't know," she said, almost unable to choke out the words.

"Expose the monsters who did this to you and God may take mercy on your soul," the priest intoned.

"No one did—" Hortensa's protestation was cut off as her head went into the basin again. Cass watched in horror as the donna struggled a second time. A bell tolled repeatedly from the nearby Campanile. It filled Cass with terror, as though the bell were calling them all to their judgment. The priest pulled the donna's head above the water once more, this time holding her by her hair.

"Last chance to confess and save your soul," he thundered.

The crowd jeered. A rock flew through the air, colliding with

Hortensa's chest. She gasped and doubled over. Onlookers clapped and stomped their feet.

Hortensa didn't beg again. She didn't even speak. Her head disappeared beneath the surface of the water for the third time. Limbs flailed. The crowd cheered. And then, Hortensa's body went limp.

"Stories exist of those

who were determined dead, buried,

and subsequently resurrected."

—THE BOOK OF THE ETERNAL ROSE

sixteen

The body was lifted roughly from the tin basin, carried to the edge of the platform, and dropped unceremoniously onto the hard wood. Around Cass, the crowd shouted and stomped their feet. A shrill voice pierced the dull roar: "Serves you right, vampire."

Cass was carried forward by the mob, close enough that she could see the sweat on the faces of the other accused women. They were now on their knees begging for mercy. Their pleas were weak through their sobs, like lambs bleating before the slaughter.

Cass stared at Hortensa, at the heap of soggy satin and tangled blonde hair that had only a minute ago been a woman. She knew there was nothing she could have done, but a sense of loss still gripped her. Hortensa was gone—murdered while her husband stood by and watched—and with her went one of Cass's chances at clearing Luca's name.

She couldn't bear to see any more. She turned away as the priest grabbed the second woman by the silver-laced straps that bound her wrists behind her back. Cass forced her way through the mob, swimming against the current of people still pushing toward the platform, ignoring the explosions of jeers and taunts.

Feliciana stood at the edge of the piazza.

"Are you all right?" she asked, seizing Cass by the shoulders. "I thought you were going to get trampled."

Cass didn't know if she was all right. She had never seen anyone executed before, and she couldn't get the image of Hortensa out of her mind, how inhuman the woman looked with her pale limbs splaying out underneath the bunched fabric of her dress. Like a broken doll, cast aside.

"Come on." Cass realized she was shaking. She looked around, but didn't see Falco anywhere. He had left her. A fist clenched and unclenched in her stomach. Clearly, she had disappointed him. He didn't know she sought only a chance to ask Hortensa why she had lied about Luca. When Cass had pushed her way toward the platform, he must have thought she wanted to watch the executions, that she believed in vampires.

She wasn't sure what she believed anymore. She didn't want to think she had unwittingly followed Hortensa into a party full of vampires, escaping just barely with her life. But the alternative—to believe as Falco did—meant accepting that the Church was executing people for no reason. Cass didn't want to believe that either.

She retreated into the palazzo with Feliciana, covering her ears with her hands to block out the jeering of the crowd and the shrieks of terror from the women on trial. *Some trial. If you confessed, you were executed. If you maintained your innocence, you were executed.*

Inside, Madalena sat primly on a divan in the portego, sipping from a small gold-rimmed cup. "Herbal tea," she said. "You should ask for a cup. It soothes the nerves."

Cass had problems that were going to require more than herbal tea to fix. "I hope it soothes your temper, as well," she told Madalena. "You didn't need to get so angry."

"Me? What about him? What about *you*?" Mada replaced her teacup in her saucer. "What can you possibly see in that peasant?"

"Probably what all women see in him," Feliciana blurted out.

Cass twisted around to give Feliciana a severe glare. Feliciana dropped her eyes, dipped somewhat ironically into a curtsy, and retreated.

Cass inhaled and turned back to Madalena. "He isn't usually like that," she insisted. "He was very upset."

Mada sniffed. "He said terrible things."

"It's true he does have some . . . *disagreements* with the Church," Cass admitted. That was putting it mildly. She wondered what Mada would say if she knew that Cass had witnessed Falco's gruesome nighttime activities back in Venice: the stealing and selling of corpses. "But he hardly ever loses his temper. Perhaps he's having difficulties here in Florence."

"Perhaps I shall *make* difficulties for him here in Florence," Mada said defiantly.

Cass sighed. Madalena had been kind enough to invite her along to Florence, and Cass was squabbling with her already.

"You're right." Cass sat down next to Mada and reached for her hands. "He was completely inappropriate. He was wrong." She believed the first part. Falco *had been* inappropriate.

"Can I get some more tea, please?" Madalena called out to no one in particular. She fussed with her top skirt. She was obviously still in a terrible mood.

"Falco *did* offer to wrangle us an invitation to tea with his patroness," Cass said hopefully. "Signorina Briani? Apparently she's very well connected."

Madalena's expression softened slightly. "Your Falco works for Belladonna?"

Cass furrowed her brow. "Belladonna?"

"If it's the same woman, her name is Bella Briani, but everyone calls her Belladonna because she is so exquisitely gorgeous. She's a legend, even in Venice. I'm surprised you never heard the name."

The butler hurried into the room with a second teacup and a painted ceramic pot. He refilled Madalena's cup and left the steaming pot between them.

Cass twisted the fluted edge of her cup so that her lips avoided a crack in the rim. "Just one more piece of news that never made it to San Domenico."

Madalena's eyes brightened. "Apparently, when Belladonna was younger, about our age, she took a fall from a horse and hit her head. Everyone thought she was dead, even the physicians. They put her body in a coffin and entombed her in a cemetery out in the country."

Cass stared at Mada fiercely. "If this is another one of your vampire stories . . ."

"Just listen, Cass."

Cass sipped her tea and fell silent. She'd had enough of monsters and vampires for the day, but at least Mada seemed to be cheering up.

"So there is Belladonna in a deep sleep in her coffin." Madalena paused for emphasis. "And then comes the cemetery caretaker, who just happened to remember that the girl was buried with a collection of jeweled rings."

Feliciana had told Cass a similar tale when she was younger: of a beautiful young woman, prematurely buried. At the time, Cass had believed her, but later she had thought Feliciana was just trying to scare her.

"So the caretaker breaks into the tomb with a machete . . ." Madalena made a slashing gesture with her arm. "He had to cut right through her finger to get at the ring. And what do you suppose happened?"

"What?" Cass asked, even though she knew what was coming.

"The girl woke up. Quite suddenly, too, if the stories are true." Mada smiled. "Can you imagine? The caretaker thought she was a vengeful spirit. He ran off, leaving the tomb door open behind him. No one ever saw him again."

"And Belladonna?" Cass asked.

"Rumor has it that the experience preserved her somehow. She's perfect in every way except for the loss of her finger."

"That's quite a story." Cass ran her fingers beneath the collar of her dress. The lace was beginning to itch.

"It's real," Mada insisted. Her face darkened again. "It's as real as the vampires haunting this city."

Cass looked away. Before meeting Falco, she had simply believed what others around her believed: vampires were real. The Church had the best interests of the people in mind. Murderers were executed or imprisoned. Innocent people were not.

Now all of those beliefs were being called into question. But she didn't want to admit this to Madalena. Mada wouldn't understand. Cass took another sip of her tea and set down the cup and saucer.

"So," she said, trying to keep her voice light, "should I tell the *peasant* that you aren't interested in having tea with this famous Belladonna? I could always go alone." She knew this wouldn't sit well. Madalena never missed a social function.

"You'll do nothing of the sort," Madalena said, her voice sharp. "Your aunt entrusted me to look after you here in Florence and I intend to do so. You can tell your peasant friend whatever you like. I'll simply request an invitation to meet with Belladonna through Father."

Hooves rattled on cobblestones, and Cass rose to look out the front window. The Alioni carriage slowed to a stop. Signor Rambaldo stepped down from the compartment as though he had heard Madalena's request and come immediately to appease her. Marco was right at his heels.

Madalena barely let the men get inside before she began cajoling her father about sending a message on their behalf.

Signor Rambaldo rubbed his graying beard. "Signorina Bella Briani, you say?"

"You've heard of her, Signore." Marco sat down on the divan next to Mada, tossed his hat onto the table, and called out for some tea. "She's supposed to be the most beautiful woman in all of Florence. Except for you two ladies, of course." He winked at Mada.

"I'll see what I can do, love." Signor Rambaldo bent to kiss Madalena on the forehead. The butler appeared with additional teacups.

Mada's dark eyes sparkled as she refilled her own cup of tea. "He'll set it up," she whispered to Cass proudly. "I know he will."

As usual, when it came to his only child, Signor Rambaldo did not disappoint. The girls received an invitation to an afternoon tea with Signorina Bella Briani the very next day. Cass was secretly relieved that she didn't have to ask Falco for a favor. The thought of being in his debt made her nervous.

She fidgeted as the Alioni's carriage bounced and jolted through the streets of Florence. She sat on one of the compartment's padded benches with Siena while Madalena and Eva occupied the other. The carriage cut through the vast Piazza della Signoria, the center of Florentine politics. Cass recognized several famous sculptures from her studies decorating the square's periphery, including Michelangelo's *David* and Cellini's *Perseus*. She couldn't get over how clean Florence was. No piles of trash and rotting food like on the Rialto.

Siena peeked over Cass's shoulder out the window and giggled at the sight of a crowd of peasant women using the gigantic *Fountain of Neptune* as a washbasin. The carriage continued, passing several churches and smaller piazzas on its way out of the city center. The compartment jostled slightly as the horse reached the end of the stone cobbles and transferred onto a soft dirt road.

Madalena wrinkled her nose as the buildings gave way to greenery. "Why do you suppose Belladonna lives all the way out *here*?"

Patches of forest had cropped up on both sides of the road, absorbing some of the sound from the wobbling wheels and pounding hooves. Still, there were plenty of villas dotting the landscape. "It's hardly remote, Mada." Cass pointed out the window at the houses that were visible through the breaks in the trees. "Perhaps she doesn't want to live in the center of town, where she can watch executions from her bedroom. Or perhaps she likes trees."

The howl of a dog sounded, off in the distance, followed by a chorus of yips and barks. Mada made a face again. "Perhaps she likes wild animals."

The carriage passed a small church, with twin bell towers framing a central dome of gold leaf and red clay shingles. It was more of a chapel, probably built for only the wealthy who lived out here past the edge of the city. Most of Florence probably attended Mass at the Duomo.

The horse slowed.

Cass hung her head out the window. "*Santo cielo*," she murmured as Villa Briani came into view. She heard Siena gasp behind her.

The stone walls rose three stories in the air, the flat roof adorned with a gold-trimmed parapet. Watchtowers complete with battlements extended above the roof on two opposing corners. Wisps of ivy crawled across the entire front of the villa and framed the large arched windows.

The lawn leading up to the villa was expansive, with neatly clipped hedges framing both sides of a path of marble stepping-stones. Beyond the hedges, flowers bloomed in large terra-cotta pots, and a pair of starlings did battle in a marble birdbath. Sapling trees bowed in the gentle breeze.

This wasn't a villa. It was a castle. Falco had mentioned that his patroness was wealthy, but this estate made Madalena's family palazzo on the Grand Canal look like a shack. Cass was surprised Falco hadn't gone on about his glamorous new place of work. Then again, he never seemed that taken with the trappings of nobility. She remembered how he had made himself at home in her aunt's villa, strumming away on Agnese's priceless harp as if it were a carved lute he'd bartered for at the market.

Madalena seemed stunned into silence. In a daze, the girls descended from the carriage and moved as one across the circular stone path to the front door. A butler dressed in brilliant red satin breeches and a blue doublet piped with silver trim opened the door before Cass could even knock. He introduced himself as Signor Mafei. The ends of his silky blond hair fell into his face as he dipped into an impressive bow. Cass always thought of butlers as senior members of the staff. She had never met one close to her own age, yet the man before her didn't look any older than Luca.

"Bongiorno," he said. "Signorina Caravello and Signora Cavazza, I presume? My mistress is in the garden. Please follow me."

Once inside, Siena and Eva curtsied and immediately excused themselves. Signor Mafei ascended a circular staircase made of the same gray stone as the villa's exterior. Cass and Madalena followed him up into a wide portego with a high vaulted ceiling. Brilliant gleaming swords and breastplates sat on marble pedestals. Statues of Roman goddesses stood in each corner of the room. Cass recognized Minerva, Diana, Juno, and Venus. Vibrant portraits covered all four walls, most depicting a raven-haired woman who looked slightly older than Cass. The woman had porcelain skin and jet-black hair that dangled scandalously past her shoulders in wide curls. She looked almost feral, with cat-shaped eyes and pouting, predatory lips. Cass wondered if it was Belladonna's daughter. Falco had not mentioned that his patroness had children.

Her stomach tightened as she stared at the paintings. Had this breathtaking girl factored into Falco's decision to move to Florence?

No. That was crazy. These paintings weren't even his work. She could tell from the brushstrokes, from the bright compositions, which made everything about the woman seem idealized.

No one could be that perfect.

Cass and Madalena followed Signor Mafei into the dining area, which was painted a deep jade and furnished in dark wood paneling. A large Oriental rug covered most of the floor. Beyond the dining area was a narrow hallway, which terminated at another set of stairs, this one leading down into Belladonna's garden. Signor Mafei gestured to the stairs and then bowed again. "She is expecting you."

Cass turned to thank the butler, but he had already disappeared.

Unlike Agnese's garden, which was well tended, neat, and very small, Belladonna's garden stretched vastly in all directions. It was bordered by the back of the villa and a high stone fence on the other three sides, giving Belladonna complete privacy from her neighbors. A series of terraces had been cut in front of the longest section of wall, each level filled with different plants. A waterfall cascaded down over the middle of the terraces. Cass had never seen so many brilliantly colored flowers. There were lilies, laurel, myrtle, and other plants that she couldn't begin to identify. Roses in unusual blends of oranges and yellows and pinks were threaded through an arched wooden trellis that shaded a round table from the sun. Great stone angels flanked both sides of the trellis. Each winged statue wore a ring of roses around its neck. The blossoms were as big as Cass's hand, and she couldn't resist reaching out to stroke the petals of a giant coral-colored bloom as she approached.

Madalena was already curtsying to the small group of women relaxing around the table. Cass hurried to join her. Before settling into the empty chair next to Mada, she quickly scanned the group of women, trying to identify the mysterious Belladonna. One was pale in every way—her skin, her hair, her watery blue eyes. The other two were darker: one with a sagging brow and a face sharp with lines, one with streaks of gray in her hair. They were all pretty, but none of them was unusual or stunning. Cass dropped her gaze to the women's hands, looking for both a flower-engraved ring and a missing finger. The pale woman had her hands folded demurely in her lap, but the other two seemed to have all digits intact. Impossible to tell whether they were wearing rings, because of the lace gloves that they wore.

"Ladies."

A voice that drizzled like honey came from behind Cass. She twisted around and felt her jaw drop slightly.

A woman in a brilliant turquoise-and-silver gown stood at the bottom of the stairs, jewel-encrusted cuffs glinting in the sun, curls of dark hair hanging in ringlets around her chin. It was, unmistakably, the girl depicted in the paintings.

"I am Signorina Briani, but you may call me Bella if you like." She looked hard at Cass and Madalena with her feline eyes. "*Mi dispiace*. I don't mean to stare, but I was trying to guess which of you knows my artist in residence Signor da Padova."

Cass almost swallowed her tongue. *This* was the legendary Belladonna? It wasn't possible. Falco and Madalena had both made it sound like Signorina Briani was close to forty. The woman before them was just a girl, a few years older than Cass at most.

Cass stood and curtsied quickly, still half in a daze. "I am Cassandra Caravello," she said. "I am acquainted with Fal—with Signor da Padova." It was so odd to call Falco by his formal name.

Madalena introduced herself and gushed for a few moments about Signorina Briani's beauty. The signorina looked amused, but reached in to give Mada's gloved hand a squeeze before arranging her gossamer skirts and taking the empty seat at the table. She introduced her companions, but Cass forgot their names almost immediately, instead thinking of them as Pale, Gray, and Scarlet, because the woman with the sharp face wore a dress almost the exact same shade of red as Madalena's.

Signor Mafei, the handsome butler, brought them each a cup of tea. Cass couldn't keep from sneaking peeks at Belladonna out of the corner of her eye every few seconds. This couldn't be Falco's patroness. There had to be some mistake.

Bella laughed and all of the other women joined in. Cass forced a laugh too, although she hadn't heard the quip. She tried to focus on Belladonna's syrupy-slick voice, but all Bella seemed to be talking about was herself: her jewels, her newest treasures from abroad, her flowers, which apparently bloomed even in the winter. Cass's mind kept wandering. How could she possibly look so young? How could she possibly be so gorgeous? Even Madalena looked plain here, a peasant girl next to Belladonna's Venus. Her skin was practically glowing. She was perfect.

Well, *nearly* perfect. Cass's eyes went to Belladonna's hands, but they were tucked away in elbow-length silvery gloves. Was she really missing a finger? Cass felt a bizarre urge to tug at Bella's gloves, to expose her single imperfection.

A fist of jealousy tightened inside of her. Falco had told her that he had gone to Florence to make a name for himself, so that he would someday be worthy of Cass. But could his eagerness to be close to Belladonna have a different—more selfish—cause?

Bella laughed again and her circle of admirers did too. Madalena, normally threatened by women who were more beautiful than she was, seemed to be hanging on Belladonna's every word. Cass felt like she was watching a circle of rodents being hypnotized by a cobra. She found Belladonna's icy perfection repellent.

A soft breeze rustled the nearest bush, loosening a couple of waxy green leaves that danced across the silken tablecloth and landed in her lap. Cass brushed them from her skirts. A rose petal had also ended up in her lap, and she couldn't help but marvel at its coloring—pink on one side, purple on the other.

"Lovely, aren't they?" Belladonna said. "They're called Janus roses, since they have two faces."

Cass noticed Gray and Scarlet staring at her resentfully. She let the petal flutter to the ground. "I've never seen roses like this. And the blooms are so large. Do you put something special in the soil?" Cass asked politely.

Belladonna smiled. "I do," she said, "but it's a secret. I'm very proud of my flowers, you see." She reached up to pluck a large pink-and-purple Janus rose from the side of the wooden trellis. She tossed it in Cass's direction. "They have the most exquisite fragrance."

Cass flinched as the bloom landed heavily on the table. Everyone was still watching her. No one but Belladonna had spoken. Hesitantly, Cass reached toward the rose. She lifted it to her face. The scent was intoxicating—like sharp perfume and sweet sugar.

Something tickled her hand. She gasped. A hairy black-and-brown spider was making its way toward her wrist. She shrieked, dropped the rose, and frantically swatted at the creature. The spider ended up on the tablecloth. The other women squealed, leaning back in their chairs as the spider made its way across the table.

Only Belladonna sat calmly. Regally. She extended a gloved hand

and gently picked up the spider by one of its tiny legs. Cass suddenly felt afraid, although she couldn't say why. The tiny spider tried to wriggle free, but Bella's delicate grip prevented it from escaping.

"You shouldn't fear my little helper, ladies," Belladonna said softly. She rose from her seat and carried the wriggling spider over to a cluster of rosebushes. She set the spider down on an open blossom. "Spiders protect my roses from harmful insects." Belladonna spun a slow circle, her eyes tracing the periphery of her garden. "Many of nature's creatures protect me and my exquisite flowers."

The other women murmured uneasily as the spider disappeared into a sea of petals. Cass was breathing hard. Everything looked a little blurry. The rosebushes tangled together like a drawer full of precious jewels. Beyond them, muted yellow and white lilies waved in the breeze.

She raised a hand to the lily pendant around her throat. Belladonna's mesmerizing garden—and her beauty—had almost distracted her from her true purpose. Luca. The Book of the Eternal Rose. But she could hardly ask to peruse Belladonna's library in the middle of tea. Perhaps later Signorina Briani might offer her and Madalena a tour of the villa.

Cass sat back in her chair and tried to focus on the conversation. At least she was finally beginning to understand the Florentine accent. She hated asking people to repeat themselves. Scarlet mentioned the scourge of vampirism, and Belladonna launched into her own story of nearly being attacked one night as she returned home from a party in the city center.

"I wear this everywhere now," she said, "even with gloves." She held up her left arm so they could see a slender chain of silver encircling her wrist. Two tiny bronze keys dangled from the chain. She gave Cass a curious look. "Is Venice also overrun with vampires? I've heard the islands are crawling with ghosts and specters that sneak in and out of buildings with the tides."

Cass frowned. If the Order truly consisted of people opposed to the Church, she would have assumed Belladonna would denounce the priests and their trials as Falco had done, but she seemed emphatically to believe in vampirism and the recent attacks.

Before Cass could reply, Scarlet said, "Venice, eh? I heard one of the most recent to go to the drowning platform was a Venetian donna." She clucked her tongue. "How do you suppose she got *herself* attacked?"

"The same way all the ladies do, I'm sure," Belladonna said drily. "By looking for something prettier than her husband to play with. Honestly, I think some of these girls actually *want* to be fed upon. An unusual fetish."

"Speaking of pretty things to play with," Gray started, "isn't your new artist Venetian as well?"

Belladonna's lips curled into a grin. "Yes, he is quite a find, isn't he? A recommendation from a business associate."

Cass felt her cheeks heating up. She quickly dropped her eyes and pretended to be fascinated by the pattern of lace on her cuffs.

"Though your physician is quite handsome too," Gray said.

Belladonna smiled. "And he's promised to make sure I never get buried alive again."

This made Cass look up again. So the story was true.

"Is he still caring for Tatiana de Borello?" Pale asked. "I was wondering if her condition had improved."

"Poor Tatiana." Belladonna fixed her eyes on Cass and Madalena. "You mustn't breathe a word of this to anyone," she said. "A young girl's life hangs in the balance."

Mada leaned closer. Cass fought the urge to look away; Belladonna's catlike eyes troubled her.

"Tatiana, the dear daughter of one of my closest friends, is clinging to life after a vampire attack. She's pale as death and her heart beats much too quickly. My physician informed the priests that she doesn't bear the marks, but that was a lie to spare her life. No one knows how or when she was bitten, but her parents have locked her away in their palazzo. As long as the priests believe she is unmarked, she won't be called to trial."

"But what if she turns into a vampire?" Mada asked, eyes wide.

"They're keeping her tied down, dear, just in case," Belladonna said. "Bound with silver. But if she were going to change, chances are she would have done so already. It's been days. My physician thinks the bite may have infected her differently."

Differently? Cass wasn't sure what Belladonna meant. According to legend, if a vampire bit you, you either died or transformed. She shuddered at the thought of there being a third, perhaps even more gruesome, possibility.

After another half hour of idle chatter, Pale excused herself, saying she needed to be home before nightfall. Cass did her best to dawdle, sipping slowly at her tea, hoping the other women would make their good-byes. Scarlet left soon after Pale, and Gray was, by this time, struggling to conceal her yawns.

Cass let her eyes wander over Belladonna's palatial villa, scanning each arched window for any hint of Falco. Did he live here? Did they take their meals together, sharing light banter across a table laden with delicacies?

Stop it. That kind of thinking would serve no one, and get Cass nowhere. She needed to focus on finding the Book of the Eternal Rose.

"I'm afraid I must walk you back to your carriage soon," Belladonna said abruptly, startling Cass from her reverie. Were she and Madalena being tossed out? "I have a meeting this evening," the signorina continued. "But I insist that you both come back tomorrow, and bring your husband and father too, if they would like," she told Mada. "I'm having a little party, and I would love to talk more with both of you. Especially you, Cassandra. Signor da Padova speaks quite fondly of you."

Madalena arched an eyebrow at Cass. Cass ignored her. "We became friends when he did a portrait of me," she said cautiously.

"I see." Belladonna's lips twitched. "I honestly think he's grown as an artist, just in the few weeks he's been here." She rose from her seat. "Of course I work the poor boy to death," she added.

"Would it be possible to see your library?" Cass blurted out. "Just for a moment? I've heard you're quite the collector."

"Certainly, dear," Belladonna said. "In fact I can show you Signor da Padova's most recent painting at the same time." She clasped her hands together as she headed for the stairs.

Belladonna led the girls quickly through the villa, giving Cass and Mada scant time to marvel over the paintings, sculptures, and other odd bits of beauty scattered throughout the cavernous rooms.

"Where does that door lead?" Cass gestured toward a large wooden door at the end of the hallway, carved from top to bottom with images of Greek goddesses.

"To my chambers." Belladonna smiled slowly. She adjusted the neckline of her dress. "But only certain guests get invited there."

Cass blushed at the insinuation. It was odd that Signorina Briani was so beautiful and wealthy, but wasn't married. *Maybe one man isn't enough for her*, Cass thought.

Then they turned a corner and entered the library, and Cass couldn't keep her jaw from dropping. Belladonna had more books than Cass had ever seen in one place before, perhaps even more books than the Doge of Venice. She quickly began to scan the shelves from a distance. Was the Book of the Eternal Rose tucked away in this room?

Her eyes didn't get far before they settled on a large painting above the fireplace, just as Belladonna proclaimed proudly, "There it is." It was Falco's work—Cass could see it in the muted real-world colors and the sharp brushstrokes. It was a painting of Belladonna, dressed in voluminous gray skirts and a low-cut emerald bodice, her breasts peeking out over the lacy neckline.

Cass dropped her eyes. It wasn't the revealing dress that bothered her. It was the way Bella's body was arranged, reclined on a bed, with one hip rolled forward, hair hanging down over her exposed collarbone. Cass thought back to the night in Tommaso Vecellio's studio, where she and Falco had shared their first kiss. He had insisted on painting her. His soft hands had seemed so purposeful as he arranged her body, as if his growing feelings had determined the tilt of her head and just the way a lock of damp hair should fall over the bare skin of her throat. Cass forced herself to look at the painting again. She wasn't imagining things. Falco had positioned Belladonna's body in exactly the same way.

"All pages pertaining to meetings, theories, subjects, and trials must be maintained in a single place, carefully guarded by the leader of the Order."

—THE BOOK OF THE ETERNAL ROSE

seventeen

Cass thought about the painting for the rest of the evening. She woke early the next day still thinking of it. Over and over, she replayed her terse conversation with Falco's patroness in her head. "What a . . . lovely background," Cass had managed to say when Belladonna had asked her opinion. "Such a unique color scheme."

"That piece was actually painted in my bedchamber." Belladonna had seemed very pleased to relay this fact. According to her, Falco had insisted on the location because the light through the southern windows was best for sitting. Belladonna had then raised a gloved hand to her forehead, adding that she had spent several excruciating days posing for the painting, saved from a cruel death from boredom only by Falco's witty conversation.

"Signorina Cass. Am I hurting you?" Siena had finished lacing Cass into her favorite topaz gown and was now brushing her hair.

Cass snapped back to reality. She had unconsciously balled her hands into fists. "No. Why do you ask?"

Siena pulled Cass's silver-plated hairbrush gently through a tangled area. "You're making the most dreadful faces."

"I'm sorry, Siena. I was just . . . thinking about something." Cass took in a deep breath and uncurled her hands. She didn't know if she was mad at Falco for painting his patroness exactly as he had painted Cass, or if she was angry with Belladonna for her baiting, suggestive remarks. All she knew was that she was in an exceptionally foul mood. Were it not for the chance to scour the library once again in search of the Book of the Eternal Rose, she might have decided to skip Belladonna's party altogether.

Siena patted her shoulder awkwardly in a feeble attempt to soothe her. "Has there been any word from Signora Querini?"

"No," Cass said. "No news of Luca." She'd received just a single letter from her aunt since she'd arrived in Florence. The short note said only that Agnese was getting on fine without Cass and that she would send word if Luca's status changed. Just over a fortnight remained before his execution.

"You must be so worried," Siena said. After a pause, she ventured, "Perhaps coming here was a mistake."

Cass didn't answer. She wished the little room at Palazzo Alioni had a mirror. She felt different since coming to Florence. Older. More tired.

Outside her window, the piazza was growing crowded: another trial, and another execution, had been scheduled. This time, a pair of girls no older than Cass were to be drowned up on the wooden platform. Cass had seen them being dragged into the square when she first woke up. They had the same honey-colored hair and heart-shaped faces. Sisters, undoubtedly.

Now, as she listened to the shouts and roars from the assembled crowd, she was surprised to feel tears pressing behind her eyelids.

She blinked them away. "Could you latch the shutters?" she asked. Even her voice sounded old and unfamiliar.

"But this room is so dark without—"

"Light a candle," Cass snapped. "Light two."

Wordlessly, Siena went to the window and pulled the wooden shutters tightly closed. When she turned around, Cass saw spots of red blooming on Siena's cheeks.

"*Mi dispiace*, Siena," Cass said, rubbing her forehead. "I didn't mean to be so harsh. Please forgive me. I'm not feeling very well today."

"That's all right," Siena answered softly, dropping her gaze.

Cass's bad temper persisted throughout dinner. She picked listlessly at her food and did her best to avoid eye contact with anyone. Madalena tried to ease the obvious tension on the carriage ride to Belladonna's villa. She chattered the entire trip, commenting on parts of Florence and lamenting repeatedly Marco's inability to attend the party because of yet another business meeting with her father's associates.

"He comes back to the palazzo so late and then falls right asleep. I can't believe he and my father decided to attend a meeting instead of a party at Villa Briani." Mada fussed with her lavender overskirt. "What do you think, Cass?"

Cass thought Madalena was being overly dramatic, as always, but she refrained from saying so. "Maybe things will calm down soon and you can spend more time together," she offered. She had more important things on her mind, like how she could sneak away from the party to search for the book, and whether Falco would be present. Was he still angry with her? Was *she* still angry with him? She didn't know.

Siena and Eva sat quietly next to the girls, conversing in whispers. Feliciana had stayed at Palazzo Alioni to prove herself to the mistress of the house. The regular washwoman was still sick, and Signora Alioni didn't want her anywhere near the palazzo until she was feeling better. Feliciana had quickly offered to spend the evening scrubbing linens and chemises.

The city streets gave way to dirt roads and scattered estates. Cass fixated on the twin clock towers of the little church that sat almost directly across the street from Belladonna's winding drive. The towers grew, and then the magnificent stone villa appeared through the trees. Once again, Cass couldn't help but suck in a sharp breath. The sun was just beginning to set, giving the whole structure a magical, otherworldly look.

The girls stepped out of the carriage and into a festively decorated portego, with ribbons adorning the Roman sculptures and large vases of Belladonna's vibrant roses sitting on every flat surface. Siena and Eva excused themselves and headed toward the kitchen, where most of the Villa Briani staff would be located. Cass handed her cloak to the butler and loitered in the portego, watching the well-dressed Florentines chat and mingle. The necklines were higher and the pearls were smaller than what she commonly saw in Venice, but it was nonetheless obvious that Belladonna's friends were extremely wealthy.

At the far side of the room, a string quartet performed and a few guests—including Pale and Scarlet from tea the previous day—were beginning to dance. Cass sighed. Belladonna had made it sound like this evening would be another intimate gathering, but half of Florence appeared to be in attendance.

Falco appeared in the doorway that led to the back of the villa, and Cass felt drawn to him like a fly to a spider's web. Then she thought of Belladonna posed exactly as she had been, and hesitated. Should she ignore him? Did she have a right to be angry? Was she just upset at the whole world? Her feelings were all tangled up.

A decision was made for her: Falco began to move in her direction. Cass turned to offer Madalena a word of explanation or excuse—certain that she would disapprove—but Mada was deep in conversation with a pair of men Marco's age, and just as Cass touched her shoulder, one of the men asked Mada to dance.

Perfect. Cass retreated into a corner, hiding behind a sculpture of Venus where Madalena wouldn't see her, and where she and Falco could converse in relative privacy. When Falco got closer, they both opened their mouths to speak at once.

"Your twin, I presume?" Falco said, gesturing toward the Venus.

Cass realized she and the sculpture both had their arms folded across their midsection. She dropped her hands to her side. "I just—"

"Come with me." Falco didn't wait for her to answer. He placed his hand on the small of her back as if he were merely helping her navigate the crowded portego. Once he hit the hallway at the back of the room, he twined his fingers through hers and whisked her into a small study, latching the door behind them. The walls of the room were painted dark gray and the furniture was made of a sturdy mahogany. He turned to her. "Now, at least, we can speak in private."

Cass's whole body felt simultaneously shivery and warm, as it always did when she and Falco were alone together. She avoided looking at him. "I just want you to know, I stayed at the execution only because one of the victims was Hortensa Zanotta, the woman who accused Luca of heresy back in Venice," she said. "She was my best chance to prove his innocence." She risked a glance at him.

Falco's face tightened. "Of course," he said stiffly. Then he sighed, and rubbed at the scar under his eye. "I'm sorry, Cass. I said things I didn't mean. It's not fair of me to expect you to share my beliefs when we—"

"Come from two different worlds?" she finished softly.

Falco groaned. "Don't do that." He took a step toward her. "Are we really so different?"

"Aren't we?" She could hardly breathe. He was so close. She could see silver threading through his blue eyes. Impulsively, she reached out with one hand to brush his hair away from his face.

Falco grabbed her without warning. He spun her around him so that her body was pressed up against the wall. Cass's heart leapt into her throat. She knew she should protest, should turn away.

But she didn't.

She surrendered. To Falco. To what she wanted more than anything. His mouth teased her, tasting her tongue and lips. She pulled him closer, her nails digging into the fabric of his tunic. He pinned her hands above her head as his mouth found the spot where her jaw met her throat. She exhaled hard. Her body threatened to slide right down the wall, but she didn't push him away. She couldn't. She angled her head to expose more of her neck. She felt his warm mouth, his soft tongue tracing circles on her skin.

"Come with me to my quarters," he murmured.

Cass's eyes snapped back open. No raised eyebrow, no lopsided smirk. He was serious.

"I can't. I—"

"You can," he insisted. "You want to. No one has to know, Cass." His breath was hot against her lips. And her face. Her whole body was burning, like lightning was sizzling beneath her skin.

And then there was a burst of loud applause from outside the room.

Cass slipped out from between Falco and the wall, her heart thudding like the hooves of a runaway horse. "What was that?" she asked, not caring in the slightest.

She had come too close. Too close to giving in, to letting go. *No one has to know.* She had actually been considering it. Images tumbled through her head. Falco carrying her to his bed. Her fingers ripping his doublet from his chest. His hands tugging at the laces of her bodice. The two of them lying together, skin to skin.

"Cass." He took a step toward her again. She dodged him, turned and escaped into the hallway, fanning her cheeks with one gloved hand. She didn't want him to see the look on her face. She didn't turn to look and see whether he had followed her.

Belladonna stood in the middle of the portego. "Esteemed guests. If you will all follow me into the dining room, the birthday feast can begin."

So. A birthday celebration. No wonder so many people were in attendance. Bella had neglected to mention that little detail when she had invited Cass and Mada to return.

Falco materialized at Cass's side. She didn't have to turn her head; she could feel his heat next to her. "We'll talk more later," he murmured. "I'll find you. I promise." He melted into the crowd just before Madalena reappeared, giggling about a conversation she'd been having with a young duke.

In the dining room, the two girls found tiny placards with their names inked in swirling letters. They had been seated just a few chairs down from Belladonna herself. Midway through the feast, Signor Mafei interrupted the meal with a wrapped package that had just arrived via messenger.

Belladonna's eyes lit up. "I suppose one never does outgrow a love of presents." She turned to Cass abruptly. "How old do you think I am?"

Cass felt her face go bright red. She twisted and untwisted the napkin in her lap, wishing she could melt into the swirling colors of the Oriental rug beneath her feet. Because of the stories she'd been told, she knew Belladonna had to be at least thirty, but could she really say that without offending her? Cass decided to play it safe. "You don't look but a few years older than I am," she said. "Twenty perhaps?"

Belladonna smiled widely as some of the guests seated close enough to hear Cass tittered and winked at each other.

Cass felt more embarrassed than ever. It was as though everyone were laughing at a joke whose punch line she had misunderstood. Her stays were pressing down on her chest, and the high collar was squeezing her neck, trapping her breath deep in her throat. "Are you going to open it?" She gestured at the gift, hoping to divert the guests' attention.

"Does everyone think I should?" Belladonna read the rolled parchment attached. "It's from Don d'Agostino."

The guests sitting closest to Belladonna all nodded their approval. Madalena leaned in to Cass and whispered something in her ear about how handsome Don d'Agostino was. "If I weren't so mad for Marco . . . ," she said, giggling, and Cass realized she was a little bit tipsy.

Belladonna set down her knife and fork and dabbed primly at her mouth with her napkin. She tugged at the brown paper wrapping, folding it back to reveal a sturdy crate. Lifting off the top, she tilted the opening toward the far end of the table so that everyone could see the contents. Cass had been in the middle of taking a drink of wine and nearly dropped a half-full glass of sweet burgundy in her lap. The entire crate was tightly packed with books, their spines a rainbow of vivid colors.

"Do you like to read, dear?" Belladonna asked Cass curiously. "You look as though I've uncovered a crate of gold."

"I do," Cass admitted. "My aunt has quite a collection, but yours outstrips it in every way."

"What is your favorite?" Belladonna asked. The rest of the table had fallen quiet. Even among Belladonna's learned friends, it was unusual for a young girl to be so interested in reading.

"I enjoy the writing of Michel de Montaigne," Cass said carefully.

Belladonna's dark eyes brightened. "He is a favorite of mine as well. *'Age imprints more wrinkles in the mind than it does on the face.'*"

"It does for you ladies, anyway," the man sitting across from Cass said with a chuckle.

As the guests finished supper, the servants cleared plates and filled cups of coffee and tea. Cass seized the opportunity to have some coffee. She liked the earthy Spanish beverage that the pope had only just declared acceptable. Of course, Agnese abhorred it, as she did almost anything that was new or different.

A man dressed in white, whom Cass presumed was the cook, waddled into the room with a huge cake balanced precariously on a silver tray. The cake was several layers high, and decorated with what looked like real flower petals.

"Before we enjoy this lovely dessert," Belladonna said, "there is one other gift I'd like to share with you." She signaled one of the serving boys and spoke some low commands into his ear. He nodded and hurried from the room. Everyone waited expectantly, looking around with amused glances.

A minute later, Falco shuffled into the room with a large rectangle under his arm. Was it Cass's imagination or did he look pale? The serving assistant came behind him carrying an easel, practically nudging Falco forward. Cass raised an eyebrow at him, but Falco refused to meet her gaze.

Belladonna tapped her fingers on the long table and the room went silent. "Close your eyes," Belladonna commanded.

Everyone but Cass obeyed.

"You too, Signorina Cassandra," Belladonna said drily. Cass, flushing, squeezed her eyes shut.

"This is the best sort of gift: one I commissioned for myself," Belladonna said. Around Cass, the guests laughed politely.

"Ready? Open your eyes."

Falco's newest painting of Belladonna stood at the head of the table. It was a reworking of Botticelli's *Birth of Venus*. Instead of lovely Venus, it was Belladonna who stood mostly nude in the painting, her right breast and thigh covered by her dark swirling mane. Instead of a seashell, she was springing forth from the blooms of a rose.

The guests broke into applause. Cass found herself applauding along with them, although she felt dazed, as though her head had detached from her body. She couldn't stop staring at Belladonna's bare legs and uncovered left breast. *I wonder how long she posed for that*, Cass thought. *Saved from a cruel death from boredom only by Falco's witty conversation.*

Falco stood next to the easel, transferring his weight from one foot to the other. Belladonna was praising his virtues—work ethic, attention to detail—to the rest of the dinner party guests.

The cook began distributing the cake, but Cass was no longer hungry. She knew she should be happy for Falco. After all, this was the whole reason he had left Venice, to make a name for himself. But she couldn't help but think of what sorts of projects he'd be doing next, of more long hours in Belladonna's bedroom. Perhaps next time Bella would just pose completely nude.

Cass leaned close to Madalena. "I think we should leave," she said softly.

"Oh, please, Cass," Mada said. "Stay for a while." Correctly interpreting Cass's change of mood, she said, "The painting doesn't *mean* anything. What sort of woman actually asks to be painted as Venus? She's obviously in love with *herself*."

"I don't care about the painting," Cass lied. "I just have a little headache, that's all." It was true. The nape of her neck and her temples were stinging. Perhaps Siena had braided her hair too tightly. "And there are entirely too many people here."

"Well, you should have Bella's handsome house physician whip you up a tonic," Mada said.

Cass recalled how the ladies from tea had gossiped about Signorina Briani's attractive doctor. The doctor, the butler, Falco. Cass wondered how many other young men boarded at Belladonna's villa. Perhaps she collected attractive staff the same way she collected books.

When Cass frowned, Madalena added, "Just let me have a few more dances." She stared at her with wide, pleading eyes.

"All right," Cass relented. "Go dance. I'm going to rest in the library." Bella's portrait there didn't seem so bad now that Cass had seen this latest work. She still hadn't made eye contact with Falco. He was being mobbed by other guests eager to discuss his techniques and sitting fees.

"I'll be quick," Mada said. She stood up from the table and left on the arm of a man with close-cropped black hair and piercing green eyes. Cass stood too. She weaved her way through the milling guests.

Her head began to hurt worse, blood pounding an uneven tempo in her ears. The guests were loud. Too loud. The airy violin music had sharpened into scalpel blades, each stanza cutting a bloody path across her skull.

Cass found the library and collapsed into a chair. The room was quiet and dim, the only light coming from a scattering of dying orange embers still flickering in the dark fireplace. She turned her back to the wall, refusing to look at the painting of Belladonna draped just as *she* had once been. What she needed to do was take advantage of this moment and search for the Book of the Eternal Rose. She would, just as soon as her headache faded. Burying her head in her hands, she pressed her fingertips hard against her temples to slow the throbbing.

"Signorina? Are you all right?"

Cass looked up. The silhouette of a man stood in the doorway. Undoubtedly, the handsome house physician. He didn't sound young, though. Maybe the gossiping hags from tea had been exaggerating.

"It's my head," she said. "It's pounding. Is there something I can take for it?"

As the man came closer, his features began to sharpen. Cass dug her fingernails into the armrest of her chair. Her stomach plummeted, and for a second she thought she might faint.

It was the man from the terrible workshop in Venice, the place where she and Falco had discovered the tin basins filled with dismembered body parts. It was Angelo de Gradi.

He had followed her to Florence.

"Nature works in circles.

Trees lure prey and hide predators.

Predators leave behind carcasses

so that they might be absorbed

into the soil and feed the trees."

—THE BOOK OF THE ETERNAL ROSE

S he recoiled in her chair. "What do you want?" she asked. De Gradi was blocking the doorway entirely. She looked around for an alternate escape route.

He stared at Cass. Deep lines formed in his tall fore-head. "I was told a woman had taken ill. I'm a doctor." He took a step toward her, narrowing his eyes. "Have we met before, Signorina . . . ?"

"I'm better now, thanks," Cass said quickly, without giving her name. She jumped up and pushed roughly past de Gradi and out into the corridor. She needed to find Madalena.

Halfway down the corridor, Cass glanced over her shoulder. De Gradi wasn't following her. She had never been officially introduced to the man who collected body parts and also served as Signor Dubois's physician, but she had thought certainly that he knew of her and the trouble she had tried to cause for Dubois at Madalena's wedding. Could it possibly be a coincidence that he was here, now, in Florence?

Cass fled back to the portego, which had grown even more crowded now that the sun had set and several guests had come inside from the garden. She didn't see Madalena anywhere. Ribbons of smoke billowing from the tall red candles in the windowsill stung her eyes. She blinked hard.

Even in the dim lighting, the dresses and doublets of those in attendance glimmered like precious stones—bright sapphires and rubies spinning around the room. Cass's headache hadn't gone away, and the jumping flames and whirling colors weren't helping. Worse, the candle smoke was melding with the scent of sweat and perfume, almost making her gag. She needed fresh air. She had to get out of the villa.

She'd just step outside onto the lawn. She knew she should find Siena and ask for company, but it wasn't as if she were going to wander far.

Descending the spiral staircase to the first floor, Cass saw a pair of lanterns and a box of tinder on a table just inside the door. She lit one of the lanterns and slipped out into the night, following the walkway of stepping-stones that led across Belladonna's lawn. The sky was full of stars, and she could just barely see the outline of another villa off to the west. It was late, and there was no candlelight glowing from its windows. Whoever lived there was likely tucked safely into bed.

There were other villas across the main road: tall houses of marble and stone that flanked the little church, which sat nestled back from the street. Still, they looked plain in comparison to Villa Briani's splendor.

Cass stood in the grass, inhaling deeply. She was grateful for the occasional wisp of wind that blew through the damp curls at the nape of her neck. The pounding in her head was fading away.

She was surprisingly unafraid, all alone, wrapped in the starry darkness. The trees, the flowers, even the elaborately manicured hedges cast soft shadows in the light of her flickering lantern. Cass realized she hadn't had the nightmare about Cristian since leaving Venice. She didn't know if it was the change of scenery or the reappearance of Falco that had driven away those terrible nightly visions. Either way, she was grateful.

She glanced back at the front door of the villa. Was it possible Angelo de Gradi honestly didn't know who she was?

Cass shook her head at her own stupidity. She had panicked for nothing. There was no reason for de Gradi to recognize her on sight. She had never given him her name at Dubois's masquerade ball, and it wasn't as if he could have identified her beneath the starling mask. He had no idea she knew so much about his activities in Venice, that he was paying peasant boys to steal bodies from graves and then dismembering the corpses in his Castello workshop.

But what was the corpse collector doing in Florence if he hadn't followed her here? Dubois was still in Venice—as far as Cass knew. Had de Gradi come here on business for the Frenchman? Or was he working for Belladonna now?

Maybe Venice had run out of dead. Between the scourge of "vampires" in Florence and the persistence of the plague, there was certainly no shortage of fresh corpses here.

An idea occurred to her: Falco had undoubtedly crossed paths with de Gradi during Belladonna's birthday party since the two were former business associates. He had to know why the physician was in Florence. Cass resolved to ask him.

Then she thought of the paintings he had made for Belladonna, and her headache came pounding back.

Something rustled in a grove of trees that ran along the northern edge of the property. Cass turned toward the noise, nearly dropping her lantern as a deer materialized from the inky blackness. It ambled to the edge of the lawn and bent down to nibble at the base of a freshly clipped hedge. Cass stifled a laugh. Belladonna seemed so protective of her plants. Eating them was probably not permitted.

"I won't tell," Cass said out loud. She had never seen a deer before, and she was spellbound, mesmerized by the graceful creature.

The deer raised its head and looked at her. Just for a moment. Then it turned, shaking its white tail as it loped back toward the wooded area.

"Wait!" Cass cried out. She took a small step forward. She wanted to admire the deer some more, to rest a hand on its flanks.

There! The deer paused at the edge of the trees, watching her from one deep brown eye. As she drew near, it turned and fled into the patch of darkness. Cass raised her lantern and stepped into the trees, careful to stick to the small path that had been cut amidst them.

Feathery branches brushed against her dress. The blackness fell around her like a curtain. Her lantern sliced away only the tiniest sliver of night, but Cass sensed that the deer was gone. She turned around to head back to the party.

And then she saw the eyes.

Yellow ones. Shining like copper pieces in the dark. Not one pair. Three. They were moving. Circling between her and the safety of Villa Briani.

Something growled, a deep throaty noise. She backed away slowly, farther into the darkness. The yellow eyes followed her. A snarl. The sound of snapping teeth. Cass resisted the urge to run. She didn't know what the eyes belonged to—dogs or something much worse—but anything on four feet would easily outrun her if she tried to flee.

She continued backing slowly away from the animals, clutching her lantern as if it were a weapon. The trees thinned out, and Cass could see by the moonlight what was hunting her.

Wild dogs. The leader, deep gray, had its hackles raised and its sharp white teeth bared. Two lighter dogs, more brown in color, crouched low behind it.

Her heart beat painfully in her throat. The dogs were blocking her path back to the party. The closest neighboring villa was dark. Would anyone even answer if Cass made it to the front door without being attacked? Quickly, she considered other options. The chapel was across the road, just beyond a short stretch of meadow, and church doors were always unlocked. She inched her way backward, careful not to move too quickly. She must not let them know she was scared; she must not let them think she was prey.

The leader of the pack snarled again. The other dogs advanced. Cass knew she was running out of time. The animals were flanking her on both sides now. Any second they would attack. If she surprised them, could she possibly make it across the meadow to the church before one of them closed its jaws around the back of her neck? Three more steps, then four. The little chapel was so close . . .

Just then, she noticed a change in the gray dog's posture. It was crouched lower, as if it were getting ready to—

The dog propelled its muscular body into the air. For a second, its dark underbelly obscured the moon. Cass's breath turned to glass. She flung her lantern at the dog. The metal bounced harmlessly off its hindquarters and the candle inside went out. But the dog, distracted by the fire, landed clumsily several feet from its target.

Cass was already running for the church doors. Damp grass tugged at her ankles. Without realizing it, she had started to scream. She heard snarling behind her. Panting. She could almost feel jagged white teeth nipping at her ankles. She launched herself at the arched wooden door, slamming into it with full force. It didn't open.

No. Impossible. She banged violently on the door, but no one answered. The skin on her knuckles split. Where was the priest? Who had locked the door? Why couldn't anyone hear her?

The gray dog lunged at her again. This time, all Cass could do was shield her face with her arm.

Sharp teeth gouged her flesh. She cried out in pain, balling her other hand into a fist and lashing out at the dog. Her hand connected with the side of its head and it released her with a yelp. Hot blood soaked the sleeve of her dress. Spots floated before her eyes, and then all she saw was the bristled underbelly of another dog. Jaws snapped shut around the biceps of her left arm. The first dog lunged again. Cass screamed as loudly as she could, the kind of scream that would have drawn fathers and soldiers and maybe God himself if any of them had been in attendance.

No one came.

The blood continued to darken her dress, and the summer air turned to ice.

The night went gray. Cass thought she saw Luca's face floating above her head. His soft brown eyes considered her gently. No, it wasn't Luca. It was Falco who looked down at her. The faces merged and mingled. Luca. Falco. Luca. Falco. And then the face became someone else's entirely.

Someone else's eyes. Someone else's lips telling Cass to *stay awake, stay awake, stay awake.*

Cass reached toward the face, but her hand closed around air, as if it were only a mirage looking down at her. Her breath caught in her throat. The face, the night sky, and the world slowly faded into nothingness.

"The bite of a dog has been

known to cause fevers,

madness, and death."

—THE BOOK OF THE ETERNAL ROSE

nineteen

Reality returned in fragments. Cass's vision was hazy. She tried to rub her eyes, but couldn't. Both wrists were bound at her sides, and her left arm was throbbing. She thrashed, trying to free herself. White-hot pain surged through her, stealing away her breath.

She lay still, panting, trying to piece together what had happened, where she was. Memories teased at her consciousness: the dogs, their teeth sinking into her flesh, the warm blood soaking through her gown.

Bulky bandages now covered her left shoulder to her wrist. She tugged at her hands again, more gently, trying to work her right one through the circle of twisted cloth that tethered her to the bed.

"Help." Her voice cracked. She cleared her throat and tried again. "Help!"

A figure moved toward her, blurry in the dark. "*Grazie a Dio*, you're awake," a man said. "I feared you had lost too much blood."

His voice sounded familiar but Cass couldn't place it. "Why have you tied me up like an animal?" She wrestled against her bonds again. "I demand that you free me this instant."

"Calm down, Signorina," the man said. He bent closer, leaning into the light.

Cass's muscles went rigid. It was the doctor she had met at Palazzo della Notte. Her eyes flicked down to his hand. His fingers were currently bare, but he had worn the ring of the Eternal Rose the night she met him, hadn't he? Her head was full of jagged thoughts, her whole life up to that moment a shattered mirror. Suddenly, Cass didn't feel certain of anything.

"I am Piero Basso, Belladonna's house physician." He nimbly undid the knots holding Cass's wrists down at her sides. If he recognized her, he made no sign of it. "You were delirious, screaming about the Devil, clawing at your own face. That is why I bound your hands."

He massaged each of her wrists, and her skin stung as blood surged back into them. Leaning over, he lit an additional taper, and as he did, his features came even more into focus. It had been dark at that wicked party and Cass hadn't seen much of him, except to notice the little things—his hair, his smile, his catlike movement—that reminded her of Falco. As he hovered just above her face for a moment, she saw that his skin was even darker than Falco's—a deep bronze color that she had seen only on people from the southernmost islands of the Venetian Republic. Perhaps he was from Crete, or one of the tiny islets in the Aegean Sea. His hair was dark, almost black. And he had eyes to match—like two pieces of shining obsidian, so dark that Cass couldn't tell where the iris stopped and the pupil began.

She raised her head, ignoring the pain that throbbed just behind her eyes as she did. The room was small and dark. Thick curtains obscured the windows, so Cass had no idea what time it was. The bed was soft, though, and the blankets were comfortable. A velvet canopy was stretched above her, with flaps tied back on the corners that could be loosened for privacy.

Piero had crossed the room to the washing table just inside the door. He was stirring something in a metal cup. At Palazzo della Notte, he had mentioned working for a woman who demanded a physician day and night. Cass had assumed it was someone chronically ill, like her aunt. But if Signorina Briani was sick, she certainly didn't show it. Where had Piero been when Cass had her headache in the library? Why had de Gradi been the one to tend to her?

"How are you feeling now, Signorina?" Piero asked. "Are you still having visions?"

Cass didn't remember any visions. She just remembered retreating down the wooded path, running from the dogs. She remembered the church, the locked door, and the teeth ripping into her arm. And then the blood.

"You found me outside the church?" she asked.

Piero nodded.

"How?"

"I had come into the garden to take a break from the dancing." Piero handed the metal cup to her. Cass looked dubiously at the cloudy gray liquid. It looked like something the servants used to clean the silver. "For pain," he explained. Piero took her left hand in his. "I heard you screaming," he said. "Like the Devil himself was chasing you." He bent her arm just slightly to examine her bandage. Pain shot through her, stabbing, racing from her fingertips to her breastbone.

Cass bit her lip to keep from crying out. She downed the medicine in one gulp. "Is my arm all right?"

"I had to repair one of the vessels," he said. "But I couldn't close the wound entirely. It will need to stay bandaged for a while."

"What do you mean, couldn't close it?" she asked. She couldn't help but imagine the mangled flesh that lay beneath the dressing. Torn skin, exposed bone.

"Wild dogs carry all kinds of sickness," Piero said. "To sew closed your wound would mean locking that sickness deep inside your flesh. Once the sickness drains out, the wound will heal on its own." He tossed his hair back from his face.

Caspita. He looked like Falco when he did that. Or maybe she was just delirious. Cass closed her eyes.

"It could take some time, I'm afraid," Piero continued. "A week or more."

Cass opened her eyes again, startled. "What?" She couldn't lie in bed for a week. Luca was depending on her.

Piero nodded. His dark eyes cut straight through her like steel spikes. "Was it only dogs that attacked you?" he asked gently.

"What do you mean, *only* dogs?"

"Some people believe that vampires can take many different forms."

"They were dogs," she said curtly. Why was all of Florence so eager to accuse women of consorting with vampires?

Piero nodded. "I believe this is yours." He held up a dusty silver necklace. Her lily. "Lovely flower. How fitting."

Cass's hand went to her throat. "It must have fallen off," she said.

Piero polished the necklace on one of his cuffs. Wordlessly, he reached behind her and fastened the pendant around her neck. "Rest now. I need to attend to my mistress, but I'll be back soon to check on you."

"Is the party still going on?" Cass settled back against the pillows.

Piero smiled. "It is afternoon. You have been asleep for fifteen hours."

Fifteen hours! Madalena and Siena must be frantic. "I came to the party with my friend, Signora Madalena Cavazza," Cass said. "Does she know where I am?"

"She was informed of your injury last night. She and your hand-maid wanted to stay with you, but Signorina Briani persuaded them to return home. They could have done no good here, weeping and trembling at your bedside. But I'll have Signor Mafei send word to them that you've awakened."

"She's staying with her aunt. Palazzo Alioni, just off the Piazza del Mercato Vecchio."

Piero smiled again. "Yes. She made certain that I knew. Can I have the staff bring you anything? Some food? Something to drink, perhaps?"

Cass hadn't realized how dry her mouth was. Her whole throat felt like it was coated with dust. "I'm very thirsty," she admitted. "It's quite warm in here, isn't it?"

Piero shook his head. "You're suffering from fevers. I'll have someone bring you something to drink."

Several minutes later, a tiny blonde girl, who might have been Siena's younger sister, brought Cass a goblet of ale. "I'll just leave the pitcher here on the table," the servant said, curtsying quickly. She scurried out of the room like she was afraid that whatever affliction Cass had was contagious.

Cass downed three goblets before her throat started to feel normal again. The pain in her arm had faded to a dull ache. She lay back on the pillow and tried to rest, but sleep didn't come. She wondered whether Mada and Siena were panicking. She wondered whether Falco knew she was there, an invalid, Belladonna's unwilling prisoner.

Cass had a feeling Belladonna hadn't told him. If she had, surely he would have come to look in on her. And what about the lady of the villa herself? Shouldn't Bella at least pretend to be concerned about a young noblewoman who was injured at her birthday party? Then again, Cass wasn't really in a hurry to see her. Shockingly, her room had four full walls and none of them was draped with a painting or tapestry of Belladonna's face. Perhaps that was why Falco had been hired. He *did* say she had hired him to paint something for every room of her villa.

Cass flung her covers back with her good arm. The room was bigger than her room at Palazzo Alioni, but the air was warm and thick and the gloom was suffocating. As soon as she twisted her body so that her feet touched the floor, she was overwhelmed with lightheadedness. She sat back down on the bed until the fog cleared from her head. Slowly, with her uninjured arm out for balance, she made her way over to the window and peeked through the heavy drapery.

She was in a bedroom at the back of the villa, overlooking the garden. She was delighted to see Falco and his easel below her. He appeared to be painting a picture of Belladonna's roses.

Cass fumbled her way to the dressing table and consulted her reflection in the mirror. It was a lower-quality mirror than what she was accustomed to in Venice, distorting her image slightly. *But not distorting it enough,* Cass thought. She was a disaster. Someone had dressed her in a pale blue chemise made of fabric so thin, she could clearly see the outline of her breasts. Had it been Piero who had removed her soiled gown and washed her body? Had he chosen the revealing garment for her? Cass cringed as her freckled cheeks went pink in the mirror. Best not to think about it too much.

She turned away, using her good hand to push a tangled clump of partially braided hair back under her sleeping cap. Then she searched through the armoire next to the table until she found a thick velvet dressing gown. Returning to the bed, she struggled to wrap the gown around her as best she could, leaving her injured arm dangling inside the robe. She worked the belt into a loose knot, using her mouth and free hand to cinch it tight.

She peeked out into the hallway. A pair of girls in blue and red were dusting a large painting of Belladonna riding a dapple-gray horse. They gave Cass a curious look as she edged into the hall, but didn't say anything. Cass nodded as she headed past them.

She descended the stairs toward the garden where she had seen Falco. She just wanted to talk to him, tell him what had happened, ask him about de Gradi. She knew his mere presence would comfort her.

The bright flowers swam before Cass's eyes, a sea of color that beckoned to her. It was madness, but she swore the roses turned ever so slightly in her direction as she descended the stairs. She had to go slowly and periodically lean against the banister to fight attacks of dizziness. By the time she emerged into the garden, Falco and his easel were gone. A group of boys in plain beige gardening uniforms squatted on their hands and knees, trimming the grass with large shears.

"Excuse me," Cass said. The boys all looked up at her as if she were speaking a foreign language. One of them gaped at her bizarre appearance. Cass ignored them. "I'm looking for Signor da Padova, the artist," she said.

"He's gone," the tallest of the boys said. "The mistress called him away to do some work inside."

Of course. Cass imagined Falco and his patroness holed up in her bedchamber working on something even more scandalous than a painting depicting Belladonna as a half-naked Roman goddess. She pushed the thought out of her mind, thanked the tall boy, and turned back toward the villa, feeling unaccountably frustrated.

Piero's medicine had soothed her slightly, but now that she was up and moving, her arm was tingling and burning. Again, Cass was dying to see what was beneath the bandages. But she was too afraid to look. She realized that she might have died if Piero hadn't helped her.

She realized, too, that she had neglected to thank him for saving her life.

She turned back to the boys, who were clipping small tufts of grass to an even height with an almost mathematical precision. "I'm sorry to bother you again," she said. "But do you know where I might find Piero Basso, the house physician?"

"His lodgings are on the first floor." Once again, it was the tallest boy who responded. "Next to the butler's office."

There was no entrance to the first floor from the back of the villa, so Cass would have to ascend the stone stairs leading away from the garden and travel through the house to the main spiral staircase. She paused at the top of the back stairs for a moment, watching as a bank of clouds rolled in from the west. The air felt cooler. A storm was coming. She ducked back into the villa and made her way to the main stairs.

Cass paused for a moment at the bottom of the staircase and reached out for the banister to steady herself. It looked as if the walls were moving. Not spinning or running away from her, but pulsing, almost as if the villa itself were breathing.

She closed her eyes and opened them again. The walls went still. She stood between the rectangles of sunlight that filtered through the front window for a moment, getting her bearings.

The main hallway ended in a T. There were arched doors on both sides of her. Tiny gargoyles were carved into the stone above them. She knocked gently on the door to her right. No one answered. She tried the knob. Locked. She repeated her soft knock on the door to her left. Again, no response. She placed her hand on the doorknob, expecting that this, too, would prove locked.

But the door swung open, and Cass peeked into the room. A small bed was nestled against the far wall, its covers disturbed, as if someone had risen from it quickly. Next to the bed was a teetering stack of leather-bound books. A candle burned on the washing table just inside the door; Piero, if indeed he was the one who lived here, would be back soon. Still, Cass crept forward into the chamber.

"Dottor Basso?" She cleared her throat. "Piero? It's Cass." She wasn't sure why she said it. She didn't really think the physician was hiding in the rumpled coverlet or behind the stack of books. Still, it didn't seem right to creep into someone's chambers unannounced.

She entered the room and closed the door behind her. Her eyes gravitated to the stack of books. She didn't think the Book of the Eternal Rose would be lurking in a lowly physician's room, even if he did wear the ring of the Order, but it wouldn't hurt to give them a quick look.

Tiptoeing over to the bed, she knelt down to examine the leather-bound volumes. Gingerly, she lifted the top one from the stack. There was no name or title embossed into the deep brown cover. She peeked at the second volume. Also blank. A rustling sound from the shelf near her head made her jump, and the whole tower of books spilled onto the floor.

Accidempoli. It had probably just been a mouse scurrying inside the wall. Wincing in pain, Cass hurriedly tried with her good arm to restack the books as they had been. A page pulled loose from one of the bindings, a diagram that caught her eye. It was a crude sketch of a person, with wide vacant eyes and a shock of long hair framing her cheekbones. She was mounted on a table, her hands and feet splayed out and bound, a Y incision carved into her midsection. Cass shuddered. The drawing reminded her of the dissected dog she and Falco had found in the workshop on the Rialto.

Except this wasn't a dog. It was a girl, just like her.

Cass turned to the front of the book. Was Piero doing the same sort of research as Angelo de Gradi? She tried to remember if she had seen his name among those listed on the parchment she had found in her parents' tomb. De Gradi, Dubois, da Peraga. She saw these names as if they were inked in blood. But Basso? She wasn't sure. Falco had said most of the Order members were wealthy. Perhaps the tradesmen and physicians were engaging in experiments that the wealthier Order members were funding.

But to what end?

The first page was dominated by a drawing of a skeleton, whose bones were identified in the margin. The next page was just a leg, its three bones enlarged to show detail. Cass flipped again and again. She paused at the drawing of an arm. According to the sketch, there were three bones in the arm. Cass was lucky the dogs' powerful jaws had not snapped them all like twigs.

Cass kept flipping pages. Interspersed among the diagrams were pages of foreign symbols and notations about illness and vitality.

She knew she should stop reading, that she shouldn't be snooping through someone's private notes. She knew how furious she would be if she caught anyone reading her journal. Her stomach clenched. Somewhere, Cristian still possessed a volume of her most personal thoughts. Cass slammed the book shut and reordered the crooked stack as she had found it.

She turned to a set of shelves next to the bed. Maybe she would find the ring he had worn to the Palazzo della Notte. Then she would know for certain he was a member of the Order. Among a jumble of medical equipment were a hairbrush, a vial of perfume, and a syringe. Cass eyed the silver syringe and attached long steel needle with curiosity. What sort of injection required a needle so thick?

The shelf below that one held a single sheet of lush vellum, with withered rose petals pinned to the page. There were scrawled notes next to some of them—strings of letters and numbers that Cass didn't understand.

She turned to go back to the stack of journals when she heard the rustling sound again. At the back of the shelf, almost totally concealed beneath a silk pillow slip, was a rectangular container made of glass. Cass folded back the fabric and shrieked, stumbling back from the shelves and sending the stacks of journals tumbling to the floor again. She had uncovered a cage.

A cage filled with spiders.

"Careful, Signorina. I wouldn't want you to faint right onto my bed. It would look bad for us both."

Cass whirled around. Piero was standing in the doorway. How long had he been watching her? "I—I'm sorry," she stuttered. "I didn't mean to disturb—I came looking for you."

"You came looking for me? I like that." Piero crossed the room in a few strides, his thick-soled boots as quiet as slippers on the stone floor. "No need to be scared." He draped the pillowcase back over the top of the cage. "Spiders are not nearly so frightening as the reputation that precedes them." His dark eyes lingered on her.

"But why do you keep them?" She bit her lip. "Are they poisonous?"

"All spiders are venomous," he said. "In most cases, however, their venom is weak, so it doesn't make people ill. My colleagues and I have found it to be just the opposite, in fact. We believe spider venom may contain medicinal properties."

"Really?" Cass couldn't imagine anything good coming from the hairy-legged little beasts.

He nodded. "Many medicines come from plants. Is it so hard to believe they might also come from animals or insects?"

"And your . . . books?" She stopped herself at the last second from saying *journals*. "Are they for studying? I was looking for something to read."

"Believe me, don't concern yourself with my books," he said. "They don't make good bedtime stories. Full of foul humors."

"I know about humors," Cass said, raising her chin. "My father studied medicine. But the texts he studied were very different."

"If I'd known you were going to spend such a long time in my chambers, I would have been there to entertain you." Piero smiled, but there was nothing amusing about the way he looked at her—as though he wanted to devour her.

Cass found his gaze too intense; she had to look away. Thunder boomed outside the window, and she flinched.

"Are you all right?" Piero asked, his hand coming to rest gently on her forearm.

"I'm fine," she said quickly. "Just in pain."

Softly, he touched her face. "You have a fever," he murmured. "Let me help you back to bed and then I'll prepare your medicines."

Before Cass could protest, Piero bent down and scooped her into his arms. He headed for the hallway.

"You don't need to carry me." Cass was blushing furiously. "I'm not an invalid."

"I believe you said something to that effect last night as well." Even though she refused to look at him, Cass could hear the smile in his voice. "And then you fainted."

She gave up and let Piero carry her through the first floor and up the winding staircase to her room, praying that they wouldn't accidentally bump into Falco. She did feel a little unsteady. She didn't know if it was her condition or seeing the spiders that had caused it.

In her room, he set her down gently on her bed and started to remove her dressing gown.

"No," Cass said quickly, willing herself not to start blushing again. "I'd like to keep it on. I'm a little chilled."

Piero looked concerned but nodded. He tucked her beneath the covers, adjusting the pillows behind her. A piece of Cass's hair fell in front of her eye. She and Piero reached for it at the same time, and their fingers brushed. Cass felt a spark move through her. She dropped her hand awkwardly into her lap. Piero tucked the shock of hair back into her cap, his fingers lingering on her jawbone for a second.

Cass thought back to the party she had crashed at Palazzo della Notte, at the way Piero had pursued her as if she were prey. She remembered the way Hortensa had willingly given herself to the masked stranger, the alleged vampire. But Piero was no vampire. He had saved her.

"Rest, Signorina Cassandra. The butler sent word to your friend and handmaid, and they will come tomorrow for a visit." He blew out the candle that sat on her washing table. "I'll be back much sooner, with more medicine to ease your pain." He smiled at her again.

After he had gone, Cass lay beneath the sheets, listening to the rain on the rooftop, trembling in a way that had nothing to do with her fever. Piero was part of the mystery, she could feel it. He wrote of experiments and spoke of humors. He owned a ring engraved with the six-petaled flower. Cass had to get close to him, even though he scared her. One way or another, he was involved with the Order of the Eternal Rose, and she would do whatever it took to get him to tell his secrets.

"Mandrake was used frequently
by the Ancients, as both an analgesic
and a sedative. In large doses it
has been known to cause delirium."

—THE BOOK OF THE ETERNAL ROSE

twenty

C ass woke from a dream, disoriented by the darkness. Her chest went tight for a moment until she remembered she was at Belladonna's villa. There was a faint padding noise, and she saw a flash of movement as the blackness distorted around her. Someone else was in the room.

"Piero?" she croaked out. "Is that you?"

A candle flame sparked to life. "Sorry to disappoint." Falco's teasing grin materialized in the soft yellow glow.

Cass smiled and then immediately winced. Why was it that she couldn't do anything except lie like a block of marble without her arm starting to throb? She adjusted the pillow behind her back. *Mannaggia.* She felt as broken-down as her aunt Agnese.

"Should I send for Dottor Basso?" Falco asked, sounding as if it were the last thing he wanted to do. He knelt down with the candle so their faces were just inches apart. "You were thrashing about in your sleep. Is it the pain?"

Cass shook her head. For once she couldn't remember her dream, which was undoubtedly a blessing. "I'm fine." Her arm was aching, but she didn't want Piero. She didn't want anything to steal away these precious moments with Falco.

For a moment, neither of them spoke. Falco set the candle on the table next to the bed. He traced the hollows under her eyes, skimming a finger across the bridge of her nose. "You look so pale," he said. "Like a ghost. I can't believe I could have lost you. What were you doing all alone in the woods?"

Cass told him about de Gradi accosting her in the library, how she'd panicked and fled the villa. "Did you know that he was here?" she asked.

Falco wrapped the fingers of her right hand in his. He sat next to her on the bed. "He's heard about the trials, about the people drowned and then dumped in graves outside the city." His mouth tightened into a hard line. "Easy pickings. He's been . . . encouraging me to go back into my former line of work." Falco added quickly, "I said no, of course."

Cass felt her stomach seize. Thinking of what he had done in Venice for money still made her queasy. "How many bodies can de Gradi possibly need? Surely Venice has its fair share of the dead."

"I suspect there are other reasons for his presence in Florence," Falco said. "He's the one who told me about the showing at Don Loredan's. Maybe he knew Belladonna would be there; he seems to be quite enamored with her."

"She seems to be quite enamored with *you*." Cass did her best to keep her voice light.

She was hoping Falco would deny it, but he merely shrugged. "As you've probably noticed, she's quite fond of most pretty things. She seemed quite taken with *you* at her birthday dinner."

"True, but she's not posing nude for hours in my company."

Falco laughed. "She might if you asked nicely. She's not particular when it comes to her admirers." He reached out and ran the back of his hand down the side of Cass's face. His voice lowered. "She's nothing compared with you."

Warmth bloomed in Cass's chest. Falco's gentle touch never failed to melt her. Did he really find her more beautiful than his stunning patroness?

Falco lifted her chin and leaned forward. His lips grazed her cheek. "There's something hard about her, like she's part sculpture. Unreal," he murmured. "You are all softness, and all real. You are ten times as beautiful as she is."

He leaned in even closer, and then hesitated. Cass knew he was waiting for her to close the almost-nonexistent gap between them. She didn't do it. She couldn't. She had come to Florence with the noble intentions of clearing Luca's name. And what, exactly, had she accomplished? She'd betrayed Luca yet again and almost gotten herself killed.

But maybe she had crossed paths with Falco for a different reason, a higher purpose. He could help her. He could be her eyes while she was trapped in bed.

She pressed her forehead against his cheek, but turned her lips away from his mouth. His face felt cool against her damp skin. "I need your help," she whispered.

"My lovely tormentor," Falco said softly. "How can I be of assistance?" Cass could hear the hurt in his voice.

She couldn't bring herself to look at him. "The Book of the Eternal Rose—" she started to say, and then gasped as something flickered in the corner of her vision. In the dim light she could just barely make out the door to her room. It was open, only a sliver, but Cass swore she saw a face in the hall. Was it Piero coming to administer medicine? Signorina Briani coming to check on her? Or was someone spying on them?

She sat up quickly, pulling her covers tight around her. Her arm throbbed in protest, and Cass bit back a cry of pain. The face disappeared from view.

"What is it?" Falco asked.

"I saw someone," Cass faltered. "A face, looking through the door."

Falco stood and took the candle from the bedside table. He strode across the room. "The door is closed," he said. He pulled it open and peered out into the hallway. "The whole villa is dark. Could you have imagined it?"

Cass sighed. Was she really so terrified of giving in to Falco's affections that she was hallucinating?

She was suddenly seized with a terrible idea: was she getting sicker? Perhaps her fevers were attacking her brain.

"I—I don't know," she admitted. "But I need you to find that book for me."

"Cass," Falco said, watching her with concern. "I'd better go. You need your sleep."

"I do not need sleep. I need the Book of the Eternal Rose." She sighed in frustration. "I know you don't believe me. Just promise that you'll at least skim the books in the library for me." She should have gone through them the night of the party, headache or no. Even if she did feel strong enough to make it to the library, she might not get a chance with Piero watching over her at all hours of the day.

Falco nodded. "Fine. I'll look for your book. And I'll come visit you again tomorrow night." He placed a hand on her head, and then pressed his lips to her cheek again. "I promise."

This time, when she slept, she dreamt of Falco.

Madalena and Siena came to visit early the following day. Cass had just taken another draught of pain medicine, so when Mada glided into the room in a brilliant blue dress with a matching hat and gloves, Cass blinked hard, wondering momentarily whether her friend was a vision. But then Siena and Eva followed, hanging back from the bed as Madalena approached with a pitiful look on her face.

"Oh, Cass," Mada said. "I feel just terrible. You wanted to leave the party, and I insisted you stay . . ."

Cass rubbed her eyes. Madalena was pacing back and forth across the stone floor, and for a moment it looked as if there were two of her. "I'll be all right, Mada," Cass said. But she wasn't sure if it were true. Madalena's crestfallen expression made Cass wonder whether Mada knew something Cass didn't. "Piero said I just need to rest."

Mada's lower lip trembled. "People die from dog bites, Cass!"

"Thank you for reminding me," Cass said. Madalena's form blurred. Cass closed her eyes. She didn't know if it was the medicine or the pain that was making her see things. Or something worse. She inhaled deeply. "I don't suppose there's been any word from my aunt, has there?"

"No, but I plan to send a message to her as soon as we return to the palazzo," Siena piped up. "I just wanted to be able to tell her that you were all right."

Whether she was truly all right was still a matter for debate, and Agnese didn't need any bad news; her constitution was hardly fit for it. "Please don't," Cass said. "By the time the letter reaches her, I'll be healed, and you will only worry her for no reason." Her arm was starting to tingle again. After the tingling came the burning, and after the burning came the throbbing.

"But Signora Querini would want to know . . . ," Siena trailed off.

"You have kept many things from my aunt that she would have wanted to know," Cass reminded Siena. "If you really want to help me, you'll get me out of this skimpy chemise and into a proper sleeping gown. If I'm going to be trapped here for days, I would prefer to be decent."

Madalena was already going through the armoire. She held up a cotton nightdress. "This ought to work," she said breezily. "Looks like something old Agnese herself might wear." Together with Siena, Mada stripped Cass out of her sheer blue chemise. They had only just gotten her dressed again when Piero barged back into the room.

"Did you sleep well, Signorina?" he asked, barely glancing at Siena and Madalena as he approached the bed.

Was it her imagination, or did the words contain a challenge? Had it been his face at her doorway in the middle of the night? Had he seen her with Falco?

Kneeling down, Piero took Cass's left hand and straightened out her arm. She flinched, first from his warm touch and then from the pain. "Your bandages need changing," he said, pointing at a light pink spot seeping through the top layer of cloth. He turned to Madalena and the handmaids. "Ladies, I can assure you, the occasion doesn't merit an audience."

Cass felt sick. Maybe Piero could give her a tonic to make her go to sleep. She flashed back to the attack, saw the dog's canines sink deep into her flesh. Penetrating. Tearing. She wasn't ready to see what lay beneath the bandages. At the same time, she was desperate to know how much damage had been done.

Piero left to gather the necessary supplies for the dressing change. Siena and Madalena both leaned in to hug her and promised they would return for a visit the following day.

"How's Feliciana?" Cass asked, trying to delay their departure.

"She's fine," Siena said. "She's worried about you, of course."

"We all are," Mada blurted out, and then quickly corrected herself. "We *were*, I mean."

Cass could think of no further questions, no way of detaining her friends, so she forced a smile and assured them she'd be home, and healthy, very soon.

Piero returned with a black cloth bag, an armful of plain white fabric, and an empty basin. As he organized his equipment on the table next to her bed, Cass tried to imagine what she might see when the bandages came off: flashes of bone and blood, blackened flesh. Her stomach churned, and she whimpered slightly.

"Are you all right?" Piero hurriedly set down a small silver vial from which he had been pouring.

Cass shook her head. She squeezed her eyes shut to hold back the tears.

Piero's normally teasing voice turned soft. "What is it? Are you hurting?"

She couldn't bring herself to voice her fears, but Piero seemed to understand. "You're afraid, aren't you?" he asked, and she nodded, feeling like an idiot, mentally berating herself for being so weak.

"The pain should be tolerable," he said. "There will be some stinging when I actually clean the wound, some pressure when I reapply the bandages."

Mannaggia. She was so worried about what her arm might look like that it hadn't even occurred to her that the procedure might hurt. She felt the blood draining from her face.

Piero pulled a pair of vials from the black bag and mixed their powders together in a silver tumbler. He added a splash of ale from the pitcher at Cass's bedside. "I can give you something," he said. "Mandrake and feverfew. It should calm you and keep the pain at bay, perhaps even put you back to sleep. Although it may cause unusual dreams," he cautioned.

Cass accepted the tumbler. "Thank you," she said, sipping the potion slowly. It was mild-tasting, like a thickened version of herbal tea.

Piero turned back to his table. Cass watched as he cut a square of white cloth into strips with a scalpel blade. He piled the pieces of white neatly on one side of the table. The sharp smell of vinegar filled the air. It was a common wound cleanser, but it always made her eyes water. Finally, as Cass watched, Piero removed the stopper from a tiny pot of salve. "Theriac," he explained.

Cass knew theriac well. It was an expensive cure-all, prepared from more than sixty different ingredients. Powdered herbs. Flower petals. Crushed viper skin. There were as many different recipes for the medicine as there were apothecaries. Cass's own father had tried his hand at a theriac elixir when she was a child. For a few months, she and her parents had all choked down a spoonful of his concoction with the morning meal. Luckily, he had eventually run out of one of the ingredients and his interest in the medicine had waned. Cass had likened the taste to a mixture of canal water and chimney soot.

"What is her condition?"

Cass flinched at Belladonna's voice. The woman strode into the bedroom without so much as a knock or a cough. She was dressed in a low-cut indigo dress with a black lace overskirt. Ignoring Cass, she spoke only to Piero.

"She's in pain," Piero said, without looking at her. "And she's lost a lot of blood."

Belladonna's eyes met Cass's for only an instant. They were like two hard stones—no trace of the warmth or charm she had exhibited at her birthday party. "Not too much blood, I hope." She turned to leave, pausing at the doorway only to add, "Keep me informed."

"Friendly," Cass said. Her mouth seemed to take a long time to form the word.

"She's just worried about you." Piero hovered above Cass with his scalpel, preparing to cut away the soiled bandages. He was still talking, but his voice had slowed down. Everything was slowing down. Cass swore that even her heart slowed to a stop beneath her rib cage. She was sinking into a gentle pool. No, a well. Down. So far down. "Piero," she murmured, lifting her good arm toward the light.

He peered over the side of the well, smiling. Could he see her? She didn't think so. It was dark. So dark. But she could see his face, backlit by the daylight behind him. Only he didn't look like Piero. He looked like Falco.

"Shh," Piero-Falco whispered. "Just relax."

She blinked, and suddenly he was down in the well with her. She sensed bandages falling to her bedsheets, but she couldn't see her arm anymore. It was too dark. Her eyelids were heavy. It was time to sleep.

~

The elixir of mandrake and feverfew helped Cass sleep so soundly that when she woke up, she felt better than she had in days. She was able to eat for the first time since her attack, and she also managed to drag herself out to the garden to get a bit of sun. When it was time for her to go to sleep again, she begged Piero for another dose.

"Did it give you strange dreams?" Piero asked.

Cass thought of the well, and the fact that Piero had become Falco. "They were unusual," she said cautiously. "But not unpleasant."

"I suppose another dose wouldn't hurt, then." His hair fell forward over one eye. "You do seem to be in exceptional spirits."

She took the silver tumbler and drank willingly. She hoped Falco—the real one, not the one from her dream—would be able to sneak into her room for another visit.

When she drifted off, she had the same odd sensation of sinking straight down into her mattress, just like going into a well. Again Piero-Falco appeared at the top of the well. Cass called out to him and he reappeared by her side. "How did you do that?" she asked.

He smiled but didn't say anything.

"Are you really Falco?" she asked.

He didn't answer.

Cass tried to stand but couldn't. She was completely surrounded by water. "What am I doing here?" she asked. "What am I looking for?"

His eyes flashed dark for a moment and he became someone else, a stranger. But then he ran his fingers through her hair, pushing her tangled tresses back away from her neck. Cass relaxed. She would know Falco's gentle touch anywhere. His lips grazed the soft skin of her throat, and her whole body went soft. She was melting. She was liquid. She was fading away . . .

And then there was a crash, and a dripping sound. Cass groaned and opened her eyes, one at a time. Her eyelids felt heavy, as though they'd been weighted overnight. What was dripping? Why was it so bright? Had Falco come to visit her last night as he had promised?

"*Mi dispiace,* Signorina." A terrified servant girl was wiping the surface of the bedside table. She had knocked over a goblet, and a puddle of pale liquid was slowly raining itself over the edge of the table down onto the floor. Cass glanced over at the clock on the wall. It read one thirty, but that was impossible. Cass never slept so late. And she still felt tired.

The servant went to the window and opened the curtains. "We thought maybe you were going to sleep away the entire day."

"Is it really midday?" Cass asked. She wanted to sit up, but her body, too, felt weighted.

"That it is," the servant said. "Your friends came for a visit, but Dottor Basso told them you were sleeping and turned them away."

Could she possibly have slept fifteen hours again? If so, why did she still feel exhausted? Her limbs were anvils. Cass knew she'd fall right back to sleep if the shades were drawn again.

The servant left and returned with a tray containing sliced fruit and a bowl of tomato soup. Cass took a spoonful of the deep red broth. Her fingers were shaking. For a second, she saw two hands, holding two wobbling spoons. The soup was far too salty, and its color reminded her of blood. It even smelled like blood. She dropped the spoon and pushed the whole tray to one side.

Piero came into the room with her medicines. She tried to sit up, but her head still felt like it was full of wet cloth. Her soft mattress drew her down into its depths, like the ocean welcoming an anchor.

She managed to turn toward Piero. He was cloudy at the edges, his hands disintegrating into fog. For a second it seemed like he was floating. Hovering. Cass blinked hard. She rubbed her eyes. Piero stood on the floor, just as he should.

"I think the mandrake is making me see things," Cass said.

"What do you mean?" Piero looked concerned.

"I'm not hallucinating," Cass said quickly. "But objects look hazy instead of clear. Sometimes my vision seems to double."

Piero nodded. "It happens. How is your pain?"

"Better," Cass admitted. She looked down at her newly bandaged arm. "But I can't believe I slept all day and still feel so weak."

"You do look pale." Piero touched a hand to her cheek. His fingers felt so warm against her icy skin. "I think it's best if you continue to rest," he said.

"More sleep?" Cass heard the pinch of frustration in her voice. "But Madalena and Siena—"

"Can wait until you're feeling stronger," Piero interrupted her. He handed her a cup of cloudy gray liquid. "No mandrake," he said. "Just something to keep the pain away." Cass drank it, despite its foul smell. He was a doctor, after all. He would make her well.

"Dreams are a portal to
our fears, a harbinger of what may
come to pass. Thus we must
cull the most valuable insights of our
sleeping minds, unafraid,
or risk life's greatest
mysteries eluding us forever."

—THE BOOK OF THE ETERNAL ROSE

twenty~one

But Cass didn't get well. Over the next few days, she grew sicker and sicker, despite Piero's constant attentions. Her temperature fluctuated. Her muscles weakened until she could not get out of bed without assistance, and, although she did not tell anyone, she began to have all sorts of hallucinations, especially just as she was drifting off to sleep. One night, the walls of her room pulsed with faint reddish light, expanding and contracting as if she were trapped inside the villa's beating heart. The next night, the ivy that ran wild over the back wall of the garden twisted its way through the tiny crack in her shutters. Vines writhed past the heavy curtains, growing toward the bed where Cass lay helpless, reaching out to her like grabbing hands.

She became convinced the Book of the Eternal Rose was nearby, but that it was slowly disappearing, a page at a time, that if she didn't find it soon, it would be nothing but an empty leather-bound cover. As ludicrous as the idea was, she couldn't shake it. Often after Piero administered his mandrake, Cass saw scraps of paper floating in the air. Each time she reached out to catch one, the parchment disinte-grated into dust.

Then Cass would grow tired and fall into the well, only now in-stead of Falco coming for her, the man who appeared in the well was a vampire, with Piero's face and Falco's voice. He would materialize beside her and she would try to scream, but what came from her lips was a pathetic gasp of air, almost a sigh.

Slowly, he would lean close to her, with lips of blood and eyes that were as yellow as the moon. And then he would talk to her in Falco's voice. Cass hated this the most, the way Falco's words emerged from the lips of a monster. But when Falco told her to relax, she did. And when he told her to hold still, she would. She'd wince as his fangs punctured her skin, but it didn't hurt. Not really. And then he would brush his lips against hers and leave her there in the well. In the morning, she always awoke in her bed, the salty taste of her own blood throbbing on her lips.

She didn't know what to think. Could her visions, somehow, be real? Was the book disappearing? Was she being visited by a vam-pire in her sleep? Cass didn't even know if she believed in vampires. Several times, she almost confessed her fears to Piero, but something held her back. What if she was right? Piero might denounce her to the Church.

Each morning, Cass raised a hand to her neck, searching for the telltale wounds that might indicate that her hallucinations were more than just bizarre fantasies brought on by fevers or medicines. On her sixth morning at Belladonna's estate, she thought she felt a pair of nicks, directly above where the pressure of her blood pumped in the right side of her neck. She ran her fingers across the spot repeatedly. There might be a bite mark there. Cass couldn't tell for certain.

The mirror was all the way across the room, and Cass didn't feel strong enough to stand. She glanced around for a closer reflective surface. Her breakfast tray was made of tarnished pewter. The best she could do was angle a spoon awkwardly at her throat. She contorted her head this way and that. No luck.

Someone coughed delicately from the doorway.

"Mada!" Cass dropped the spoon on the bedside table. "I'm so glad to see you. I thought you'd forgotten about me." Cass didn't mean for the words to come out so bitterly.

"I make the trip here every day after breakfast, Cass," Mada said, in a tone of reproach. "The last few days you've been sound asleep and I couldn't bring myself to wake you." She raised her eyebrows at the spoon. "What, exactly, were you doing?"

Cass knew she could trust Madalena. She ordered her friend to close the door, and then, after Mada had taken a seat on the bed, Cass told her everything: the dream, that she wasn't getting better, that she woke up weaker and more fatigued each day. She told her everything except that the vampire spoke in Falco's voice. Mada didn't need another reason to be suspicious of him.

"There are tiny red marks on your neck," Madalena admitted. Seeing Cass's expression, she added, "But maybe you've been picking and scratching at it. How could a vampire get into your bedroom?"

Cass sighed. "I don't know. It all sounds ridiculous, but . . ." She fiddled with the coverlet. She had a suspicion she didn't know how to voice; she didn't want Mada to accuse her of being jealous. But finally she decided to risk it. "Belladonna 'came back from the dead,' didn't she? And she doesn't seem to age. And even among her servants, no one looks much older than either of us. *And* we know she's the leader of the Order of the Eternal Rose . . ." Cass rubbed at her neck again. "What if everyone here is a vampire?" she blurted out. "What if one of her servants is drinking from me in my sleep?"

Madalena's eyes widened. "Do you—do you really think she might be a—" Mada couldn't even choke out the word. "And her servants too?"

"I don't know," Cass said. "It's possible, isn't it?"

Madalena stood with sudden resolution. "That's it. Enough. We've got to get you out of here."

Cass shook her head. "I'm too weak to stand. I can hardly *go* anywhere."

"I'll bring my father back. Or Marco. They can carry you to the carriage."

"I can't leave yet, Mada," Cass said. "I need to *know*." She also needed to find the Book of the Eternal Rose.

Madalena rubbed her forehead. "What can we do, then? There has to be a way to protect you."

Cass tried to think past the pounding in her skull. "Where is Siena?"

Mada waved her hand in the direction of the hallway. "She was supposed to be seeing about getting us some tea."

"Listen. The two of you will spend the day here with me, perhaps go for a stroll around Belladonna's garden. But tonight, you'll send Siena home in the carriage alone." Cass's throat went dry. She swallowed back the taste of sawdust. "If you spend the night, you can hide behind the curtains and see whether there really is someone sneaking into my room." Cass blushed. She knew she was asking Mada for a lot. And it was ludicrous, wasn't it? The thought of a vampire prowling Belladonna's villa, feasting on her in her dreams.

Madalena turned ghost-pale. "But what if you're right? What if we're both attacked? Then I won't be any help to you at all."

Immediately, Cass realized she had asked the wrong person for help. The mere thought of vampires was almost enough to make Mada faint. She wouldn't be able to hide quietly behind the curtains while a vampire drank from Cass. She'd shriek like she was the one being attacked and pull out the vial of holy water she wore around her neck. They'd both end up dead, or worse.

Siena was the better choice. She was quiet, and she could be fierce when the situation called for it. Siena had once attacked Falco with a frying pan back on San Domenico. He and Cass had been making plans in Agnese's dark kitchen when Siena came upon them whispering and thought Falco was a kidnapper or a murderer. She had clocked him a good one. His head hurt for days. "Siena will do it," Cass said. "She's done this sort of thing for me before."

Madalena arched an eyebrow but didn't ask for details. "I'll find her," she said, gliding from the room. She returned with Siena a few minutes later and Cass explained the plan once more.

When the sun set, Piero brought Cass another draught of mandrake and feverfew and began to re-dress her wounds. Cass felt him cutting through her bandages. The cool vinegar splashed on her arm, which was throbbing a lot less than usual. "How is it?" she asked thickly. She was already beginning to sink down into the well.

Piero didn't answer right away. "The wounds are healing," he said. "My main concern now is your lingering fevers. But you've had no more visions?"

"No," Cass lied. The mandrake had made her so drowsy that Piero was no more than a shapeless form. Her visual disturbances were probably the result of the medicines he was giving her. Cass refused to entertain any other possibility.

As she dozed off, the vampire visited as usual, gently stroking her hair as he drank from her.

"Why me?" Cass asked him, tilting her head so that she could look into his yellow eyes.

The vampire lifted his lips from her neck. The blood had painted them black in the darkness. "You're helpless," Falco's voice whispered. "Why not you?" He kissed her on the forehead. "Sleep now," he said, but he shook her good arm as he spoke.

Cass turned away from him, snuggling her arm beneath her pillow. The vampire shook it again . . .

"Signorina Cass!"

Cass's eyes flicked open. Siena was standing over her, pale and wide-eyed, shocks of blonde hair coming loose from her usual smart braid.

"I'm awake," Cass mumbled. She pulled her arm out of Siena's grasp. It took her a few seconds to remember why Siena was still there. She sat up in bed. Her hand went to her neck. She felt it immediately: an almost-imperceptible bump.

"Did you . . . did you see someone?" Cass asked.

Siena sat on the edge of the bed. "It wasn't a vampire. It was Dottor Basso. After he bandaged your arm, he left. You fell asleep. You were so still. I wasn't even sure if you were breathing." If Siena chewed her lower lip any harder, she was going to draw blood. "He returned with a black case and a large needle. Signorina Cass, he drew blood from that spot on your neck. Several syringes full. Why would he drain your blood in secret?"

Why, indeed? It was common to use leeches for bloodletting, at least in Venice. Cass had seen the slimy creatures attached to Agnese's papery skin multiple times. Was there a medicinal reason Piero was drawing her blood? If so, why was he taking so much blood that it was keeping Cass pale and bedbound? And why would he do it in secret? Was Piero *trying* to give her visions? Was he trying to make her think she was being feasted on by vampires?

"I'm not certain," Cass said. She didn't want Siena to panic. "He's probably just trying to balance my humors. You've seen Dottor Orsin draw blood from my aunt quite frequently."

Siena shuddered. "With leeches. Not with that horrible long needle."

"Leeches are pretty horrible too," Cass said, rubbing the spot on her neck again. Her fingertips came away smudged with red, and she could almost feel her heart accelerate in her chest.

"I think we should take you back to Palazzo Alioni," Siena said. "Even if Dottor Basso isn't doing something wrong, I just don't like the feel of this place. It feels . . . alive, somehow."

Cass didn't have to ask what her handmaid meant. She had started to feel the same way, like the villa was imbued with a malevolent presence. There didn't seem to be enough servants to maintain the estate, yet everything was always pristine and perfect. And then there were the walls that sometimes pulsed with life and the flowers that turned to look at her.

But Cass wasn't ready to leave. Now that she knew what Piero was doing, she could refuse the mandrake. If she had to, she could confront him about the bloodletting. Somehow everything was connected. Luca. The Order. Belladonna. Piero and his spiders. She could *feel* it. If she stayed, she could explore the villa in depth; she could find the Book of the Eternal Rose. If her head cleared, everything might begin to fit together.

"Don't worry, Siena," Cass said. "I'll just refuse the sleeping medicine. Piero won't treat me against my will. If he does, I'll scream and then . . ." What she was going to say was that Falco would come running, but bringing up his name would make Siena think of Luca, and Cass didn't need more guilt. "Someone will come and find me. At least I'm not turning into a vampire, right?"

Cass was hoping Siena would crack a smile, but her face remained as worried as ever. "Then I'll stay here with you," Siena declared, looking as if she'd rather take a turn on the drowning platform behind Palazzo Alioni.

Cass wanted to say yes, but it seemed unfair. Even as a handmaid, Siena would be expected to sleep in the servants' quarters, and Cass spent most of each day dozing. Siena would be basically alone at Villa Briani. "There's no point in that," Cass said. "You wouldn't be allowed to sleep in the same room with me. Signorina Briani would probably put you to work dusting all of her portraits."

Siena couldn't keep a flash of relief from showing, but quickly her expression turned sober again. "There's something else, Signorina Cass. As Dottor Basso bent down to move your hair away from your neck, I'm not certain, but it looked as if he—" She stopped, obviously uncomfortable.

"What?"

"It looked as if he kissed you. You're not—" She fumbled over her words. "The two of you aren't—"

"Lord, no!" Cass covered her mouth with her hand and quickly prayed for forgiveness. But of all the things Siena could have said, this was the most unexpected. Siena must be mistaken. Piero was learned and handsome. He didn't need to go around kissing girls while they were unconscious. "Maybe you saw wrong," Cass continued quickly. "Maybe the angle made it *look* as if he kissed me."

"Maybe," Siena said doubtfully. "I just hate the idea of you all alone here. Promise me you won't let him give you any more medicine."

"I promise," Cass said.

It was a promise she intended to keep. The next night when Piero came with his bandages and mandrake, Cass pretended to sip at the cup as he watched. Then, as he resumed his work, she glanced around the room. *Mannaggia.* There was no good place to pour it. She could dump it over the far side of the bed and onto the floor, but what if Piero heard the splash of liquid hitting the tile? When he glanced toward the window, Cass dumped the syrupy liquid underneath her covers. She flinched as a bit of it splashed onto her skin.

She pretended to fall asleep, just as she had the past few days when Piero changed her dressing. She noted with satisfaction that the thickness of her bandages was decreasing, the pain easing. Her arm was healing.

Piero closed the shutters and drew the thick curtains. Cass opened one eye, just a sliver, as he slipped out of her bedchamber. Now to wait. She listened to the villa creak and groan, to the mice scurrying in the walls. A pair of owls hooted back and forth outside her window.

She worried she might not make it, that sleep might steal her away even without the mandrake. She felt leaden, her limbs and eyelids heavy. She wished Falco would visit. Perhaps he had come the previous few nights but found her sleeping and left. Or perhaps he had stayed, sat by her bedside, and watched her while she dreamed. Maybe that was why the vampire spoke with his voice, instead of Piero's.

Just as Cass gave in and let her eyes flutter closed, she heard her door creak open.

"Cass?" The whisper was faint, but it was a whisper that made her whole body go warm.

"Falco?"

He moved with catlike grace through the darkened room, kneeling by her bedside. "I'm surprised you're awake. I've looked in on you the past couple of nights, but you've been sleeping so soundly, I couldn't bring myself to disturb you."

"Are you so busy that you can't stop by during the day?" Cass hated the way she sounded. Plaintive. Needy.

Falco pressed his lips to her cheek. "The signorina has been keeping me excessively busy." He paused. "She looks in on you a lot too. Last night, I saw her watching you sleep."

The thought of Belladonna watching her sleep made Cass's skin crawl, but she bit back a sarcastic response. She didn't want Falco to think she was jealous. "I'm just glad you're here now." She reached out her hand to touch his face, and then his hair. He was real. He wasn't a dream.

"Is there anything I can bring you? You must be bored out of your mind."

"Did you have any luck locating the Book of the Eternal Rose?" Cass asked hopefully.

Falco shook his head. "I pored over every volume in the library for you. There is no Book of the Eternal Rose."

"I bet she keeps it in her chambers," Cass murmured. "You've been inside her room, right?"

"And I never saw any book." He raked his hands through his hair. "What makes you think it even exists?"

"Because Luca said—"

Falco didn't let her finish. "Of course," he said shortly. He didn't bother to hide the bitterness in his voice. "Sometimes I wish . . ." He shook his head, his words fading into the darkness.

"You wish what?" There were so many things Cass wanted him to say: he wished he had met her before she was engaged, he wished he had stayed in Venice to fight for her.

"Forget it," he said, his voice still tight. "I shouldn't have gotten upset. You focus on getting stronger. I'll keep looking for your book."

Cass threw her good arm around his neck. "Thank you," she whispered, pressing her lips to his cheek. "I feel certain it's in Belladonna's chambers. If you could just peek around the room the next time you're *painting* her in there."

The Book of the Eternal Rose was in the villa—Cass could feel it. But it was just out of her reach. She counted back in her head how many days she had been at Villa Briani. A week, assuming she wasn't missing any days. That meant Luca had less than a fortnight until his execution. Falco had to help Cass—he had to. Otherwise Luca would die.

"Just know that I'm always thinking of you, all right?" He brushed his lips against hers, stood up, and started back toward the door. "Sweet dreams, starling," he said, ducking out into the hall.

Cass let her eyelids flutter closed for a moment. She wanted to scramble from the bed and run after him. But she couldn't.

The door squeaked again. She assumed it was Falco again and almost called out to him.

But it wasn't Falco.

It was Piero.

Soundlessly, he crossed the floor to her bedside. She hoped he couldn't see that her eyes were open, just barely. Turning slightly, she watched as he hovered in front of the table, pulling items from a black bag. Tinder snapped. A candle flamed to life. Something silvery scattered the faint light. Cass squinted: a steel syringe, just as Siena had said.

Now was the time for Cass to cough or speak or otherwise let Piero know she was watching him. But she wasn't quite ready. She didn't know what more she was hoping to find out.

No. She did know. She wanted to see whether he would try to kiss her, thinking that she was asleep.

Cass closed her eyes. She felt him sit down next to her on her bed.

"Cassandra," he whispered.

She didn't answer. *Breathe. Inhale. Exhale. Don't twitch.*

The air grew heavy around her as Piero bent low. His warm hands tilted her chin. His breath tickled her skin.

She couldn't stand it anymore. She opened her eyes. "What are you doing?" she demanded, sitting up, pulling her covers up to her chest.

Piero jumped up from the bed, startled.

"*Santo cielo.* You scared me." He narrowed his eyes at her. "Why are you awake? Did you drink all of your mandrake?"

"No, I didn't." A quiver made its way into Cass's voice. She inhaled, gathered her courage. "You've been draining my blood while I've been sleeping."

"That's ridiculous," he said, with a harsh bark of laughter. "Why would I take your blood? You lost too much of it in the attack. I told you so myself."

"There are punctures on my neck from where you draw it out," she said stubbornly. She looked at the bedside table, expecting the syringe and needle to be sitting there, but the table was empty except for Piero's black bag. "Where's the needle?"

Piero considered her with his penetrating eyes. "You told me you weren't hallucinating." His voice sounded almost accusatory.

"I'm not," she insisted. "Open your bag."

Piero showed her the inside of the black velvet bag. There were a few glass vials of herbs, a pot of theriac salve, and a silver flask. No syringe. No needle. Could she have mistaken the flask for a syringe?

"I don't understand," Cass said.

Piero reached out to touch her forehead with the back of his hand. "Poor thing," he murmured. "So confused."

"I am *not* confused. There are marks on my neck." But as she felt around with her fingers, she couldn't seem to locate the nicks she had felt earlier.

"Let me see." Piero pushed all of her hair back behind her shoulders. He angled her head so that he could get a look at the side of her neck. With one hand, he rubbed the skin of her throat rhythmically, at first softly, but then more deeply. Cass didn't want his touch to feel good, but it did.

"I see no marks," he said. "Poor Cassandra. Your arm is healing but I think your body is still sick." He reached his other hand around to the back of her neck, gently probing her stiff muscles. "You're weak. You're imagining things."

He was so close to her that she could smell him. A combination of sweet and sharp scents, a hint of something medicinal, like the balsam her father used to smell like. It all made Cass feel very young and small and alone. Piero was still massaging her neck. She was just starting to relax when his fingers grazed a tiny sore spot.

"There," she said, her whole body going rigid. "Right there."

Piero leaned closer. "That?" He ran his fingertip over the spot. "Nothing more than a spider bite." He gripped her chin and stared hard in her eyes, as though daring her to challenge him. His voice hardened. "Or it *could* be the bite mark of a vampire, I suppose. As a physician, I would be the one most qualified to decide. I can give you a more thorough examination in the light of day, if you desire." He paused, letting his threat sink in. "Do you desire it? The penalties for vampirism in Florence are very grave."

Cass balled her hands into fists under the coverlet, so Piero wouldn't see. She trusted Siena implicitly. She knew the marks on her neck were from repeated bloodletting. But if she publicly accused Piero, he might diagnose her with a vampire bite. The Florentine priests would take her away.

She would be Hortensa on the platform. Flailing, drowning. Tossed aside like a broken doll. Piero Basso had the power to sign Cass's death warrant.

"Think carefully, Signorina," he said, drawing away. His mouth was smiling, but his eyes were hard.

"The essence and vitality
of youth are contained
in the blood of the young."

THE BOOK OF THE ETERNAL ROSE

twenty-two

Cass lay in bed, staring up at the ceiling, replaying Piero's words in her head. How dare he threaten her. How dare he *lie* to her about taking her blood. She wanted to leave him, to leave this whole villa and return to the safety of Palazzo Alioni. But that would be giving up, and she was no quitter. She had told herself, repeatedly, that she would do whatever it took to find the Book of the Eternal Rose and free Luca.

There had to be a way to persuade Piero to tell her the truth, or better yet to trick him out of some information. If Siena was right and he had truly kissed her while she was unconscious, then he obviously found her attractive. Could she use that to her advantage? Could she go and find him in his chambers and feign romantic interest in him, as a way to learn more about the Order? Cass didn't think so. For one, he was smart and would see through her ruse. And even if he didn't, she was weak and wouldn't be able to escape if things got out of control. Plus, she really didn't want to touch him more than she had to. Just the thought of him caressing her in her sleep made her want to have a bath.

So then what? She decided that perhaps she could play to his controlling side. She could pretend to be terrified of him. She'd find him, apologize for her paranoia, and beg him not to report her to the priests. She could even offer to let him take more blood from her while she was conscious, as a show of subservience. The thought of the long needle in her neck made her stomach lace itself into knots, but it might be a way to get Piero to admit that he had been bleeding her.

Even if he refused, Cass could throw herself on his mercy until he at least pretended to forgive her outburst. Then, she could suggest they have a glass of wine together. If she could get him to drink with her, she just might be able to cajole secrets from his lips. Everyone got chattier when they were drunk, didn't they?

Energized by her plan, she struggled to her feet and slipped into her shoes. Her feet moved awkwardly, heavy as stone. A half step at a time, she crossed her room to the doorway. She stopped to light a candle, but the box of tinder was empty. She would have to make her way in the dark. She headed toward the main staircase, her right hand pressed against the wall for balance. Her muscles trembled in protest beneath her skin, but Cass ignored the burning. Thirty paces down the corridor was the elaborately carved wooden door leading to Belladonna's chambers. The Book of the Eternal Rose was beyond that door—Cass could feel it. But the door was locked, and the key was likely one of the two threaded onto Belladonna's bracelet. There was no way for her to enter. Approaching Piero for information would have to suffice for tonight.

Cass leaned back slightly as she began to descend the stairs to keep from pitching forward into the dark. A shadow danced at the periphery of her vision. Someone below had lit a candle—one of the servants, no doubt. Guided by the faint light, she made her way around the corner, leaning heavily on the wall for support. The door to Piero's chambers was open. Cass saw a pair of candles burning on the shelf next to his bed.

"Piero?" She pushed the door all the way open, but the room was empty. What could he possibly be doing out of bed in the middle of the night? The floor beneath her feet suddenly felt unsteady.

His quarters were tight, and the only place to sit, other than the bed, was a plain wooden stool that rested in front of the shelves. Cass didn't want to go near the shelves. Her skin twitched again at the thought of the cage full of spiders. Still, the room was starting to break apart. If she didn't sit somewhere, she knew it was only a matter of time before she passed out.

She lowered herself to the stool, which wobbled dangerously beneath her. She rested a hand on the lowest shelf for support, averting her eyes from the covered cage.

Her fingers landed on parchment. It was the journal Cass had flipped through the previous day. She noticed some of the pages had been torn out. The anatomy sketches were still there, but the mysterious symbols and notes were gone. Her other hand bumped something farther back on the shelf, a fluted glass vial with a stopper made of cork. It had a symbol stamped on the top of it, a triangle with a T inside of it. Cass twirled the vial in her good hand. Dark liquid sloshed around in the container. Perhaps it was some sort of medicine. *Made from spider venom.*

She returned the vial to the shelf. Glass clinked against glass.

Casting a quick glance at the door, Cass bent down so that her face was level with the lowest shelf. It was completely packed with glass vials.

Cass lifted a second vial up close to her eyes. The cork stopper was marked with three overlapping circles. The fluid inside this one looked a deep red.

Like blood.

Cass replaced the vial in the spot where she had found it and picked up a third. This one was stamped with a lily insignia. Her fingers flew immediately to her necklace. Was she holding a container of her own blood?

"Traditional wisdom speaks of four liquids, or humors, found within the body. It is these four fluids that determine the nature of a human being, from health to temperament."

—THE BOOK OF THE ETERNAL ROSE

The next evening Cass again pretended to take the mandrake draught, and again poured it out when Piero wasn't looking. She hadn't waited for him to return to his chambers the previous night—after seeing the vial of her own blood, she'd fled back to her room, needing time to puzzle through what this meant. Not only was he draining her blood, but he was *saving it*.

Now she lay awake, expecting him to sneak back into her room with his needle and syringe. Turning on her side, Cass stared at the dark curtains that blocked every drop of starlight that might have squeezed through the shutters. The whole house seemed shrouded in a haze of sleep. Even the malevolent presence she sometimes sensed lay dormant. Everything was quiet.

Perhaps she was just finally healing. Perhaps all the flashes of foreboding were connected to her fevers, which were finally going away. The ache in her arm was fading, and for the first time since Piero had rescued her, Cass felt well enough to realize just how alone she was.

And then she heard the door to her bedroom creak ever so softly as it swung open. Her whole body went tense, and her heart battered itself against her ribs as she thought of what she would say to Piero, how she might defend herself against him and his bloodletting. Her stomach roiled as she thought about the vials of blood that stood in neat rows on Piero's shelf. But she quickly realized that the dark form creeping across the floor wasn't Belladonna's physician.

"Falco," Cass said. Her heart was still pounding, but for a different reason. "Did you find it? The Book of the Eternal Rose?"

"No." His hair fell forward as he leaned down to brush his lips against her forehead. "But the entire villa seems to be empty. I thought we might sneak into Bella's chambers and do a little investigating." He winked. "It'll be like old times."

Cass sat up so quickly that her head went fuzzy and the room began to rotate. "You have the key?"

Falco held up a tiny scalpel, which Cass knew he sometimes used in his painting. "Who needs a key?" he asked. He dropped the instrument into his pocket and took both of her hands in his.

Cass waited for the dizziness to fade and then let Falco help her to a standing position. The floor was ice beneath her. Her left leg wobbled as she slid her feet into the dyed leather shoes she had worn to Belladonna's birthday party. She cursed under her breath, tightening her grip on Falco's hands until her legs felt steady.

"Do you think you can make it?" he asked. "I could go and search alone, but I might not find anything, and I know you won't be satisfied until you see for yourself."

"Just go slow with me," she said sharply. So Falco still didn't believe her and was doing this only to appease her, or maybe to prove she was wrong. Well, she would be the one proving him wrong. Cass knew the book was in Belladonna's chambers.

Falco lit a candle from her washing table, and with Cass leaning slightly upon him, the two stepped through the doorway into the hall.

The house was dark and quiet. Falco led her down the long corridor toward Belladonna's chambers, holding the candle out in front of her so that she might navigate the occasional statue or pedestal shrouded in blackness. Beside her, he moved as if he needed no light at all, as if he'd spent his entire life walking the halls of this villa instead of just the past couple of months.

Something tugged at her ankle, and she raised a hand to her mouth to stifle a scream.

"What is it?" Falco pulled Cass in toward him, his other arm out as a barrier between her and any possible threat that was lurking in the dark.

She looked down and realized it was only a braided tassel on the edge of an Oriental rug that had gotten caught on her shoe. "Nothing," she whispered. Shaking her head, she freed herself from the tassel and continued down the corridor.

Carvings of Venus, Victoria, and Diana looked out from the wide arched door that led to Bella's chambers. Cass leaned forward to press her ear against the wood. The room beyond was completely silent, but what if Bella was simply asleep?

"You're sure she's not here?"

"I saw her leave with a group of men not long ago," Falco said.

Cass's mind filled in the details he didn't. *A group of men from the Order.*

She held the candle while Falco made quick work of picking the lock. He grinned crookedly in satisfaction when the mechanism disengaged with a telltale click. Pocketing the scalpel, he pushed open the door.

Resting her free hand on Falco's lower back for support, Cass followed him into the room. The flickering flame illuminated only a small circle of the darkened chamber, but again Falco moved around with ease. He took the candle from Cass and toured the room while she stood just inside the doorway.

"Here we have the bed." It was a giant canopy bed made of dark wood, with long shimmery turquoise flaps that hung loose over the mattress. Falco pushed aside one of the flaps and lifted the pillows so Cass could see there was nothing beneath. He ducked down and peered under the frame. "Nothing on the floor."

"What?" Cass had stopped listening for a moment. Even in the dark she could see Falco's latest painting of Belladonna, the one of her springing forth naked from a rose, hanging on the wall opposite the bed. Cass forced herself to look away. Her eyes had adjusted to the dark, and she could clearly identify the outline of a washing table, a dressing table, and an armoire.

Falco turned a corner into the large adjoining bathroom. It was empty except for a pair of mirrors and a circular bronze basin for bathing. "See, there's nothing here."

Cass returned to the main chamber. "What about the armoire?"

"I think she keeps it locked," he said.

Cass remembered Belladonna's silver bracelet with the keys dangling from it. "So then work your magic again," she said.

Falco frowned across the room at the tiny golden padlock that glimmered in the faint light. "It's a much smaller lock. What if I break it? Then she will know someone was in here. I could lose my position."

"Falco," Cass hissed. "Who locks up their clothing? There's obviously something important in that armoire."

"My position is important," he muttered. "And if you cared for me, you'd think twice before asking me to risk it over some crazy conspiracy idea." But he crossed the room to the armoire and held the candle next to the lock.

"I am *not* crazy." Cass realized she had curled her hands into fists. Her fingernails were digging crescent moon impressions into the flesh of her palms.

Falco jiggled the lock and the metal twisted apart.

"That was fast," Cass said.

He turned toward Cass, his face a mask of worry. "I didn't do anything. The lock was already open."

Cass tugged on the armoire's handles, and the doors swung open. She didn't care who had unlocked it. She only cared what was inside. Both halves were lined with shelves. "Hold the light for me," she said. Energized, she began at the top, feeling behind each hat, each folded bodice and skirt, each silken chemise. Nothing. She moved to the other side. Cuffs. Collars. Strings of pearls and jeweled hair clips neatly laid out on a bed of velvet. And then, an empty shelf.

Cass grabbed the candle from Falco and held it next to the shelf. She could see a faint outline of dust, with a clear spot in the middle. A large, rectangular clear spot. A spot that might fit a sheaf of papers, or a book.

"It's gone." She couldn't keep the despair from her voice. Her heart shriveled inside her. "Someone beat us to it."

Falco raked a hand through his hair. "What's gone? There's nothing there, Cass. That's probably just the shelf where she keeps whatever she's wearing right now."

"Is she wearing something rectangular?" Cass pointed out the lines in the dust.

Falco shook his head, but didn't respond. He shut the armoire and rethreaded the padlock. He tried to close it, but couldn't. "Whoever opened this before us seems to have stripped the mechanism."

"You believe that someone broke in here, but you don't believe me about the book?" Cass felt the sudden urge to reach out and shove him. Why was he being so stubborn? She hadn't disbelieved any of the story when Luca had told it to her.

A board creaked above their heads. One of the servants was awake.

"Let's get out of here before we get caught." Falco took Cass's arm and led her out into the corridor. He locked the door. "Come on," he said. "I'll walk you back to your room."

"I don't want to go to my room," Cass said. She pulled away from Falco. "I need to find that book. Perhaps someone took it out to add pages to it. I'm going to keep searching." She knew it was pointless, hopeless, that whoever had stolen the book was long gone, but she couldn't just let Falco tuck her into bed. Luca was going to die. Didn't Falco understand that? "Why don't you believe me?" she whispered, her voice breaking apart at the end.

Falco punched the wall lightly. "Do you know how many commissions I've gotten since the night of Bella's birthday party? *Five.* And some of them are for multiple paintings. She's changing my life, Cass. I realize she's friends with de Gradi, but that doesn't mean she's involved with his experiments, or even if she is, it doesn't mean they're doing anything wicked." He stroked the side of Cass's face with the back of one hand. "You were attacked by dogs. You've been feverish and sedated. I'm not judging you for believing some nonsense about an Order or a book, but—"

"It's true!" Cass slapped his hand away from her and stepped back from his reach. She wanted to punch the wall just as Falco had. "There *is* an Order, and there *is* a Book of the Eternal Rose, and when I find it, it will probably be full of horrible things about your precious Belladonna." She was practically screaming, but she didn't even care. Tears pushed at the backs of her eyes. "And after I use it to save Luca, I will let you see it so you can see just how wrong you were."

Falco's jaw tightened. "I feel sorry for you, Cass. But eventually you're going to have to accept the fact that da Peraga is going to die." His eyes flashed dark in the flickering candlelight. "Sometimes I wish that day would hurry up and get here, so that I could have my starling back."

Cass stumbled backward like she'd been slapped. The candle wobbled in its holder and then tumbled to the floor, bathing her and Falco in darkness. "You bastard," she whispered.

"Cass." Falco seemed to realize he had gone too far. "What I meant—"

"I don't care what you meant." She pointed away from herself, confident Falco could see her gesture in the gloom. "Just go. Now."

"Fine." His voice was ice. "I need a drink anyway." He spun on his heel. A few seconds later Cass heard his footsteps thundering down the main staircase. The front door opened, and then slammed shut.

Cass's body slid down the wall until she sat crumpled in a heap on the stone floor. She tried to hold in the tears, but couldn't. Her body shuddered with sobs as she thought about what Falco had said. How could anyone be so cruel? Luca would never say such a thing. Luca would probably tell Cass to forget about him and go be happy with Falco if he knew of her feelings. Cass sniffed. For the first time, she wished Falco could be a little more like her fiancé.

After her sobbing began to subside, she wiped at her eyes and then turned toward her bedroom at the far end of the hallway. It seemed impossibly far away. And she had meant what she said about continuing to search for the book. Even though she knew it was gone, her only other choice was to resign herself to the fact that Luca was going to die. She really would go crazy if she gave in to that line of thinking.

Suddenly, the hallway brightened, just slightly. Cass blinked hard, wondering if she was imagining it, but then she heard the front door fall shut with a soft click. Falco must not have gotten that drink after all. Perhaps he was coming back to apologize. She swiped at a few leftover tears and then used the wall to get herself back on her feet. She padded to the top of the staircase to see if it was indeed Falco returning.

But it was Piero who was skulking around the lower level. Cass watched as he set something on the side table—it looked like a chalice of some sort—and then slipped into his room. He was back in the hallway a moment later, with a cloak hanging over his arm. He stopped just inside the front door to fasten the garment around his clothes and lift the hood. The flowing fabric obscured every inch of his body. Piero grabbed the chalice and ducked back out into the night. Where had he come from at such a late hour? Where was he going?

Cass crept her way down the staircase a half step at a time. Forcing herself to hurry, she made her way to the foyer and peered outside. The moonlight clearly illumined Piero, heading across the lawn, his black robe flapping in the breeze. Wherever he was going, he was going on foot.

She glanced around the foyer. A pair of cloaks hung from hooks. No doubt they belonged to some of Belladonna's servants. Cass snatched the one closest to her and slung it over her shoulders. It was ridiculously large. The sleeves dangled over her hands; if she put up the hood, it would surely cover her entire face. Gathering the excess fabric in her good hand, she headed out the door.

Ducking down behind one of the giant flowerpots to catch her breath, Cass watched as Piero crossed the road and headed into the field of tall grass that led to the church. The night air pierced her lungs, sharpening her senses. Her pain was still there, a faint pulsing in her bandaged arm, but her legs felt steady. Cass took a deep breath, stood up, and followed him.

She hurried as best she could past the grove of trees on her left. *Yellow eyes. Running. Hot breath.* Her legs buckled as the memory of the dogs almost undid her. *Locked door. Teeth. Blood pooling on stone.* She breathed in crisp air and kept going. The road was damp, and her feet sank slightly into the mud as she crossed it. Then she started through the field, wincing as an occasional nettle pricked her through the thin soles of her leather shoes. A short line of carriages stood off to the side of the church, the horses stamping their feet occasionally. The drivers were clustered in a tight circle, talking quietly and passing around a flask.

When Cass was about twenty paces from the church, a pair of

hooded figures appeared around the far side of the building. She bent low in the tall grass, hoping the black cloak would help her merge seamlessly with the night.

The two people kept their heads ducked as they murmured to each other. *Telling secrets,* Cass thought. Secrets she desperately needed to know. Almost like a single entity, the two forms disappeared into the church.

If Cass put up the hood on her cloak, could she pass for one of the robed guests? It was worth a try. Another figure, body obscured by loose fabric, entered the church. There was a meeting going on, perhaps a meeting of the Order of the Eternal Rose.

Cass tiptoed up to the wooden church door, the door that had remained firmly closed when she had so desperately needed sanctuary. Fear swelled inside of her. She was positive that the door that had just allowed the mysterious hooded figures to enter would stick fast when she tried to enter. Exhaling deeply, she curled the fingers of her right hand around the cold black handle. The door easily opened under the pressure of her hand. She pushed it just a crack and peered inside.

The entrance hall was dark.

Cass said a silent prayer and slipped inside. As her eyes adjusted to the blackness, she noticed a faint red glow coming from the direction of the altar. Wisps of incense smoke curled in the air. The sweet, flowery smell reminded her of Palazzo della Notte. Was there a connection? There the attendees had worn masks. Here everyone wore hoods draped low.

The robed figures had all taken seats in the long wooden pews. Cass slid into the very back row, which was empty. Pressing her palms together, she bowed her head so that a casual observer might think she was deep in prayer. She peeked out from beneath the hood of her cloak.

The church was cross-shaped, its high, arched ceiling covered with peeling frescoes. Someone had pushed the main altar back against the wall and dragged a large baptistery carved with angels and roses into the transept—the area where the two arms of the cross intersected. A lone figure in black rose up from the first pew. The lithe form almost seemed to float as it stepped gracefully into the baptistery. Cass didn't see the ripple of holy water. The baptistery pool was empty. Or was it? The faint light, the smoke—Cass couldn't trust her vision from the back of the room. She slid to the end of her pew and made her way slowly up the side aisle, keeping her hood pulled low. She ducked into an alcove where she could get a clearer glimpse of the proceedings without being seen.

The pool was indeed empty. If the figure were to be baptized, where was the water? And why not do it on a holy day instead of secretly, in the middle of the night? Cass was struck by the most horrible thought: that she was about to witness the baptism of a vampire. But then the figure loosened the belt of its cloak and flung the garment to the floor of the chapel. Cass barely stifled a gasp.

It was Belladonna. And she was naked except for her silver bracelet and a pendant that hung down between her breasts—a six-petaled flower inscribed inside a circle.

A deep murmur ran through the crowd.

"Witness the power of young blood." Belladonna turned a slow circle. "As most of you know, I just celebrated the fortieth anniversary of my birth."

Cass nearly choked. *Fortieth?* Impossible. It was what she had originally thought, but that would make Belladonna almost twice as old as she looked. Cass stared at her, both horrified and fascinated by her nakedness, at her milk-pale skin and soft curves.

Cass's eyes drifted, coming to land on the tiny stump of middle finger on Belladonna's left hand. Had Belladonna really reawakened from the dead? What if the story was wrong, and Bella hadn't been in a deep sleep? What if Belladonna really was a vampire?

A pair of hooded figures—men, clearly, by their broad shoulders and stiff gaits—approached the baptistery. Belladonna's body relaxed, and for a second Cass thought of what she had seen at the Palazzo della Notte. Her cheeks went hot. Perhaps the Order was just about sex, some noble-class alternative to a brothel.

Belladonna turned to the hooded figures and kissed each of them. One nearly lost his hood as she wrapped her lean arms around his neck. Cass caught a glimpse of high cheekbones and blond hair. It was the butler, Signor Mafei—she would have sworn to it.

The two men at Bella's sides each raised a silvery chalice in the air.

"Behold," Belladonna called out, "an offering in the name of the Eternal Rose." The men tipped the containers, and dark, viscous liquid poured down over Belladonna's hair, splashing off the angles of her elbows and spattering the marble basin of the baptistery and sending an occasional droplet out toward the floor.

Blood.

Cass could smell it. She instinctively drew back, but the cloaked figures leaned forward as a group, murmuring and moaning, arms outstretched. They were reaching for Belladonna.

No. They were reaching for the blood.

Cass felt as though she might be sick. What was happening? Her vision went momentarily dark. She couldn't faint—not here. She took a deep breath and the room came back into focus. She stared at the ruby liquid as it spattered off Belladonna's skin, as the black-robed figures clamored for it. Could it be her own blood the mob was fighting for? Some of it, perhaps. There was too much to have come from a single person—unless someone had been drained completely dry.

As the last drops of blood poured from the chalices onto Belladonna's bare shoulders, the people grew quiet again. The glistening fluid began to darken and coagulate on her skin, masking half of her face, obscuring one of her breasts as if she were wearing a dress that had been partially torn away by a madman.

Belladonna raised one spattered arm to her face and inhaled deeply. She dragged her wrist across her mouth, licking her lips.

"Divine," she said. "I can sense the power. Who is it I am tasting?"

"The young Tatiana de Borello," a man said. Cass recognized Piero's voice. "Sadly, the humors in her blood were of inferior quality. I saw to it that she passed away just an hour ago."

Tatiana de Borello. Cass had heard the name before, at Belladonna's afternoon tea. Tatiana was the young noblewoman one of Bella's guests had asked about. Cass shivered, remembering how everyone—even Madalena—had seemed hypnotized as Belladonna described the girl's illness.

Belladonna reached out and touched her fingertips to Piero's hooded face. "Certainly the blood of someone so young will have *some* beneficial properties."

She turned back to address the masses. "Devoted followers of the Eternal Rose. We are increasing our efforts and drawing nearer to

the creation of an Elixir of Life. Once we have created a pure specimen of the fifth humor, we will be able to produce enough elixir for
all of us."

A ripple of excitement moved through the crowd. Then a man
burst out, "From what, exactly, are you creating this magical pure
specimen? And what of your sister chapter, your *loyal supporters* in
Venice? Will there be no elixir for us?"

Cass knew this voice too. Her heart stopped. Angelo de Gradi.

Belladonna's face twisted into a frown. "I have been telling you
for years, Dottore, that the fifth humor can be procured only from
the blood. Not by slicing away at livers or spleens. My own father,
who dedicated his life to seeking out the research of those before
him, made this clear before his death. His words are inscribed in the
Book of the Eternal Rose. Have you never gotten a chance to review
its pages?"

Cass sucked in a sharp breath. If someone had stolen the book,
Belladonna didn't yet know it was missing. Could de Gradi have
taken it?

"I have, but—"

Belladonna silenced de Gradi with a wave of her hand. "Blood is,
as you know, *difficult* to obtain, and sadly there seems to be great
variation among our subjects as to its quality." She narrowed her
eyes. "But we will succeed."

Apparently the Order believed in the fifth humor, and in Florence they were going as far as to steal blood from the living for their
research. The parties at Palazzo della Notte suddenly made perfect
sense. Attractive men luring lonely and bored women away from
their husbands. Drugging them. Drawing off their blood and sending
them home weak and confused, marked as victims.

Belladonna gestured to Signor Mafei to help her with her cloak. He draped the garment over her shoulders, and she cinched the belt around her waist. "And yet, Dottore, you still persist in your barbaric methods of trying to extract humors from the tissue of the dead. Wasting time. Wasting blood. What makes you think we here in Florence owe you anything?"

Cass's head was spinning. Angelo de Gradi hadn't purchased corpses to study anatomy and improve medical techniques. He had been cutting up bodies to try to create the fifth humor.

"Begging your pardon, Bella, but the dead have always been in good supply, and far more compliant than the living," de Gradi said. "I should like to observe young Dottor Basso's *persuasive techniques*. Then again, perhaps there is safety in tradition. Wasn't the Order almost destroyed from within during your father's time at the helm?"

Belladonna stared at him coldly. "You would do well to not speak ill of my father, Angelo."

De Gradi backed slightly away from the baptistery pool. The rest of the Order members still encircled him closely, perhaps hoping there might be a chance to bathe in *his* blood if he kept talking.

"Did not Signor Dubois donate generously to your cause while he was living here in Florence, back when you were just a girl?" de Gradi asked. "Was it not his gold that helped pay for your physicians?"

"Joseph's money did not go as far as you presume," she said. "And I no longer need his fortune." She tugged on her belt again. "One can only imagine what he might squander the elixir on. Imagine, eternal life for Venice's *finest* courtesans."

The group tittered, and the tension seemed to ease.

"Bella," de Gradi said, almost in a playful tone. "Rather than talk of finances, perhaps we should talk of common interests. Does not the Book of the Eternal Rose say it was a Venetian woman from whom your father once isolated a near-perfect specimen of fifth humor?"

Belladonna raised an eyebrow. "Are you implying the women of Florence are inferior to the Venetians?"

"Not at all." De Gradi bowed. "Your beauty makes such thinking unimaginable. I was merely suggesting that the purest fifth humor may come from a Venetian bloodline. If the good Dottor Basso would share his notes, Signor Dubois and I could continue your research in Venice."

"I'll consider your proposal," Belladonna said, with a wave of her hand. She stepped out of the baptismal pool and spread her arms wide before the crowd. "Brothers and sisters, what is left is yours."

Cass watched in disbelief as the hordes of robed figures leapt from their seats. They pressed forward, crawling into the baptistery, clawing at the smears of dried blood, even rubbing their faces against the sides of the marble pool. Hoods were falling, and Cass knew that if she got closer, she might be able to identify some of the members writhing around in the baptistery.

But she was revolted, and could not force herself any closer to the blood fest.

Belladonna strode down the center of the church, with Piero and Signor Mafei flanking her. With her, Cass knew, lay additional answers. Discreetly, she ducked out of the alcove and headed down the side aisle, straining to make out what Belladonna was saying.

"It's disgusting, don't you think?" Belladonna asked. She paused at the threshold to the entrance hall, gesturing again at the crowd.

Cass tucked herself back in the corner of the nave, keeping her hood pulled low. "The way people lose control over a little blood."

"It's only natural." Piero shrugged. "You yourself know the benefits of fresh blood. To what else can we attribute your exquisite youth and beauty?"

"I don't claw and fight to get at it," Belladonna pointed out.

Piero's voice seemed to contain a smile. "That is because you have your faithful shepherds to bring it to you."

"If the magistrates of Florence were witness to this, the whole Order would be strung up as vampires," Signor Mafei said.

"Convenient, isn't it?" Belladonna said. "The Church and their obsessive worry about the undead. A most opportune way to hide our tracks and dispose of our unwanteds. Poor girls. They can't even defend themselves without admitting to what they think happens at our decadent little *parties*. And their husbands and fathers would likely execute them for those crimes as well." Belladonna smiled. "*Grazie a Dio* for lust and fear. Without them our work would be much more difficult."

Signor Mafei opened the church door, and wind rushed in.

Cass realized she was shaking violently. She pressed her body against the wall of the church. Everything was starting to make sense. The Order of the Eternal Rose was using the city's fear of vampirism as a cover for stealing blood. They were extracting humors from the blood and attempting to create the mythical fifth humor, long rumored to be instrumental in extending human life.

But apparently not all blood worked. It had to possess a certain quality. It had to be the *right* blood.

Angelo de Gradi had suggested that it might have to be Venetian blood.

No wonder Piero had been draining her.

And what if her blood *didn't* contain the required properties? How much time did she have before the remainder of her blood would be taken forcefully from her? How long before it was Cass, and not Tatiana de Borello, who was being poured over Belladonna's perfect skin?

"Prior research suggests the four bodily humors are blood, black bile, yellow bile, and phlegm. It is rumored that recombining them in the proper proportions might yield the fifth humor."

—THE BOOK OF THE ETERNAL ROSE

twenty-four

C ass stayed crouched in the back corner of the nave for
several minutes. The other members of the Order at
last began to file out of the church, murmuring to each
other as they made their way down the aisle.

The temperature seemed to have dropped several degrees. She
gathered the oversized cloak tightly around her as she continued to
piece together everything she had heard, as she struggled to believe
it. Piero had saved her life. If it weren't for him . . .

If it weren't for him, my blood would have been wasted, she
thought. A puddle on the stone doorstep in front of this very church.
Clearly it was her blood he had saved from the dogs, not her.

She swallowed back the taste of bile. She thought of the party at
Palazzo della Notte where she had first laid eyes on Piero. He wasn't
the one who had lured Hortensa upstairs. Signor Mafei, perhaps?
How many other men were doing Belladonna's evil deeds? How
many other women had fallen prey to the scheme, enticed by prom-
ises of seduction only to be drugged and bled without their knowl-

edge? Perhaps *all* of the women who found themselves on the drowning platform had been victims of the Order. It was perfectly horrible.

But it was perfect.

Cass realized the church was almost empty. Just a handful of black-robed figures still clustered around the baptismal pool, clawing at the remaining minuscule spots of blood. The wispy smoke from the scarlet candles faded into the gloom. She remembered how the doors had been locked the night of her attack. The last thing she wanted was to end up trapped inside. She rose quickly from her hiding spot, but her legs wobbled beneath her, and she sank back to the floor.

Tears stung her eyes. Her arm didn't hurt, not too much. It was her heart, her whole being that ached. The realization that her parents might have accepted—supported, even—something so depraved sliced through her.

Willing away the surge of darkness that threatened to overcome her, she tried once more to stand. Slowly, with one hand on the back pew for balance, she struggled to her feet and returned to the entrance hall. She flung open the heavy door and let the rush of air pull her out into the night. The door slammed shut behind her.

She glanced across the vast field to where the outline of Belladonna's villa loomed. She wasn't going back there. Not ever. She needed to return to Florence, to Madalena and Siena. But she was at least a couple of miles from Palazzo Alioni, with no real guarantee that she'd be able to find it even if she did walk all the way to the city.

A chuffing sound made her turn her head. There were still two carriages parked on the road along the side of the church, undoubtedly belonging to the Order members who were still lingering inside. Cass crept toward them. Both drivers stood in front of the lead carriage, passing a silver flask back and forth.

She quickly circled behind the second carriage. It had a rack on top for supplies as well as a deep wooden compartment built into the back. Were the owners going into Florence? Probably, but there was no guarantee. She opened the door to the compartment and peered into the black space. It was big enough for a pair of trunks.

Or a person.

Cass glanced back toward the front of the church. The wooden door was swinging open. There was no time to think. She used her good arm to pull herself up and into the compartment, gathering her cloak around her to protect her skin from the rough wood. Folding her knees up toward her chest, she pulled the door shut from inside, tucking the hem of her cloak in the latch to prevent it from engaging and trapping her inside.

Santo cielo! What had she done? What if these people lived farther away from Florence than Belladonna? What if they decided to shuck off their cloaks and tuck them into the luggage compartment? They might think she was a robber and stab her.

But Cass couldn't change her mind now. If she tried to slip out, she would be discovered. Besides, almost any destination would be preferable to Villa Briani. She struggled to make out the sound of approaching footsteps, but her blood was drumming in her ears and her heart was rattling beneath her breastbone, blocking all noises from the outside until the door to the riding compartment opened with a rusty groan. She held her breath.

Voices sounded. A man and a woman. Their words were muffled, but Cass didn't think she recognized either speaker.

Seconds later, the horse whinnied and the wheels beneath Cass began to roll. It took all of her concentration to hold her body still and keep from crying out each time the carriage hit a bump or a rock. She cradled her injured arm against her chest, trying to protect it from the compartment's hard angles.

Each time the carriage turned, Cass tried to decipher whether she was headed toward Florence, but all the bouncing around had left her hopelessly dizzy, and the darkness threatened to smother her. All she could do was hope for the best.

It seemed like an eternity before the wheels slowed beneath her and the carriage came to a stop. The door opened and Cass heard the passengers alight. She strained to hear their animated voices, wishing she could make out what they were saying. Their footsteps receded, and she was just about to open the compartment when she heard another voice. The horse chuffed and stamped its feet. The driver must be unhooking it to stable it for the evening.

Cass waited until she heard the horse plod away. Then she waited some more, just in case. Her eyes had begun to adjust to the blackness of the compartment, and she could make out the tight walls of the cramped space. Her knees were still folded up against her torso. It would feel good to stretch her legs.

She opened the compartment a crack and peeked out. More darkness, with just the faintest hint of moonlight streaming through a high window. She opened the door the rest of the way and slid her body out of the carriage. She was in the stable of a private palazzo. She crept out onto the street and was relieved to see what appeared to be Florence.

But where exactly in Florence? Cass wasn't sure. She twisted her neck from side to side and stretched her arm over her head. She knew she should be scared, that walking the streets alone was dangerous, but she was just relieved to be away from Villa Briani.

She picked a street and continued straight along it, hoping she might hit the banks of the Arno or find something she recognized. Each time she saw the tall spike of a church steeple in the distance, she hurried forward, hopeful it would be the Campanile, and next to it the beautiful Duomo, Santa Maria del Fiore.

A scratching sound rose suddenly from the silence behind her, but when she whirled around to see who was following her, she came face-to-face with the discarded paper wrapping from someone's buy at the market, blowing and twisting its way down the path. She shook her head. Would she ever stop jumping at shadows?

Just as despair threatened to overcome her, Cass saw something familiar: a wooden sign shaped like a wine goblet swinging back and forth in the breeze. *I Setti Dolori.* The taverna she had gone to with Falco.

Cass retraced that path they had taken when they left, hurrying quickly past the spot where they'd kissed. She crossed the Piazza del Mercato Vecchio, which was quiet except for a single homeless man who was fast asleep on the steps outside of the church. As she approached Palazzo Alioni from behind, Cass realized she had another problem. No one was expecting her. The servants would all be asleep and the door would be locked. She would have to sleep in the stable.

She didn't mind. Slipping inside the darkened enclosure, Cass barely noticed the stink of manure or the roughness of the hay she lay down in. Her eyes were drawn to the gaudy pair of unicorns painted on Palazzo Alioni's carriage. She was finally safe.

But she had failed.

The Book of the Eternal Rose was gone, and Luca's execution was just over a week away.

Light filtering through the high stable windows woke her in the early morning. Plucking a few bits of hay from her hair, she smoothed her oversized cloak and knocked gingerly on the front door of Palazzo Alioni. The butler looked bleary-eyed as he opened the front door.

"*Bongiorno.*" Cass headed straight for the stairs before he could even reply. She felt stronger on her feet than she had in days. Just getting away from Villa Briani seemed to have improved her condition. She slipped into her little room and hurriedly closed the door behind her. Almost without thinking, she dropped the dead bolt into place. She had never been so happy to see the stark walls and dusty painting of the Virgin.

She went to her trunk and flipped open the leather top, relieved to see the bundle of parchment about the Order, along with her journal.

Cass grabbed the journal and pulled the little chair over to the washing table. Her quill was still right where she had left it almost two weeks earlier. Sadly, the ink had dried up. She flung the journal back into her trunk with a sigh. Thumbing through the papers from the tomb, Cass took note of each mention of the Book of the Eternal Rose. Cass felt certain she had discovered the book's hiding place in the armoire with the broken lock, but who had taken it? And what would Belladonna do when she found out?

Cass understood, now, how Joseph Dubois was connected to the Order, and why Angelo de Gradi was in Florence. Dubois had financed some of the Order's depraved research before starting his own sister chapter in Venice. De Gradi was there to make sure that the Frenchman's generosity wasn't forgotten, and also to glean information from Belladonna about alternative strategies for producing the fifth humor.

She sat on the side of the bed and ran a hand through her tangled hair. There had to be a way to save Luca that didn't involve the Book of the Eternal Rose.

"Signorina Cass?" Siena called to her from the hallway. The doorknob jiggled. "Are you all right? Why is the door locked?"

Because no one in Florence can be trusted. Cass slid out of bed, undid the bolt, and opened the door.

"Signorina Cass! It's true. You're here!" Siena's face lit up.

Cass smiled too. "I can honestly say, I have never been so happy to see you." She fought the urge to wrap her handmaid in a one-armed embrace.

Siena turned from the doorway. "I'm going to get my sister and Signora Madalena," she called over her shoulder, her face flushed with excitement.

"It's still early." Cass yawned. "You don't have to wake them."

"Wake whom?" Madalena glided into the room, fully dressed, her hair impeccably braided and pinned high on top of her head. Her smile was dazzling; she looked as happy to see Cass as she had looked on her wedding day. "The butler informed me of your return as soon as I opened my eyes."

Feliciana entered behind her, carrying a tray of fruit and bread. "Look who's back." Her lips formed a perfect heart-shaped smile. She set the tray on the washing table and stepped back to scrutinize Cass. "You look so thin. Have they been starving you?"

"I felt quite ill for several days," Cass said, happy to see that Feliciana, for her part, was starting to look less emaciated. Her skin and lips were completely healed, and her hair even looked like it might be starting to grow back, just slightly. "But I'm ready to make up for it."

She realized all three of them were staring at her, undoubtedly waiting for her to explain why she had returned home at the break of dawn without telling anyone of her plans. She took a deep breath. "Close the door, Feliciana," she said. "I have something to tell you. All of you." She began to describe the events of the past night, starting with the fight between her and Falco.

Siena's eyes grew wide, and she crossed herself when Cass got to the part about Belladonna stripping naked in front of the crowd.

"And you're certain the book has been stolen?" Mada asked. Her fingers fiddled with the crucifix that dangled from her belt.

Cass nodded soberly. "And without it, Luca will almost certainly be executed."

Siena's eyes filled with tears. She fled from the room and Feliciana went after her.

Mada reached out and wrapped Cass in a loose hug. "Don't give up," she said. "Luca is one of the most honorable men I know. He can't die. The Lord will intervene."

Cass couldn't answer her. Why would God spare Luca if he hadn't spared Tatiana de Borello? Perhaps Hortensa Zanotta had committed other crimes besides falsely accusing Luca of heresy. Perhaps she had deserved her punishment. But Tatiana had been young, innocent. Like Liviana, she had died before she even had a chance to live.

Cass could not put her faith in a God that allowed the Order of the Eternal Rose to flourish. If there was the slightest chance that Luca could be saved, it would be she who had to make it happen.

"I'm returning home immediately. I'll inform Siena and Feliciana of our pending departure," Cass said, a bit of the heaviness seeming to clear from her limbs. "Unless you think your aunt might consent to keep Feliciana on for a while. There's no reason for you and Marco to hurry back with us. I know you were planning to stay on."

"Nonsense," Mada answered immediately. "I'm sure Stella will hire on Feliciana, at least for the summer. And I want to return with you to Venice, to be there if . . . you need me," she finished.

Cass shook her head, her throat thick. "I'd feel better if you stayed here. You could make sure Feliciana stays safe. Perhaps you could even continue investigating the Order of the Eternal Rose for me." Would Cass still care about the Order if Luca were executed? Yes. She wanted to know exactly who her parents had been, to what end they had forsaken her for evil. Had they ever created a successful elixir? Was that why Belladonna looked so young? Or was she maintaining her perfect skin by bathing in human blood? How many people were involved? How many supporters of the Order knew of its true purpose? How wide was its influence? Cass needed these questions to be answered.

"If you want me to stay here," Madalena said, "I won't fight you on it. But I'm not like you, Cass. I'm not as brave or as smart. I may not be able to find your book, even with Marco's help."

Cass smiled tightly. "I'm going to get my things together," she said. "Would your father be able to assist me in arranging passage back to Venice? I suppose tomorrow is the earliest I can leave."

"We'll make the necessary arrangements." Madalena patted

Cass's hand, not unlike the way Agnese sometimes did. Her voice was low, soft. It was the voice of someone who knew there was no hope. "I'll see to it immediately. Let me know if there's anything else that you need." Her skirts swished as she crossed the room to the door.

Too overwhelmed, for the moment, to even think about packing, Cass took refuge on her bed, resting her injured arm gently at her side, tunneling her face into her pillow. A twinge of pain moved through her biceps, nothing compared with the wound that tore her chest open. Would she ever lay eyes on her fiancé again? Would she carry his death around with her like she carried the death of her parents?

Cass tried to imagine Luca gone, but couldn't. Even when he had been in France studying, he had always lingered in the back of her mind, his letters arriving with almost mechanical regularity. Even though Cass had spent most of her life away from him, she couldn't fathom being completely and utterly *without* him. He was her future, a promise left to her by her parents: a life that was safe, steady, dependable.

Falco had stormed away from her after their fight. Luca would never do that. If she told him to go, as she had told Falco, he might quietly take his leave, but not without letting her know that he would still be there—always—when she needed him.

Cass had always viewed Luca's differences from Falco as weaknesses, but she was starting to realize she'd been wrong. Falco was passionate, but he was also volatile and opinionated, so quick to get angry or frustrated. Luca was simply different, so staid and calm, except when the situation truly called for it. He had spent years away from her, but he understood the woman she was becoming. That was why he hadn't pressured her about the wedding. He knew she needed time for the decision to become her own.

Madalena came to find her for dinner. Cass debated skipping it—she didn't want to face anyone else, to see their pained eyes and piteous expressions—but she hadn't eaten breakfast and she was starving. At Mada's urging, she reluctantly took her seat in the dining room. It turned out to be a mistake. While Cass was packing, Madalena had taken it upon herself to inform the rest of the household of Cass's immediate return to Florence because of Luca's impending demise.

Cass didn't want to talk about it, didn't even want to *think* about it, but everyone else did. Marco and Signor Rambaldo took turns first arguing about the injustice in denying a man a trial and then assuring Cass that the Senate would come to its senses, that this was merely a ploy to get Luca to confess. Mada nodded along with them, reminding Cass that Luca was good and God was good and everything would work out. Cass knew they meant well, but each time one of them said Luca's name, she could almost see him dangling from the tarnished chandelier, his neck purple, his throat crushed.

She tried to distract herself by staring at her lap, counting the tiny, uneven X-shaped stitches that made up the fleur-de-lis on her napkin. Seeing those Xs made her think of Mariabella, the dead courtesan she'd found strangled to death and slashed with an X in her friend Livi's tomb. And thinking of Mariabella also made her think of Cristian. Cass folded her napkin and looked at the wall instead.

Also no help. A giant mural depicting Judith holding a sword to Holofernes's neck was painted on the wall opposite her seat. Drops of blood were just beginning to fall from her silvery blade. The painting appeared to be as old as the palazzo. Cass wondered about Signor Alioni's ancestors. Why would they have wanted such a gory picture in their dining room?

After what felt like two lifetimes, the servants cleared the bowls of soup and brought plates of roasted duck and herbed potatoes. It was without a doubt the most delicious-looking food Cass had seen come up from the kitchen at Palazzo Alioni. She felt as if *she* were the one who had been condemned, enjoying a last meal on Signora Alioni's finest, only slightly chipped, gold-rimmed porcelain.

Across the table, Marco and Signor Rambaldo were still debating. "If Luca confesses to this trumped-up charge, the Senate will reconsider the sentence," Signor Rambaldo said.

"What if he doesn't confess?" Marco asked.

"Perhaps we should speak of something else." Mada dabbed at her lips with her napkin. "I hear the cook has prepared some sort of pastry for dessert."

Another course to suffer through. Cass sipped her wine, wondering whether she should plead illness and flee to her room.

Signor Rambaldo swallowed hard. "Luca da Peraga is no fool," he said, spearing another bite of potato with his fork. "He isn't stubborn enough to die. He has his mother to think about, and Signorina Cassandra."

"Cass." Mada tried again to change the subject. "Did Stella tell you she'd be delighted to keep Feliciana in her employ for the time being?"

Cass felt a momentary rush of relief. Feliciana would be safe. She nodded at Signora Alioni. "Thank you for your kindness."

Signora Alioni nodded in return. "She's a fine worker, though I fear she may distract some of the boys." She smiled and arched an eyebrow.

Marco barreled on. "Yes, Signore, but even if Luca confesses, there is no guarantee that he'll ever go free."

Madalena cleared her throat loudly and shot a meaningful glance at her new husband. "I received a message from Prudentia today," she said.

"Who?" Cass asked.

"I don't believe you've met her. She's married to Marco's cousin."

"Right," Marco said. He finally seemed to have understood that Cass could not bear to sit through any more discussion of Luca's fate. "Teodor's wife. They were planning to spend some of the summer in France, were they not?"

France. Luca had studied in France. Cass had to stop thinking of Luca or she would go mad. She forced herself to concentrate on Madalena's face. "Is that right?" she mustered. "I've heard France is lovely."

"Yes. She and her husband have been exploring Paris." Mada smiled. "Her letter goes on and on about the Notre Dame cathedral. Apparently it has the most breathtaking stained-glass windows."

"Notre Dame," Marco mused. "Have you seen it, Signore?" He turned to Madalena's father.

"I have, indeed," Signor Rambaldo said. "A stunning piece of architecture. Though to be fair, Venice has her share of beautiful structures as well."

"Is it true," Marco went on, "that there are catacombs beneath Notre Dame's courtyard? Ruins of the original settlement built by the Celts?"

"I have heard that. Crumbling walls, broken swords, perhaps some ghosts trolling the place looking for their bones." Signor Rambaldo rubbed his beard thoughtfully.

Madalena flung down her fork. "Both of you ought to be ashamed," she cried out. "I've been trying to distract Cass from morbid thoughts, and you two turn a lovely conversation about Paris into a ghost story."

"It's all right, Mada," Cass said. Her heart was going fast in her chest. The story had reminded her of something Belladonna had said at tea, the day she and Cass first met. Bella had spoken of Venice being rife with eerie specters that snuck in with the tides and stayed to haunt the city's dank lower levels.

At the time, Cass had been surprised at how superstitious Belladonna had seemed. Now, however, she knew it was all an act, and a different aspect of the story struck her: the part about *sneaking in.*

Perhaps there *was* a way to save Luca. Could Cass sneak into the Doge's dungeons like the ghosts and the tides? It was highly unlikely. Even if she could gain entry, she didn't know if she'd be able to find Luca. And if she found him, she didn't know if she'd be able to free him.

All she knew was that if she did nothing, he'd be executed in just over a week.

As a child, Cass had taken Liviana to play near the canals, and the contessa had accidentally fallen into the fetid water. Even though it was years later that Livi became ill, Cass had always partially blamed herself for Liviana's death.

And when Cass's parents had gone off on a research trip, Cass had written them letter after letter, begging them to return home early so that she might spend Christmas with them. They had attempted to make the journey back during a rough, stormy December, and had died somewhere along the way. Cass didn't know if it had been her fault, if they might have survived had they stayed away until spring, but she blamed herself anyway.

Luca had returned to Venice to protect Cass from his half brother Cristian. If he died, it would be partially because of her. Cass's conscience was heavy with the blood of others. She would not add to that burden. She would save Luca, or die trying.

"Blood left to cool will separate
into layers of black, red, yellow,
and clear. We believe each of the humors
can be extracted from these layers."

—THE BOOK OF THE ETERNAL ROSE

twenty~five

Cass left for Venice the following morning. Madalena, Marco, and Signor Rambaldo were staying in Florence, as was Feliciana, at least for the time being.

"I need to make a stop before we head to the coast," Cass said. She and Siena were sharing a carriage back to Mestre, where they would then board a ship to take them home. As much as Cass had no desire to ever see Piero or Belladonna's villa again, she couldn't leave Florence without saying good-bye to Falco. She hadn't seen him since their fight and didn't want him to think he was the reason she'd left Villa Briani and returned to Venice.

He wanted to see her too. An urgent message had arrived late the previous night. The folded parchment was tucked inside of Cass's trunk, but she recalled the words exactly: *I'm sorry for what I said. I didn't mean it. Please forgive me. I must see you so that I can explain. I will come to Palazzo Alioni tomorrow evening. If you do not receive me, I will accept the fact that you never wish to see me again.* Typical Falco—get angry first and then think later.

Still, Cass understood why he'd said what he did. She knew what it was like to speak out of turn when emotions ran high. And it had been unfair to ask for his help in freeing Luca. She knew that now, and she didn't want Falco to think she hated him. But Cass would have to hurry back to Venice to make it before Luca's execution. She couldn't wait for Falco to come to Palazzo Alioni that night.

"Of course," Siena said. She was busy twisting and untwisting the belt of her dress, no doubt worrying about Luca's execution.

Cass's own fingers were busy rolling and unrolling a piece of parchment. She had scrawled Falco a quick response note. Nothing romantic. Just good-bye and good luck and a reassurance that she didn't hate him. If he were absent or unavailable—and part of her hoped that he would be—she would just leave the message with the butler and hope that he delivered it.

She shivered a little. Signor Mafei had seemed so charming when she and Madalena had first met Belladonna for tea. But he had been there at the church, dressed in black, pouring blood just like Piero. Anyone who belonged to the Order of the Eternal Rose was sick and depraved. Evil.

Cass's heart splintered in her chest as she realized the gravity of her words. There could be no more excuses. Her parents had been evil too.

The carriage turned onto the dirt road leading to Belladonna's villa. Siena yelped as one of the wheels hit a rock. Cass glanced up and realized they were at the edge of town.

"Where are we going?" Siena frowned slightly, as if she knew the answer but couldn't quite believe it.

"Villa Briani." Cass lifted her chin toward Siena's disapproving gaze. "Just for a moment."

Siena shook her head but didn't say anything. She turned her attention back to her lap and sat silently until the carriage slowed to a stop in front of Belladonna's villa. Cass wondered what Siena was really thinking. Cass had pulled her handmaid to the side late the previous night after everyone had fallen asleep. She had told her there might be a way to help Luca escape from prison. At first, Siena had looked at Cass as if the wound on her arm had traveled all the way to her brain.

But slowly, Cass had explained the possibilities. They could contrive their way into one of Palazzo Ducale's many servants' entrances and hide away until nightfall. Then they could find their way into the Doge's prison. True, once they were there, they would have to overpower the guard to steal his keys. Cass was still working on that part of the plan.

"I'll go with you," Siena had said without hesitation, her blue eyes as serious as Cass had ever seen them.

Cass didn't know if Siena believed they could really free Luca from the Doge's prison or if her handmaid loved him enough to volunteer for a mission that might get her killed, but the offer of help had made the idea seem real. It was foolish and crazy, but if there was the slimmest of chances that Cass could actually save Luca, she had to try.

But first, she had to deal with Falco.

One last good-bye.

Cass took the driver's hand and stepped down from the carriage compartment. She felt a tremor of nervousness move through her as she made her way along the path that led to the arched front door. She could barely bring herself to knock. What if Piero answered? What if Belladonna answered, naked and covered in blood?

Idiota. Signor Mafei would answer, of course. It was only proper. And when she wasn't posing for nude paintings or bathing in blood, Belladonna did seem fond of being proper. Cass reached out and rapped bravely on the wooden door.

Sure enough, moments later Signor Mafei's green eyes studied her curiously. "Are you here to see Dottor Basso?" he asked. He looked down at Cass's bandaged arm, just the end of which peeped out from her cloak.

"Actually, I—I have a message for Signor da Padova," Cass said, hating herself for feeling self-conscious. She knew how it sounded, as if she and Falco had been lovers. But really, how was it that she felt compelled to stammer and blush about a few stolen kisses, whereas Signor Mafei could stand over her so smugly, having drugged and seduced women to steal their blood?

"I believe he's working down in the garden," Signor Mafei said. "If you want to wait here, I can see if he's available."

"That's all right," Cass said quickly. Suddenly, she was in a hurry to escape Signor Mafei's mesmerizing stare. "I'll just go say hello. I remember the way."

"But Signorina—"

Cass ignored the protest. She swept her way up the stairs and through the portego and dining area, barely glancing at the painted likenesses of Belladonna. What was it Falco had called her? Hard? Unnatural?

Cass had just started to descend the back steps into the lush garden when she saw them. Belladonna lay back on a divan, her milky, perfect skin completely exposed except for a twist of dark curls draped over her breasts and a string of strategically placed roses covering the area between her thighs. Falco sat on a stool, sketching on a large piece of parchment. Cass squinted. Bella's curvy form was coming alive through Falco's strong lines.

Belladonna said something and laughed, tossing her curls over one shoulder and exposing her breasts. Setting down his charcoal, Falco stepped over to the divan to adjust her hair. His hand seemed to linger on her bare skin for a moment. Cass told herself she was imagining it, but then Belladonna reached out and twined Falco's fingers in her own. She looked up at him passionately, and he did not pull away. He bent toward her, free hand delicately adjusting one of the rosebuds perched along the curve of her perfect legs. Cass thought for certain they were going to kiss.

Or worse.

Falco's hand reached for another bloom.

Cass backed her way up the stairs, tucking the letter she had written deep inside the pocket of her cloak. Belladonna ran a hand through Falco's hair and Cass stumbled, landing on the top step with a thud. Scrambling to her feet, she clawed at the door handle, desperate to be back inside the villa, away from the garden, away from what she had seen.

Too late. Falco whirled around. "Cass," he said. Pulling free from Belladonna, he galloped across the grass toward the stairs.

Cass finally got the handle to work. She ran inside, slamming the door behind her. Lifting her skirts with both hands, she raced through the dining area to the portego. A servant girl who was dusting the canvases turned to look at her curiously.

Cass heard the sound of the back door opening and closing again. Ignoring the servant's perplexed look, she ran back down the main stairs to the foyer.

"Cass!"

She flung open the heavy door, relieved to see the horse and carriage just where it had been.

She vaulted her body back into the compartment without even waiting for the driver to assist her. "That was quick," Siena said.

"He was busy," Cass said. She turned to the driver. "Go. Now. Please."

The driver snapped the reins, and the horse whinnied and surged forward. Within seconds the carriage was headed down the dirt drive. Cass didn't turn around. She didn't need to. She knew what she would find. Falco watching her leave.

The carriage turned onto the main road. "Is everything all right?" Siena asked.

"Yes," Cass said quickly, willing the carriage to go faster as it headed north toward the Apennines.

"You look as though you've seen a ghost." Siena furrowed her brow.

"Don't be silly," Cass said. She could hardly breathe.

Falco and Belladonna. She didn't want to believe it, but it had been right there in front of her face. The way Falco's hand had grazed Belladonna's breast as he adjusted her hair. The way Belladonna had gripped his fingers in her own deformed hand. The look that had passed between them.

That look.

Could Cass have imagined it?

She hadn't seen Falco's face, but Belladonna's had been unmistakable. Triumph. Hunger. A desire to claim what she felt was rightfully her own.

And Falco hadn't pulled away.

Not until he realized Cass was there. The nerve of him to run after her. Just days earlier he had said her jealousy was unfounded, that Belladonna was "hard" and "unreal" to him. Cass swore under her breath. She had been right all along.

Siena gave her another strange look.

"I'm just worried about Luca." Cass closed her eyes and rested her head against the wall of the carriage compartment.

The journey home mirrored the trip to Florence, only the mood was infinitely more somber. Cass was a ghost, a shell, going through the motions. She passed the time staring out the carriage window, praying that the weather would hold, that the roads wouldn't flood, that the wheels wouldn't break. Her brain registered the beauty of the forests, the mountains, and the crystal-blue lake, but her heart ached when she thought of Falco, and her mind spun obsessively around the problem of freeing Luca.

After loading all of their supplies onto the ship that would take them back to the Rialto, Cass stood at the edge of the deck with Siena, watching as the boat floated away from the shore. The sky was blue and clear. *Grazie a Dio.* If the fair weather held, they would arrive home just two days before Luca's execution. Cass would need every moment of time she had left to come up with a plan. The farther the mainland receded into the distance, the more Florence felt like a dream. Soon they would be back in Venice, back on San Domenico, where things would return to the way they should be.

Only they wouldn't.

A grizzled older man introduced himself as the ship's medic and offered to take a look at Cass's arm. Her wounds had not been cleaned or rewrapped in days, but the pain in her arm had all but faded. Still, it wouldn't hurt to see how things were progressing, just to be safe. The medic ripped off her bandages with his callused fingers. Cass squeezed her eyes shut for a moment, steeling herself for what she might see.

"You're healing nicely," he said.

She opened her eyes. The bruises on her forearm had faded to a yellowish brown. The torn flesh over her biceps had grown together, but her whole arm was ghost-pale and smelled sour. Cass wrinkled her nose.

The medic laughed. "Nothing a scrub or some sea air won't cure."

Later, after everyone else was asleep, Cass made her way to the top deck of the ship. The wind twisted the tail of her cloak as she stared out across the Adriatic Sea. Cass knew the boat's captain stood just on the other side of the snapping sails, but for the moment she felt completely alone. In a few hours, the sun would rise and they'd dock in the quay behind the Palazzo Ducale. From there, Cass and Siena would catch a ride out to San Domenico Island.

And then what? Time was slipping through her fingers. Cass felt confident she could gain admittance to the Palazzo Ducale. But what match were two girls for an armed dungeon guard?

The boat pitched, and she grabbed on to one of the ropes to steady herself. The rough fiber bit into her skin. Above her head, a torn sail slashed out at the wind. Cass watched the flapping fabric stab the sky repeatedly.

Two girls would be no match at all for an armed guard.

Unless they were armed too.

"Our research shows
that rapidly spinning a vial of
blood will produce purer humors."

—THE BOOK OF THE ETERNAL ROSE

twenty six

Weapons?" Siena asked incredulously. "You mean to hurt someone?"

They were finally home: in Agnese's villa, using the storage room that had previously housed Feliciana as a private place to talk. Cass hadn't been able to sleep or eat since she'd gotten off the ship at daybreak. She couldn't think about anything except Luca. She would do anything to save him. Surely Siena understood. Cass looked up at her from where she sat crossed-legged on Feliciana's makeshift bed. "Not if we don't have to. Just in case." Luca's hourglass was running low. Only two days until his scheduled execution, at noon, in the Piazza San Marco.

Siena paced back and forth in front of her. "Could you really do it? Stab a man?" She stared at the paring knife Cass was holding, as though it were a serpent that might lunge from Cass's fingers and bite her.

No.

"Yes," Cass said.

Maybe.

She thought of Cristian. "If my life was in danger," she amended. She tucked a tendril of hair behind her left ear, enjoying the feel of being able to bend her arm without pain. "What if something goes wrong, Siena? Are you ready to spend the rest of your life as a prisoner in the Doge's dungeons?" Cass knew she would rather die than suffer that horrible fate.

Siena didn't answer. "You should return that to the kitchen. Cook will flay the whole staff alive if even a single knife goes missing."

Cass shrugged. "I wasn't thinking of stealing. A kitchen knife isn't ideal anyway. We could buy proper daggers at the market, or a blacksmith's shop."

Siena rubbed her forehead, as if she still couldn't believe they were even discussing it. But she asked, "And what else?"

Cass glanced around the storage room. Unfortunately there was nothing of use in the boxes and trunks, not the ones that were unlocked, anyway. "Masks, maybe?" she offered. "Or veils?" There would be no chance for Cass to resume her normal life after they helped Luca escape. Even if she wasn't recognized, Luca would never be able to return to Venice without risking arrest. But it was different for Siena. Only Cass—and likely Feliciana—knew of her feelings for Luca. Siena would not immediately be a suspect. If no one recognized her, she would be able to remain Agnese's servant if she so desired.

Cass realized, suddenly, that helping Luca escape meant starting a life with him. Had it come to that? Was Cass ready to be Luca's bride? Did she have any choice?

She imagined Belladonna stripping Falco from his paint-spattered clothing. She thought of them naked in the garden, covered only by a handful of those bizarrely giant roses. Her stomach laced itself into knots.

"Are you all right?" Siena asked. "Are you . . . are you scared?"

"No," Cass said shortly. "I'm not afraid." There could be no second thoughts. She pushed Falco from her mind. Luca was her future. She would make things right. She wouldn't give up, no matter what the cost.

Dinner was a struggle. Cass knew her aunt was overjoyed to see her again, but deep lines framed Agnese's gray eyes, and she seemed to be purposely hiding her concern about Luca's situation under a veil of light questioning about Cass's stay in Florence. She wanted to hear everything. What did Cass think of the great marble Duomo? Had she gone for Mass? Had she visited the Uffizi, one of the oldest art galleries in the world? What about the Boboli Gardens? Were they as lovely as everyone said?

Cass didn't have the heart to tell her aunt that between being attacked by dogs and having her blood drained in her sleep, she hadn't had much time for sightseeing. Part of her wanted to flee the gloomy dining room immediately to avoid Agnese's incessant questioning. The truth was right there, rolling around in her mouth. Every second she sat facing her aunt, it crept a little closer to her lips. Cass knew that if she didn't escape soon, she would blurt out the whole insane plan.

But at the same time, Cass didn't know how many more conversations she would have with her aunt. The old woman's voice was music, bringing back a flood of memories: Agnese chastising Cass for falling asleep during her studies, Agnese chastising Cass for her posture, for not wearing her chopines, for falling in the muddy streets and wrecking one of her dresses, for sneaking out of the house at night, for wandering off and getting attacked at Madalena's wedding.

Cass swallowed back a lump in her throat. Living with her aunt *hadn't* been just a series of lectures. She also remembered the way in which Agnese welcomed her into the villa when Cass was just ten, the way she allowed Cass to have thirteen-year-old Feliciana as her handmaid, even though at that time Feliciana was just a kitchen servant who could barely dress herself. Cass thought of her new journal that she'd barely gotten to write in because of her injuries in Florence. Agnese had given it to her after the excitement of Madalena's wedding and the attack on Cass had settled down. She had never felt more connected to her aunt than she had at that moment.

And now she was going to sever that connection, willingly, to try to save Luca.

"You're so quiet, dear," Agnese commented. "I suppose you're still exhausted from your journey."

Cass nodded mutely, struggling to swallow a bite of fish. "The sun was rising by the time we made it home." She thought again of her plan, her secret. Agnese had secrets too, locked away in the storage room. How could she and her aunt have shared so much, but still have so much hidden from each other? She couldn't find the right words to ask about the locked trunks, but she couldn't bring herself to leave the table early either. Forcing a smile, she struggled through the rest of her aunt's questions as best she could, spinning a half-truth here and there to satisfy the old woman.

When the servants cleared the last of the dessert dishes and Narissa appeared to help Agnese back to her chambers, Cass stood in the doorway to the dining area, watching her aunt's hunched frame shuffle down the corridor.

Cass returned to her own room and sat at the dressing table, piecing through the loose parchment she had found in the Caravello tomb. The description of the "research" and "subjects" made more sense now. Not only had the Order been testing their experimental elixirs on plants and insects, but they had also been self-administering, documenting vitality, wound healing, and more. Cass glanced again at the register of signatures, scanning the list one more time to see if any additional names sounded familiar. She realized both Piero Basso and Dionisio Mafei were present. But where was Bella Briani? Why wasn't she listed? Cass again tried to make out the name at the top of the parchment. She thought maybe she could make out the looping swirl of a B. Perhaps the blurred signature belonged to Bella, the leader of the Order of the Eternal Rose.

Were all of her servants members of the Order? Were they all taking test samples of the elixir? Would Belladonna try to indoctrinate Falco eventually? Cass should warn him, but she couldn't. To try would be fruitless. Even if a message from her made it through to him, he wouldn't believe her.

Cass flipped to the next page: a sketch of a six-petaled flower, encircled by unfamiliar chemical symbols. Slipper hopped up on the dresser, curious to explore the crinkling parchment. Cass picked up the cat and held him on her lap. He seemed a little thinner than before she left. She petted his soft fur, wondering who would take care of him if she didn't come home. She held him up to her face so that their noses touched. He wriggled in her grasp before reaching his neck out to nudge her with the top of his head, something he did when he was happy.

"I missed you," she said, setting Slipper back onto the floor. The cat purred in response. Tears blurred Cass's vision. She quickly pressed her palms to her eyes to dry them.

She tucked the bundle of parchment inside the drawer of her dressing table and wandered downstairs and out into the garden. Roses crawled up the side of Agnese's wooden trellis, pinks and reds and corals melding together like fire. Cass settled onto one of the stone benches, remembering how she and Luca had sat in this same spot just two months earlier. It seemed like a lifetime ago. So much had happened between them since then. She and Luca had argued. Cristian attacked her. Luca then told her the truth about how Cristian was his half brother, and how he would never allow Luca to be happy.

Then, Luca had asked her if she'd heard of the Order of the Eternal Rose. How long had he known about the Order? Did he know their parents were members? Why did Cass's mother steal pages from the book and hide them in the Caravello crypt? Cass prayed she'd get the chance to see him again, and that he would be well enough to escape the Doge's dungeons. Only then could she ask him all the questions that had plagued her over the past few weeks.

She lay back on the bench. Looking up at the bright blue sky, she wished for the millionth time that her mother were still alive to guide her. Not the woman who was a member of a wicked Order, but the mother she remembered, with a laugh like bells and hair that smelled of lavender. The mother who used to tell Cass she was bright and beautiful and could have the whole world if she wished it.

Cass didn't want the whole world. She just wanted Luca to live. She spoke the wish quietly into the sky. Maybe a ministering angel would hear her, and take pity.

The kitchen door swung open. Cass sat up quickly, gathering her skirts around her. Siena was heading into the garden, both arms laden with parcels.

"What is all of that?" Cass asked. She glanced up at the thick glass window at the back of the villa to make sure no one was watching them.

"Were you planning to wear your favorite dress into the Doge's dungeons?" Siena asked, stacking several of the wrapped packages on the bench next to Cass. Cass marveled that Siena actually seemed to be enjoying herself. Her eyes were glittering, and her cheeks were flushed. She almost looked excited. "I bought you something more appropriate. And look." She sat on the bench across from Cass and unrolled a piece of vellum out onto her lap. It was a crude drawing. Even without anything labeled, Cass could tell what it was. A map of the main level of the Palazzo Ducale.

"How did you get this?" Cass's mouth fell open.

"I know someone who works for the palace," Siena said triumphantly. "A boy who used to fancy my sister." Siena glanced up at the rose trellis for a moment. "I persuaded him to give me a bit of information in exchange for a little gold. He said that in preparation for his execution, Luca was moved from one of the upper cells to the pozzi. He drew this rough map so that we'll know which way to go to find the stairs to the lower prison."

So. Luca was now being detained in the pozzi, the horrible underground prison. Cass had heard stories of cells flooding, of prisoners drowning in the foul water that rushed in with the tides. The only way to stay dry was to hover on the bed of stone at the center of each cell, sometimes for hours. Hordes of insects bred within the rotting larch walls, and even after the water receded, the odor of mold and canal water stayed behind.

And then the rats appeared.

"He said we should enter here," Siena said, pointing at a door on the south side of the palace. "Servants go in and out of this door until sunset. We'll have to sneak in and hide away for a few hours, until the senators go home and the rest of the palace retires for the evening." She pointed at another area on the map. "The royal wine room is here. It's kept dark and we can hide behind the casks."

Cass hated the thought of a darkened wine room—so similar to the room in which Cristian had attacked her. But she wouldn't be alone. Siena would be with her. Cass felt a rush of affection for Siena, so strong she nearly reached out and hugged her. Siena was willing to risk her life for Cass, and for Luca, a man she could never have.

"The tide will be highest around midnight tomorrow," Siena said.

"Tomorrow?" Cass croaked. The word seemed so flimsy, so near. Cass was suddenly aware of the breeze blowing in from the lagoon. Her skin turned to gooseflesh. Tomorrow was too soon. But it was their only chance. Luca would be executed the following day.

"I think our best time to enter the dungeon will be about ten," Siena continued. "That way we have time to get back up the stairs and out the same door before the water levels reach their highest point. They won't get high enough to drown us, but navigating the dungeons in high water wouldn't be pleasant." She frowned. "What if we're seen? Water or no, we won't be able to outrun the palace soldiers."

"We'll have to jump into the quay," Cass said, with more conviction than she felt. "We can hide beneath one of the docks. Once it's safe, we'll swim across the Giudecca Canal to San Giorgio Maggiore." She stopped. "Can you swim?"

"I can stay afloat if it means staying alive." Siena looked doubtful. "Can *you* swim?"

Cass had tried it once or twice as a child. Her parents had taken her on trips to the mainland where lakes and rivers were plentiful. "I think so," she said. "There's a wooded area behind the church. I'll hide some supplies there so we can spend the night. You can find passage back here in the morning."

"But I can't just leave you," Siena protested. "Luca might be ill. You might need my help."

Cass's stomach lurched. "We'll figure something out, Siena," she said. "But *we* can't go back to San Domenico. The soldiers will come for us if we do."

Siena nodded, but she looked crushed. "I could come with you," she said hopefully.

Cass shook her head. "Staying on with us might be dangerous," she said. "And we might live far away from Feliciana. I wouldn't want to keep you from her."

Siena bit her lip. Cass reached out and squeezed her hand. She knew what it was like to want two opposing things simultaneously.

"Why not wait?" Cass said. "I'll send word to you somehow, once Luca and I are settled somewhere safe. You can decide then where your future lies."

Siena nodded. She gestured to one of the parcels she had stacked next to Cass on the bench. "A servant's uniform, black and gold for the Palazzo Ducale." She pulled something sleek and silver from a package that was coming unwrapped. A dagger. Just looking at the sharp blade made Cass's insides seize up. Would she be able to use it? She didn't think so.

But she might not have a choice.

Agnese didn't make it to the dining room for the evening meal. As much as Cass had been grateful to avoid her aunt's hawklike gaze, she felt a sudden, pressing need to have one last conversation with her. After stopping to check her reflection—no, her plan wasn't visible in her expression, it only *felt* that way—Cass requested two trays from the kitchen, then headed to Agnese's bedroom.

"Come in," Agnese said in response to her knock.

Cass pushed the door open just wide enough to admit herself. Her aunt was propped up on several pillows.

"Cassandra." Agnese's smile broadened, but then quickly faded. "You're upset," she said. "I take it there's been no news of a commuted sentence."

Cass shook her head. She pulled the chair from Agnese's dressing table over to the side of the bed.

"I guess I'd hoped that perhaps . . ." Agnese's voice trailed off. She reached out to take one of Cass's hands in her own gnarled fingers. "No matter what happens, I'll see to it that you're taken care of. I can find you another match."

"Aunt Agnese!" Cass frowned. "I don't want a husband. I want Luca to go free." Fearing she'd said too much, Cass dropped her eyes.

A sharp knock sounded from the corridor. "Come in," Agnese said.

Narissa and another servant entered with a pair of supper trays. They handed one to Cass and helped Agnese balance the other on her lap. Cass looked down at the porcelain bowl of beef soup and platter of warm chunks of bread. She needed to keep up her strength, but her stomach hadn't stopped churning since Siena had come back with the daggers. Narissa tucked an embroidered napkin beneath the loose folds of Agnese's chin and draped a second cloth over her chest.

"That will be all. Thank you." Agnese turned back to Cass. "I know this must be very hard on you, Cassandra." Agnese bit into a crust of bread. "But just having you safe in Venice makes me feel stronger," she said. "I know I told you to go, but I had the most awful feelings while you were gone, like I might never see you again."

Cass set her spoon down on her tray. Had her aunt somehow sensed the danger in Florence? She felt a wrenching sense of guilt. What would happen to Agnese if Cass and Luca were forced to flee the Republic? It might not even be safe to send word that they were alive.

"You don't need to worry about me," Cass said. "You raised me to be strong. I—I will always love you for that." Cass blinked back hot tears. She rarely told her aunt that she loved her.

"Of course, dear." Agnese, looking somewhat embarrassed, reached out and patted Cass's hand. "I didn't mean to upset you. I just didn't want anything to happen to you. As I've said, you're all I have."

The guilt was practically choking her. Was she doing the wrong thing, risking her life to save Luca? "I noticed several trunks downstairs," she blurted out. "They're locked. Do they belong to you?"

Agnese stiffened. "Those are my private belongings, Cassandra. I trust you have not been snooping."

"No, no," Cass said quickly. "The door was open. Perhaps a servant was cleaning."

"That room is full of the woman I used to be," Agnese said primly. Cass waited for her to elaborate, but she didn't.

"So . . ." Cass swallowed. "The items in that room . . . they belong to you, and not to Matteo?"

"The items downstairs belong to whomever I choose, and I do not choose Matteo."

"But . . . where did all of it *come* from?"

The suggestion of a smile passed across Agnese's face. "It's a long story, and our soup is getting cold. Perhaps we should save it for another time?"

"All right," Cass said. Her heart ached. She knew there might not *be* another time.

Before Agnese had finished eating, her papery eyelids had drifted closed. Cass set both trays on the dressing table and removed the napkins from her aunt's chest. Then she bent down and kissed Agnese on the forehead. She couldn't help but wonder if this was the last time she would ever see her.

"Pure water gives life. Foul, contaminated
water takes life away. So also does pure
blood hide the secret to eternal life,
whereas contaminated blood sustains
only temporary mortality."

—THE BOOK OF THE ETERNAL ROSE

twenty-seven

The next day, just after dawn, Cass crept out to the grave-yard with the leather bundle of papers and her journal. She couldn't bear to lose either item, and at least if she locked them in the Caravello tomb, she would know they were safe. She'd figure out a way to retrieve them eventually.

She had wanted to hide away one other thing—the portrait Falco had painted of her, the canvas he had started the night of their first kiss. Even though she knew they weren't meant to be together, Cass didn't want to relinquish the memory of everything they had shared. But the painting was too bulky to conceal beneath a cloak, and she'd have a hard time explaining it to Luca someday. Reluctantly, Cass had left it where it was, nestled at the very back of her armoire behind all of her skirts and bodices.

She tucked the bundle of parchment and her journal behind one of the high coffins, locked the crypt door, and rethreaded the lion key onto the chain around her neck. She touched the lily pendant gently. "Bring me luck," she whispered.

Back in her room, Siena helped Cass into the servant's uniform. The fabric was a little rough against her skin, but Cass loved being able to forgo her stays. She selected her most luxurious cloak—the black satin one with the white fox fur collar and cuffs—wrapping it snugly around her so that people would be less likely to notice the simple apparel beneath. She slipped into a pair of soft leather shoes and grabbed one of her shorter pairs of chopines. She planned on ditching the overshoes as soon as she could do so without attracting attention.

Siena pinned Cass's hair into a secure bun and handed her a simple bonnet with a black silk veil that could be lowered as desired. Cass nodded approvingly.

Agnese was still sleeping as the two girls prepared to set off for the Rialto. Cass paused at the bottom of the staircase, just inside the front door. If only she could run up the stairs and peek at Agnese one last time. But no, it was too risky. Her aunt might wake and see everything reflected in her eyes. Perhaps, if everything worked out as it should, Cass could send her a note someday.

She inhaled deeply, trying to quell the sadness and terror that welled up in her chest. She wasn't just saying good-bye to Agnese. She was saying good-bye to the only life she knew, to whispered conferences with Siena, to teasing Bortolo for falling asleep standing up, to sneaking bits of chicken up to her room for Slipper. Cass almost burst into tears at the thought of never seeing her cat again.

But she was doing what she must.

Giuseppe rowed them across the lagoon. He raised an eyebrow when the girls requested a quick stop at San Giorgio Maggiore, but didn't question them. Cass had a package of clothing and coins tucked under her arm. She and Siena made their way to the back of the church. Cass slung her parcel from a tree branch, hoping no one would find it before nightfall.

They returned to the gondola, and Giuseppe rowed to the Rialto, where he dropped them off near Luca's family palazzo. Cass had announced loudly the day before that she was going to spend the morning circulating a petition among Luca's neighbors asking for mercy on his behalf. Not as if the Senate would care about sentiments gathered from the district if they didn't care they were executing an innocent man, but it was a proper story—just the sort of thing a distraught fiancée might do.

Instead, the girls headed to Piazza San Marco. There was no point in spending all day huddled behind casks of wine, especially when it increased the likelihood of being caught. Wandering the piazza was a good way to pass time. The area around the Palazzo Ducale and the Basilica San Marco was teeming with people dressed in brightly colored dresses and cloaks. The snap of sails and the shout of fishermen from the quay behind the piazza punctuated the buzzing chatter of vendors and buyers roaming the crowded square. Scents—the sharp jasmine of perfume and the sweetness of honey—mostly obscured the stench of the nearby canals.

Cass had never been so dazzled by the piazza before. She felt as though she were seeing everything for the first time—ironic, since she was no doubt preparing to see it for the *last* time. A dark-skinned old man hobbled by with a box of freshly baked bread for sale. She bought a loaf and some honey for dipping to share with Siena, although she found that she could choke down only a few bites.

One corner of the square was filled with foreign vendors selling costume jewelry and swatches of silk. Cass and Siena browsed the booths, pretending as if they were, like many of the people in the square, just out for a day of pleasure and fun.

"Look." Siena elbowed Cass and pointed toward the main entrance of the basilica. A conjurer was performing for a throng of people.

Cass's stomach tightened. Maximus the Miraculous. He lifted his hat from his head and bowed low before the crowd. The breeze off the water whipped through his dark hair. A stream of rose petals blew from his hat, and several women began to clap.

Cass had learned the identity of the murdered courtesan after speaking with the conjurer. For a while, she had even considered him a suspect. She didn't know whether seeing him here was a good or a bad omen.

"Let's walk by the door," Cass said lightly. The dazzling sun, the people, the shouts of laughter—all of it felt like a dream. Could she possibly be here, now, contemplating risking her life? Was she really about to break into the Palazzo Ducale, the seat of Venetian government?

They passed the door that Siena's mysterious friend had indicated. They looked out at the sparkling quay as they walked, but Cass was making plans in her head. It was only a few feet from the door to the water. When they escaped—if they managed it—they needed to hit the ground running. It would take just seconds for them to disappear beneath the water's surface.

If they were discovered, the palace would send soldiers after them on foot and in boats. They'd search the piazzas and the canals. Cass, Luca, and Siena would have to hide out in the fetid water, tucked away beneath a dock, invisible in the shadows. Then, when the soldiers spread out, they could swim to San Giorgio. The outline of the great church loomed just across the Giudecca Canal. Cass looked fearfully at the water. She could make it. She would have to.

She and Siena circled twice around the entire Palazzo Ducale: two girls out for a summer stroll. Then they once again threaded their way through the crowded Piazza San Marco. One last look at a Venice Cass might never see again.

When she was certain no one was paying her any attention, Cass slipped out of her chopines. She unfastened her cloak and draped it across the stone railing that ran along part of the piazza. A vendor would undoubtedly find them and offer them for sale.

She glanced up at one of the clock towers. Its golden hands indicated four o'clock. It was still early, but she didn't want to wait too long and risk the servants' door being locked before she and Siena made their way inside the palazzo. They would not get a second chance. "Ready?" she asked Siena, finding that although she was not wearing her stays, she still could hardly breathe.

Siena nodded. "They won't expect servants to be coming and going after sunset. We might as well get inside and find the wine room." Her hand went to the pocket of her skirt. She was feeling for her dagger. Cass did the same. It was there—heavy, wrapped in kitchen cloth. Reassuring.

They headed for the wooden servants' door, slipping through it without hesitation, as though they belonged there.

Inside, a long hallway ran the length of the palazzo. Servants milled past carrying armloads of clean linen. A pair of noblewomen walked arm in arm, probably waiting for their husbands to finish up with a meeting.

"Keep your head down," Siena whispered. "You want to be invisible."

Cass kept her eyes trained on the ornate marble floor. She mentally mapped the space. Siena's friend's sketch had been very exact, and they made it to the wine room quickly. They slid through another door, which banged heavily shut behind them.

Instantly, Cass saw Palazzo Rambaldo's wine room. Cristian. Pulling her forward. Her skin felt tight. Her heart stuttered. She reached out and gripped Siena's forearm to steady herself.

"Are you all right?" Siena asked, dropping her voice to a whisper.

"Fine," Cass said. She pushed away the image of Cristian, the idea that he might be lurking in the shadows, waiting for her.

Siena and Cass inched their way toward a back corner of the room. The casks here were thick with dust. Cass felt certain no one would come to tap them today. The floor was damp, but thankfully, there was no standing water or evidence of vermin. After crouching awkwardly for a few minutes, Cass dropped all the way to the ground, sitting crossed-legged in her simple skirt. Siena did the same.

"And now we wait," Siena said.

Cass nodded. Six hours or so. An eternity.

"We should go over the plan again," Siena whispered after a minute.

There wasn't much to go over, but Cass knew she was just trying to pass the time. They would wait until it was late, and creep out into the corridor and down the hallway. According to Siena's map, the adjacent hallway was called the Hall of the Three Chiefs. A service stairwell connected it to the lower prison. Cass and Siena would descend the stairs, find Luca, find the dungeon guard, get the key—*somehow*—and open Luca's cell.

For a long time, they sat in silence as heavy as the darkness around them. The sounds of dripping, the echoes of voices from the hall, the occasional scrabble of a rat's feet against the stone—all of it seemed amplified.

"I'm sorry," Siena blurted out suddenly. "About Luca. About how I . . . about the way I . . ."

She trailed off. Cass reached out and squeezed Siena's hand. Cass had caught Siena with one of Luca's monogrammed handkerchiefs on Madalena's wedding day. She had known instantly what the token— and Siena's mortification—had meant. Siena was in love with Luca. Perhaps she always had been, even when she was a mere scullery maid and he was just a boy who visited San Domenico occasionally with his parents.

Cass had been shocked, but not angry. Stunned, but not jealous. She thought of the feelings that had developed so quickly between her and Falco. She was no stranger to forbidden love.

For a brief instant, Cass allowed herself to think of him. She still had feelings for him. If there had been any doubt, it had evaporated the instant she saw him in the garden with Belladonna. Falco's hand lingering on Belladonna's bare skin. Bella's hungry look. The pain, the rage—it was a wave, threatening to drown her. But was that what love was supposed to be? Pain? Madness? Or was love something more like what she felt for Luca? Something that motivated a person to be selfless and even self-sacrificing.

"You can't help how you feel, Siena," Cass said gently. Her heart swelled, making her chest feel tight.

Several more beats of silence passed. When Siena spoke again, her voice was trembling. "Signorina Cass, you have been so good to me, so good to my sister. I just want you to know, in case any-thing happens, that I—" Her voice cracked. "That I love you. Like family."

Cass squeezed Siena's hand again. "Me too," she whispered. Both girls were silent for a few moments. "You can try to sleep, if you like," Cass said. "I'll keep watch."

"Sleep? I'm so nervous, I may never sleep again."

"I feel the exact same way." Cass leaned her head back against the wall. The room was completely dark. Even if a servant did come to fetch wine, the light from a single candle or lantern would not give away their hiding place.

"What do you think Feliciana is doing right now?" Cass asked after a minute. Anything to keep from thinking about everything that could go wrong.

"Probably breaking the hearts of peasants and schoolboys all over Florence," Siena said, and Cass heard a smile in her voice. "If Signora Alioni thinks she's a distraction to the serving boys now, just wait until her hair and her curves start to come back."

The minutes crawled by, expanding slowly into hours. Periodi-cally, Siena would creep from her hiding spot and open the heavy door just far enough to peek out into the corridor, to judge the time of day via the light from the hallway windows. The third time she did, she came back to where Cass sat and held out her hands. "I think it's late enough," she said, pulling Cass to her feet.

There was a damp spot on Cass's skirt from where water had leached through the stone floor, and her legs and feet were numb from sitting for so long. She tucked a few stray tendrils of hair up under her simple gray bonnet and let the black silk veil fall in front of her face. She stamped her feet to try to regain sensation in them. Siena lowered the veil on her hat too. Cass couldn't help but realize how odd her handmaid looked dressed in black instead of blue, with her pale face obscured. It was as if Siena had become someone else, a stranger. She had always thought of Siena the way she thought of Luca: steady, dependable, unchanging.

Maybe she was wrong—about everyone and everything.

They stood inside the door, listening for sounds in the hallway. Cass's heart started galloping in her chest. Siena opened the door a crack and both girls peeked out. The hallway was dim. An iron lantern hung from a peg at the end of the corridor. It would give them just enough light to navigate by.

Cass took a deep breath and slipped into the hall. Siena followed, and the two girls crept down the wide corridor. Cass's leather slippers made only the faintest *thwap* on the marble floor, but to her each footstep was a thunderclap. She was certain that a battalion of palace soldiers would rise up out of the darkness to arrest them at any moment.

Siena nudged Cass toward the Hall of the Three Chiefs. They found the service stairwell that led down into the dungeons. With trembling hands, Cass reached up and slid the lantern from its peg. She was so scared, she nearly dropped it, and Siena reached out, steadying her hand. Cass didn't know how Siena could keep so calm, but she tightened her grip on the lantern and choked back the fear in her throat.

The temperature dropped as the girls descended the stairs. The dungeon was black as death. The scents of mold and feces swirled around them, and tears rose in Cass's eyes. She wanted to throw up. She wanted to run away. She wanted to scream. Clanking and moaning filled the air. Cass wondered if Belladonna had been right, if these twisting corridors were crawling with ghosts.

She forced herself to keep going.

At the bottom of the staircase, Cass and Siena paused, listening for sounds of patrolling guards. The water, Cass noticed, was already seeping into the prison. Her leather slippers were almost completely submerged. She struggled to walk without making sharp sloshing sounds.

The pozzi was shaped like a square, its block of cells arranged so that no prisoner could look out the tiny grate in his door and see anything but a blank wall. A single corridor ran around the perimeter of the prison. Each wooden cell door was recessed in the stone walls and held closed by a lock and two thick dead bolts.

"How will we ever find Luca?" Siena asked. For the first time, she sounded afraid.

Cass didn't answer. She held her lantern up to the tiny barred window in the first door. A man lay on a raised stone platform, naked except for a tattered pair of breeches. Bruises and bite marks covered his torso.

The man sat up when he saw the lantern's light. "The water is coming," he said, leering at her. "Afterward, the vermin."

Cass lowered the lantern quickly. The water was only up to her ankles. Plenty of time. Siena gripped her elbow and piloted her forward. In the next cell, a man squatted over a silver bucket. Cass quickly passed on. Next—a man slept on the raised platform. The fourth cell appeared to be empty.

But just as she turned away, a figure launched itself at the door. "Angels," the voice rasped. "Have you come to free me?"

Cass backed up quickly, pulling Siena with her. But the man

began to bang on the door of his cell. "Angels," he cried out. "They've come to free us all!"

"Shh," she hissed. But the man continued to bang on his door, and several other voices picked up the chant: "Angels!" They screeched, clawing at their doors. "Angels of mercy!"

Just then, Cass saw light from around the next corner. A guard shouted, "Settle down, all of you!"

Quickly, she extinguished her lantern and retreated with Siena into a recessed portion of the corridor. The two girls stood with their backs against the damp wall. Boots sloshed through the water, drawing closer. Cass's heart beat three times for each footstep. She held her breath, terrified the guard might actually be able to hear her blood racing through her body.

"What are you going on about?" The guard knocked harshly on the doors he passed; abruptly, the prisoners fell silent. Only one of them spoke up—the man who had given the alarm.

"Angels," he hissed. "They've come to set us free."

The guard laughed and hawked a bit of phlegm into the swirling water.

"The only thing coming to set you free will be Death himself. Go back to sleep. Don't make me get my boots wet again or you'll pay for it tomorrow."

Cass risked poking her head around the corner, and saw the guard's lantern heading away from them. She counted to ten. Then, ducking low, she and Siena crept back down the corridor. It was getting harder to move. The water was almost at her knees.

At the next corner, Cass saw that the guard had his own elevated platform, situated against the far wall of the cellblock. As Cass watched, he stepped up out of the murk, set down his lantern, and hung a set of keys on a hook protruding from the stone wall. Dropping to a squat on the platform, the guard pulled a flask from his pocket and took a long drink.

Cass ducked back out of view.

The keys were so close. But the guard was wearing chain mail, something Cass should have considered. Their daggers would be useless—even as a threat—against a man in armor, unless they could get close enough to slash his throat. Her insides curled into knots at the thought. "I saw the keys," Cass whispered to Siena. "But first we have to find Luca."

Siena nodded. She opened her mouth to speak, then froze.

"Cass?" The word came from behind her.

She spun around. The cell was dark, quiet. A roman numeral fifteen was painted upside down over the door. Had someone just said her name? Or had she imagined it?

A shadow stirred from inside the cell. There was a liquid sound in the dark, water being disturbed.

A man's face appeared at the tiny grate. Siena covered her mouth with one hand. Cass swallowed back a gasp. He had a thick beard covering his cheeks and chin, but his brown eyes shined golden in the darkness.

It was Luca.

"Am I—am I seeing things?" Luca's voice was dry, cracked. "Is that you, Cass?" His eyes were wide and staring, as though he had woken in the middle of a dream.

Cass felt like weeping. He was here. She had found him. She wanted to throw herself through the stone and press her face to his chest. Instead, she leaned close to the grate. "We're going to get you out of here," she mouthed.

Luca rubbed his eyes, like he still thought Cass was just a dream. He shook his head. "Impossible," he whispered.

Cass reached for his face, barely managing to squeeze her fingers through the grate and touch his cheek. "I'll be back. I promise."

Reluctantly, she turned away from Luca, nearly colliding with Siena. Ducking down, Cass swept her hands back and forth in the rising water, fighting back a surge of nausea as unfamiliar slippery objects swirled through her fingers. She refused to think about what they might be. She traced a sharp crack in the dungeon floor, digging her fingertips beneath the broken stone until one of the pieces came loose. It was about the size of her hand, but much heavier. Siena mimicked Cass, and soon came up with her own jagged piece of rock.

The two girls circled away from the guard, turning two sharp corners until they had returned to the bottom of the service stairwell. They *needed* those keys, but there was no way to sneak up on him while he was awake. If they were lucky, he would eventually fall asleep.

Cass and Siena huddled in the darkness of the stairs, creeping to the edge of the cellblock occasionally to peek around the corner at the guard. He took swigs of his flask and toyed with the hilt of his sword. At one point Cass thought she heard him singing to himself. The fetid water slowly rose up to her waist, soaking her skirts, making it feel as though her pockets were filled with lead.

She chanced another glimpse around the corner. Black liquid lapped at the edges of the guard's platform. He had slumped against the wall, his chin resting on his chest.

Now was their chance.

Cass directed Siena back to Luca's cell. She had to be ready to pull open the dead bolts as soon as Cass had the keys in her possession.

Straightening up, Cass moved carefully through the thick, foul-smelling liquid. It sucked at her stockings as she advanced. Her shoes were bricks. Heavy. So heavy. Her skirts swirled around her in the mire. The blackness was a cloth bag—no, a coffin—that threatened to smother her. She clutched the slab of broken rock so tightly that she feared it might crumble to pieces before she made it down the corridor.

Another heavy step. And then another. She approached the sleeping guard. The prisoners were all quiet. Cass prayed for stealth, for invisibility. If one of them called out, she was a dead woman. Another step. Her whole body trembled. But there was no turning back.

Slowly, she maneuvered herself onto the raised platform. She hovered over the guard, trembling. He snored lightly, expelling the smell of liquor. Cass could see the stubble of beard. The network of wrinkles around his eyes. She could almost see the pulsing of blood in the thick vessels of his throat. Her own blood roared in her ears. She turned her head toward the darkness. Where was Siena? Was she ready? When Siena loosened the dead bolts, the guard would wake up. Unless . . .

Cass considered the heavy rock cupped in her hand and then thought about the dagger in her pocket. She looked back at the guard, visualizing the pulsing in his neck. She imagined sticking the blade through his throat, spilling his blood down the platform into the murky water. He was sleeping so soundly. She could do it.

Only she *couldn't* do it.

She didn't know whether to be relieved or disappointed.

The keys dangled just above the guard's head. Carefully, Cass rose to her feet. She extended her arm, for once grateful that she was taller than most every girl she knew. Luca's freedom was at the tips of her fingers. She could save him, maybe, as long as the keys didn't clank together.

But they would. She knew they would. And then the guard would wake.

Keeping one hand curled around the wet piece of stone, Cass slowly reached for the keys.

"No man can achieve

greatness without

risking his life for it."

—THE BOOK OF THE ETERNAL ROSE

twenty-eight

Just as her fingers curled around the cold metal, the guard grunted and changed positions. Cass flinched. The keys fell from her trembling fingers, landing on the stone platform with a harsh jangling sound. The guard's eyes opened.

Both he and Cass froze. His eyes seemed focused on her throat. He blinked rapidly in the dim light as he went to draw his sword. Cass realized he was staring at her pendant, that the diamond of her lily must have reflected the lantern light oddly, rendering him blind for a precious second or two. She attacked, slamming the rock down against the bridge of his nose. He groaned, flailing sideways, tipping his lantern. The flame flickered out, but not before Cass saw the guard reach again for his sword.

She brought the lump of stone down hard on the back of his skull.

He slumped forward, hands twitching. Cass cracked him a third time with the rock, and his body went limp. The hysterical desire to laugh rose in her throat. *Please don't be dead.*

Grabbing the keys, she spun and jumped off the platform into the dark, swirling water. All she had to do was get Luca. Then they could escape back into the night. The sucking mire, the foul odor—the dungeon was starting to suffocate her.

"I saw what you did," a prisoner cried out. "Set me free and I promise not to tell."

Cass ignored him, but the prisoner next to him took up the same cry. "We saw it. We all saw. You have to set us free." Fists pounded on doors. Metal slammed against metal as the prisoners swung their buckets against the grates in the cell doors. If they didn't stop, a guard patrolling the main floor of the palazzo would surely hear the commotion.

"Be quiet," she said sharply. "All of you be quiet, or I'll be dead before I can set anyone free." It was not exactly a promise—and not a lie, either.

Most of the prisoners quit their banging. The one in the cell next door to Luca pressed his face to the grate, watching her approach.

Siena was struggling with the second dead bolt. Cass used the keys to unlock the door. Leaving the keys to dangle from the lock, she pulled with Siena and the metal rod bit into the wood as the dead bolt swung loose. Luca pushed the door open from the inside.

Again, Cass was amazed at how much he had changed, how pale and gaunt he looked after only a month of being imprisoned. "You shouldn't have come," he said.

"Let's go," Cass said. She left the keys dangling from the door and used her arms to propel her body through the rising water. Siena and Luca followed. The other prisoners resumed their pounding and screeching.

Cass, Luca, and Siena ran for the stairwell, sloshing through the water. As they climbed the stairs, Cass's serving dress clung to her skin like hands gripping her, pulling her downward. She had lost one shoe in the murk and hadn't even realized it. She kicked off her other and went barefoot. Shoes would only weigh her down once they got into the water. Already, her chest felt like it would explode. She could barely breathe.

They hit the Hall of the Three Chiefs running, but before they made it to the servants' entrance, a guard turned the corner into the south corridor, obstructing their passage.

"Stop!" he called, unsheathing his sword.

Cass spun around, dragging Luca with her. There had to be another door off the long hallway. The water was just on the other side of the wall, and with it, freedom.

The corridor reverberated with shouting—disembodied noises that seemed to rise up from everywhere at once. Cass was too frightened to turn around and see whether they were being pursued, or by how many. She knew more guards would come. An image flashed in her mind: she and Siena locked inside one of the watery prison cells, huddled on her stone bed as the water level rose higher and higher, threatening to overtake them. Another flash. Luca's body falling, his neck snapping. Cass heard a scream; she wasn't sure whether the sound was in her head.

"Here!" Luca panted out. They had found another door. Luca struggled to slide back the thick iron rods that held it closed.

And then, Cass realized Siena wasn't beside her.

Whirling around, Cass saw Siena sprawled out in the hallway. She'd fallen.

No, she'd pretended to fall. As the guard reached her, Siena lashed out at his ankle. Silver glinted in the dim light. The guard stumbled backward in surprise.

"Hurry," Siena screamed. She was on her feet now, moving sideways, dagger extended. The guard was favoring one leg, but his sword was still six times as long as Siena's blade. Their dance could have only one ending.

Luca got the door open, and the warm night air rushed in, smelling of salt, of canal water.

"Come on, Siena!" Cass shouted.

Siena flung the dagger at the guard's face, spinning around as he ducked. But she made it only two steps down the corridor before he was on top of her. It was too fast. His sword flashed behind Siena like lightning. The blade came straight through her front. Siena fell to her knees. A sea of red flowed from her chest.

"No!" Cass screamed.

Siena's body flailed. Her eyes widened, as though in surprise, and her mouth opened. For a second, Cass was sure she would speak.

Then her head rolled forward, and her body went still.

Cass screamed again. She tried to pull her hand from Luca's. She had to get Siena. Save Siena.

The guard was just a few steps away now. More guards were approaching from another hall, their boots hitting the marble flooring like thunder.

"No, Cass," Luca said. He pulled her through the door and into the night.

She splintered. Part of her remained inside the Palazzo Ducale. Part of her fell to the floor like Siena. Bleeding. Dead. Floating. Spots of light blurred before her eyes. The ground vanished from beneath her feet. And then there was only water.

"The key to immortality may lie

within a chosen sect of humanity."

—THE BOOK OF THE ETERNAL ROSE

twenty-nine

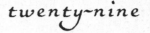

Shouts ricocheted off the surface of the lagoon, but Cass saw only darkness. All around her. Inside her. *Siena.* She choked back a sob. Tiny waves lapped against her chin.

"Shh." A voice, so soft, Cass thought it was speaking straight into her mind.

Luca.

"I'm so sorry, Cass."

Straight into her heart.

She realized his arms were around her, that their bodies were intertwined beneath the frigid water. He was keeping her afloat. Without him she would sink like a stone, falling until she could go no farther.

Siena.

Cass sobbed again, nearly swallowing a mouthful of icy water. Her vision sharpened. They were in the quay somewhere, west of the Palazzo Ducale, tucked beneath a private dock. Soft clouds of light floated along the darkened canal. Soldiers. Soldiers were searching for them.

Luca pressed his lips to her forehead. "We couldn't have saved her. This is what she wanted, for you to escape. For you to live."

"I know." But the words were hollow; they didn't mean anything. Luca didn't know of Siena's love for him. Cass wasn't going to tell him. She didn't want him to share her pain.

Her guilt.

Another sob rippled through her body, which Luca misinterpreted as shivering.

"We'll get out of the water soon," he said. "As soon as the search parties spread out."

Search parties. As if they were going to be rescued instead of executed. "San Giorgio," Cass whispered. "Sie—" She couldn't even say Siena's name. "I left some supplies there. In the woods behind the church."

"So brave," Luca murmured. "So smart. I can't believe you came for me."

"I couldn't let you die," Cass said.

But she had let Siena die. No. Siena had distracted the guard so Cass and Luca could escape. Siena was a hero. Cass hadn't *let* Siena do anything. Siena had made her own choice, and it was brave.

Luca touched his lips to the hollow beneath each of Cass's eyes. Cass realized she was crying again. "Her body," she whispered. "We need to get her body, somehow."

"After she's identified, the palace will return it to Signora Querini," Luca said.

Cass knew he was right, but that didn't close the hole in her chest. Through a blur of tears, she watched the glow of lanterns spread out. The sharp sounds of whistles and shouts began to dwindle.

"Can you swim?" Luca asked.

Cass nodded. The Giudecca lay directly across the water, with San Giorgio slightly to the southeast. Both islands were shrouded in darkness, but Cass could easily envision the façade of San Giorgio's church. She'd passed it hundreds of times on trips back and forth to the Rialto. It took only a few minutes to cross the Giudecca Canal by gondola, but Cass wasn't sure how long it would take to swim. And there was no place to stop or hide in the middle of the water. If the soldiers headed back toward the Palazzo Ducale before Cass and Luca made it to the shore, they would be discovered.

The idea should have terrified Cass, but she couldn't stop thinking of Siena. She couldn't stop seeing her pitch forward onto the floor of the corridor, blonde hair spreading out like a halo, blood flowing freely. It should have been Cass who died. How was she going to explain what had happened to Agnese and Narissa, to Feliciana?

Cass realized, suddenly, that she *wouldn't* be able to explain it. She couldn't exactly send a letter detailing what had happened that night. Siena was a hero, and they might never know it. And she, Cass, might never speak to Agnese or Narissa or Feliciana again.

"Are you ready?" Luca's arms were still around her, one on the small of her back, one on her waist. Would she sink when the water got deep? She hadn't gone swimming in years, but Luca couldn't hold her up and swim the two of them across the water. Cass would have to make it on her own.

She nodded dumbly, and then realized it was probably too dark for Luca to see her. She swallowed hard. "Ready," she whispered.

Luca grabbed her hand. Strange swirling things beneath the water grabbed at Cass's ankles as she inched forward with Luca until the edge of the dock was right above their heads. She tightened her grip on his hand and clutched at the wooden mooring post with her other.

She struggled to peel her fingers from the rough, rotted wood. She wasn't afraid. It was just that relinquishing her hold on the post felt like letting go of everything.

Siena.

Cass craned her neck to the east, back toward the Palazzo Ducale. What was happening? Was Siena still lying in a heap on the ornate marble floor? What if she hadn't died? What if Cass and Luca had abandoned her to the Doge's dungeons, to the foul, vermin-infested wells? No. It wasn't possible. The sword had passed straight through her. Cass had seen the blade emerge from Siena's chest. She had seen her eyes roll up to heaven, as if she were looking for God to take her.

"Come on, Cass." Luca guided her toward the open water.

"I can't," she whispered.

Luca wrapped his fingers around hers and tugged. The hold broke, and her hand slipped free of the wood.

The current pulled her and Luca quickly apart. Cass reached out for him, but he wasn't there. Her skirt had wrapped itself around her legs. She couldn't kick. She couldn't do anything. Her body started to sink. She tried to remember how to swim. She flailed out with her arms, and succeeded in moving forward, barely, as her dress spiraled her down.

Fighting to keep her head above the surface, she looked for Luca. All she saw was the reflection of moonlight on water and the hazy shorelines that mocked her—so close, so impossibly far.

Cass submerged briefly, then fought to the surface, blinking away murky fluid. And Luca was there, suddenly, a dark form in the water. Beyond him, to the southeast, was San Giorgio Maggiore.

She reached down and freed her legs from her skirt with a vicious rip. Immediately, she felt lighter. She kicked her feet, trying to propel herself through the water.

Luca fought the current to stay by her side. So strong despite his ordeal. He treaded water next to her, his long hair and beard making him look like a stranger in the night. "Are you all right?"

Cass didn't speak. She couldn't. The simple fabric of the servant's outfit was growing heavier with each stroke. She needed to focus, to make it to land.

"I'm all right," she gasped. "Keep going."

Luca struggled to stay with her, but the water pulled him away again. Cass tried to follow him, concentrating on the blurry form she thought was San Giorgio Maggiore's dome, but the stars were swirling in the sky, making her dizzy and disoriented. She felt as if she were going backward toward the Palazzo Ducale instead of forward to freedom.

The current tugged her back and forth. A rogue wave blew up from nowhere, slapping her in the face, pushing her under and causing her to swallow a mouthful of water.

Gagging, she expelled the foul liquid. Her lungs burned. Her throat swelled. She coughed violently for several seconds. Her vision went momentarily dark. Was she even heading in the right direction anymore? She didn't know.

It took her a minute and several more strokes of treading water to find the dome of San Giorgio Maggiore again. She reached out and propelled her body forward again, kicking with all her might. The water was cool compared with the warm night air, and her teeth chattered loudly. Her legs sank lower. Each kick was harder than the one before. She was getting tired. So tired. So heavy. Her eyelids fluttered shut. She wasn't going to make it.

"Luca," she croaked, as if her mouth were full of sand.

No answer.

Her chin dipped below the water.

And then her foot hit solid ground.

She gasped with relief, collapsing to her knees as the shore materialized beneath her. Her torn skirt and bodice clung to her clammy skin as she crawled onto the land. Stumbling to her feet, she turned to find Luca beside her.

"I knew you'd make it." He wrapped his arms around her, pushing her wet hair back from her face to kiss her on the cheek. "*Grazie a Dio*, you're all right."

In front of them stood a long stone building, the monastery connected to San Giorgio Maggiore. Tiny square windows ran the length of the wall. All of them were dark.

"Come on," she said. Luca's touch seemed to strengthen her. She caught her breath and turned toward the center of the island, toward the trees. She felt as if she were caught in a dream, as if her body were functioning independent of her brain.

With her legs trembling beneath her, Cass crossed the sandy ground in front of the monastery, holding tight to Luca's hand, until they reached the little patch of woods. Even in the dark, she found her way back to the tree where she had hung the supplies. It was exactly twenty paces from the shoreline, with thick waxy leaves that obscured the leather sack dangling from a low branch.

Wordlessly, she untied the bag and handed Luca the clothing Siena had taken from Bortolo's quarters. The elderly butler was the only member of the household even close to Luca's height. Cass pulled her own clothes from the pack. She was moving numbly, mechanically. She was too tired to speak. Too tired to think. Tears hovered on her eyelashes. There was a third set of clothing in the bag. Siena's clothing.

Luca stepped away and turned around to give Cass privacy. She wrestled out of her waterlogged dress and slipped the fresh chemise over her head. She tugged the skirt over her hips. The dry fabric felt good against her skin. She slipped her arms through the sleeves of her bodice and stopped. The ties were in the back. She had no way to lace it without Siena's help.

A sob escaped from her lips. Luca was at her side in an instant. "Cass. What is it?" he asked. "Are you hurt?"

"I need Siena," Cass whispered, feeling incredibly stupid. "I—I can't lace this bodice. I—"

"I'll help you," Luca said. With slow, fumbling fingers, Luca threaded the first lace through the highest hole. He dropped it and grabbed the lace on the other side.

Cass started to tell him it was faster if he threaded one lace through all of the holes first, and then did the same on the other side. But she stopped. There was something comforting about Luca's painstakingly slow progress, about the methodical but innocent way his hands grazed her back repeatedly.

"Thank you," Cass said, when he had made it all the way to the bottom and knotted the silk pieces in a clumsy bow. She blotted each cheek on the back of her hand.

She tried to swallow back all of the questions that rose inside of her. What would happen to her now? What would happen to them? How would they live? Where would they go?

"Come on." Luca led her back to the tree. The ground beneath her bare feet—even Siena hadn't thought to bring an extra pair of shoes—was littered with leaves and brambles. Luca lowered himself to the ground. He brushed away the vegetation, clearing a spot big enough for the both of them. He leaned back against the tree trunk. Cass realized he was wearing only breeches and a chemise, that the plain black doublet Siena had packed was hanging over his forearm. He handed the doublet to her. "You can use it as a blanket," he said. "Or a pillow."

Cass sat next to him, leaning her head on his shoulder. Even in fresh clothing, he smelled of sweat and canal water, but she didn't pull away. "I'm comfortable," she said.

Luca draped the doublet over her arms and torso anyway. "Do you think you can sleep?"

She shook her head. She didn't think she'd ever be able to sleep again.

But she did. In the morning she woke up with her head resting on Luca's lap, the spare doublet clutched in her arms. She sat up, blinking in the sunlight that filtered through the trees.

The events of the night flooded back. Siena, sacrificing her life so that Cass and Luca could go free. *I'm sorry.* Cass thought the words as hard as she could. She felt certain that Siena could hear them all the way in heaven. Surely, she had gone to heaven. No one was more pure of soul than sweet Siena had been.

Cass's chest ached. What if Agnese thought Siena and Cass had fled San Domenico together? What if Siena's body wasn't returned? She would be treated as a dead criminal, dumped in a ditch like the three girls tossed into an unmarked grave outside Florence. Another innocent victim of the Order.

The Order was responsible for everything—her parents' deaths, Luca's imprisonment, Cass's attack.

Siena.

Luca groaned softly. Cass looked over at him; he was still asleep. He had dirt and leaves in his hair, and his chemise had managed to lose a button in the night. Cass couldn't help but notice that his right shoulder was bleeding through the garment. She reached out to touch the bloom of red and he flinched.

"I don't know," he muttered, twitching in his sleep. His shirt fell open, exposing a series of jagged red scars down the front of his chest. Cass gasped. Luca opened his eyes.

He blinked hard. "What is it?"

"You're bleeding."

Luca looked down at his shoulder. "It's fine. The water carried me into a mooring post last night. I think I got caught on a nail."

"And this?" Cass reached out one shaking finger and traced down one of the scars.

Luca stiffened. He sat up abruptly, adjusting the fabric so that he was covered. "It isn't as bad as it looks," he said quickly.

"What . . . what did they do to you?" Cass's voice trembled.

"I don't want to talk about it." His voice softened. "What's done is done, Cass. We need to look forward, not back."

"The Order," Cass said, her resolve returning.

Luca looked at his hands. "Our parents spent most of their lives trying to destroy the Order of the Eternal Rose."

"No, Luca." Cass's throat was thick. "You've got it wrong. Our parents were *members*."

"I know," Luca said calmly. He lifted himself to his feet and then bent down to help her from the ground. Keeping one of her hands twined in his, he started walking toward the shore. "My father told me. But the Order wasn't always bad, Cass. It was founded almost a hundred years ago by people who believed in the advancement of science through the examination of cadavers. Those with access to the dead formed a network. They shared their research. They took the name the Order of the Eternal Rose."

Angelo de Gradi's words from the church in Florence echoed in Cass's head. He'd said something about the Order almost being taken down from within. Could he have been talking about her parents and the da Peragas? Hope flickered inside of her, but only for a moment. Cass shook her head. "Even today, de Gradi is still defiling bodies in the name of *science*."

"The goals have changed. The Order has abandoned its pursuit of scientific knowledge to chase after some mythical formula." Luca's expression darkened as he looked out over the water. "They seek everlasting life. They want to turn man into gods."

"The fifth humor," Cass said slowly. "I went to Florence, Luca. They're using blood." Breathlessly, she relayed the story of how she'd met Piero Basso at Palazzo della Notte and then later ended up watching Hortensa Zanotta's execution. She told Luca about the dog attack, about Piero drugging her and stealing her blood, about following him to the church and watching Belladonna's sacrificial bath.

By the time she was finished, the bell tower of San Giorgio had come to life. Cass counted six chimes.

"We can't risk staying here much longer, but I know a place where we can go," Luca said. "I have a friend from school whose father lives on the Giudecca. No one will come looking for us there."

"Can we trust him?" Cass asked.

"We might not have to," Luca said. "We might be able to hide away in his barn for a few days without him even knowing we're there."

"What then?" Cass asked. "Where will we go?"

Luca touched one hand to her lower back. "Wherever we need to," he said, "to finish what our parents started."

Cass glanced over. The sunlight glinted off Luca's light brown eyes. "You still want to destroy the Order?" she asked. "After everything you've been through?"

He plucked a rock from the sandy soil and turned it over in his hands. "Especially after everything I've been through." His eyes lifted to meet hers. "Everything *we've* been through."

Cass thought back to a younger Luca who had once given her a similar stone, its edges worn by water, shaped into a heart. She had never imagined that boy might desire anything besides a life of traditional nobility. Servants. Children. A position within the Senate. A doting wife. Perhaps she had been wrong all along.

Luca flicked his wrist and sent the stone flying out into the waves. Cass watched it bounce across the surface of the water. He turned toward her, tucking a tendril of hair back behind her left ear. "Don't you want the same? Will you help me destroy the Order of the Eternal Rose?"

"I do." Cass suddenly felt warm. Her heart fluttered in her chest as she looked up at him. "I will."

Luca pulled her in close. He pressed his lips against her cheek. Cass turned her head. She reached up and stroked the back of his neck as she turned her mouth toward his. He tightened up for a second and then relaxed. His lips pressed against hers, gently at first. Then harder. Cass's whole body trembled. She folded herself against him. Her hands found his hair, the muscles of his back. Everything was warmth. Light. New life.

New beginnings.

She wanted to kiss him until she ran out of breath, and then kiss him some more.

When they finally broke apart, Luca trailed his lips from her cheek to her jawbone to her earlobe. So softly, like rose petals being dragged across her skin. "Cass," he whispered, "you make me want to be better."

She buried her head beneath his chin. "You are already the best man I know." It was true. How had she not seen it? Luca had lied to her once, but it had been to protect her. He wouldn't lie to her again. And he wouldn't betray her. Not like Falco had with Belladonna. Cass trusted Luca with her life. With her heart.

He squeezed her against him and lifted her up into the air, spinning her around once before setting her gently back on the sand. "With you, I feel like anything is possible," he said. "I love you."

Cass smiled against his chest. "I love you too," she murmured, but the wind and the waves and the beating of his heart stole away her words.

No matter. Their time together was just beginning.

"Creation of the Elixir of
Life will elevate the Order
of the Eternal Rose above the Senate,
the Church, and God."

—THE BOOK OF THE ETERNAL ROSE

Epilogue

Piero turned the crank, and the metal cylinder began to whirl. Silver flashed. Glass tubes clinked together inside the mysterious apparatus. He cranked again. And again. A few more turns and the machine slowed to a stop. Piero removed a single tube. He held it up to the fire, nodding in satisfaction at the layers of fluid: a clot of darkness in the bottom, then red, then a skim of yellow, then clear on the top. All four humors, separate and pure. All four humors extracted solely from blood.

Consulting his notes, he carefully measured out the different humors with a pipette. Drops of red, yellow, black, and clear fell into a tiny crucible. Everything had to be done in just the right ratio and order, or the reaction wouldn't work. With a pair of long iron tongs, he held the crucible just above the fire. The mixture needed to be hot, but not singed. If the flames surged too high, he'd have to start over.

He heard the fluid begin to sizzle. He pulled the crucible back from the fire. With a tiny wand, he stirred the solution five times clockwise, five times counterclockwise. The liquid bubbled and then turned clear. Not pinkish. Not yellowish. As transparent and color-less as water. It was the fifth humor, another remarkably pure sample. Piero stared in wonder for a moment and then added exactly one dram of spider venom. The venom kept the fifth humor from sepa-rating when it cooled, but Piero thought it was also responsible for the potency of the newer batches of elixir. Back when they had used wine instead, the resulting compounds had only slightly increased the longevity of the roses that served as Piero's first line of testing subjects. His current test plant had been in full bloom for weeks, and there was not even a hint of wilting on any of the petals.

If the elixir worked as it should, they wouldn't have to take it daily as they had been. Perhaps every other day, and then later once a week. It would build up in their bodies and keep them from getting ill. It would keep them from aging.

Finally.

Piero didn't yet know why some blood resulted in a batch of fifth humor that was cloudy or imperfect, but what he did know was that this subject's blood resulted in the purest humor he'd ever seen. And the strongest elixir. He had been testing it not just on the roses and spiders, but also on himself. He had never felt as alive as he did in that moment.

He scribbled a few notations on a loose piece of parchment and then waved it dry. When he had finished with this subject's blood, Belladonna would insist on personally locking up his notes. Some-one had stolen the Book of the Eternal Rose right out of her cham-bers, and she was livid about it.

He found her in the garden, composing a letter on her finest vel-lum. "What are you writing?" he asked.

Belladonna looked up. "Did you get a chance to meet Cristian de Lambert?" she asked. "He used to work for Joseph Dubois in Venice, but Dubois sent him away, so he came here, hoping to work for me. I sent him back to Venice to spy on Joseph and spread fear about the threat of vampirism." Her tight lips turned slightly upward. It was the closest thing Piero had seen to a smile since the book had gone missing. "If Angelo de Gradi is right and mass amounts of the proper blood can only be found there, that could be very useful to us."

"I believe you'll find these notes useful as well." He set a few sheets of parchment on the table next to her half-composed letter. "I know you are upset about the book, but truly, we didn't lose anything crucial to our goals."

Bella's posture tensed, and for a second Piero thought she was going to pounce on him. "That book was my father's, and my grandfather's before him. I will get it back or I will die trying, do you understand?"

"Completely." Piero bowed low. He had learned it was best to appease his patroness when she was in one of her moods.

"And when I find whoever took it, I will kill that person very slowly." She watched his reaction.

Piero knew she suspected both him and the butler, Dionisio Mafei, of the theft. As members of her inner circle, they were two of the only people who knew where she kept the book. Piero hadn't stolen it, though. Why would he? He enjoyed his current arrangement too much, and as the one actually making the elixir, he knew there was no way Belladonna could deny him his share.

She seemed to notice the vial clasped in Piero's hand for the first time. "Another test batch of your favorite elixir?" Her catlike eyes tunneled straight into him.

"It is." Piero gestured at a rosebush near the center of the garden. "I've been feeding this plant for two weeks."

Belladonna's lips curled into another half smile as she studied the roses in question. Her whole garden was stunning, but this particular bush was laden with the largest, most vibrant blossoms she had ever seen.

"I cannot wait to begin taking this elixir," she said. "I do hope, whoever your donor is, that she hasn't been executed as a vampire." Belladonna laughed a cold, bitter laugh.

Piero thought of the shelf in his room, of the row of glass tubes stamped with the lily insignia. "Do not worry, Bella," he said, smiling. "I know exactly where to find her."

Acknowledgments

I have to start this page by thanking you, the reader. Getting a book published is almost like getting an invitation to a certain school of witchcraft and wizardry. Getting multiple books published is like getting *paid* to attend that school. It's the best thing ever, and it's possible only because of you. I will never forget that.

More thanks:

To my mom for her unwavering support, even though most of the time I have no clue what I am doing; Paul for always being a calming influence, and for driving me across several states to see a dolphin show that one time I was really sad; and Vicky for sending copious e-mails full of brainteasers and baby animal pictures, and for hiding chocolate all around my apartment every time I go out of town.

To Lexa Hillyer, Lauren Oliver, Beth Scorzato, and everyone at Paper Lantern. Beth, you are my backup calming influence. Thank you for not filtering my relentless 2:00 a.m. e-mails full of questions and semi-ranty tirades. Renaissance expert Eleanor Herman, once again your insights raised this book to a new level.

To Team Philomel: Michael Green, publisher, Jill Santopolo, editrix of wonder and tireless advocate for more kissing, Julia

Johnson and the rest of the editorial team, Kristin Smith, Lisa Kelly, Sheila Hennessey, Anna Jarzab, Elizabeth Zajac, and anyone else who had a part in getting the word out about this book—you guys rock!

To Stephen Barbara and the people at Foundry, Jennifer Laughran and the Literaticult, the Apocalypsies, the Blueboarders, the book bloggers, Jessica Spotswood, Andrea Cremer, Antony John, Heather Brewer, Rhalee Hughes, all of the Breathless Reads girls, Left Bank Books, Pudd'nhead Books, Main Street Books, the St. Louis and St. Charles library systems, my crit partners: Cathy, Jasmine, Jess, Ken, and Marcy. I literally could go on forever listing other industry people who have helped me along this journey. I feel incredibly lucky to be part of a community that is so invested in the success of its members.

To everyone else who put up with my insane schedule: Connie for the late-night gossip and iced coffee, Julie for the bookmarks and inviting me to the hipster bar (I'm gonna go one of these days, I swear), Ben for going to the gun range with me when I needed to shoot things, Jeff for going out to eat with me when I needed to eat things, and all of my amazing colleagues at Award Winning Teaching Hospital, especially Debbie Hoog for taking me on a vicarious trip to Florence.

Adam, you continue to be my Kryptonite and not mentioning you here would just be wrong. We'll always have Golden Tee.

Finally, the interwebz can be a scary place for a new author. You blog, you tweet, you pin, you post, but is there anyone listening? Or are you just shouting into the ether? Extra-special thanks to Monica Lopez, Nikki Wang, and my amazing group of cyber-pals, for being a constant reminder that I'm not all alone in this.